THIS BOOK IS IN MEMORY OF

 Nicole Hudson

and

 Cleo Simpson

MY MOTHER CHOSE HIM

by

ShaRae Simpson

DORRANCE
PUBLISHING CO
EST. 1920
PITTSBURGH, PENNSYLVANIA 15238

Dorrance Publishing Co
585 Alpha Drive
Suite 103
Pittsburgh, PA 15238
Visit our website at *www.dorrancebookstore.com*

ISBN: 978-1-6461-0210-5
eISBN: 978-1-6461-0545-8

MY MOTHER CHOSE HIM

Chapter 1

"**M**y God, My God," is what Ms. Wallace said as she looked at her daughter Diamond's bruised face. Slightly hunched over, she barely made it in the house. "What happened, baby?" asked Ms. Wallace as Diamond went and laid on the couch. The girl couldn't even talk, her mouth swollen, from many blows to the face from the man who loved her so much. So, when her mother asked her, "Who hurt you?" all Diamond could do is look at her and cry. What she wanted to say was this: "Who hurt me? That crazy-ass man you put me together with. He did this, and he's been doing this and it's all your fault." But the words wouldn't come out. Ms. Wallace went to turn the lights on, only to see her baby a mess with cuts and bruises covering her face. Ms. Wallace then got up and walked to the bathroom to get some wet towels. Coming back to wipe remaining bloodstains off her daughter's face. When she was done she asked, "Diamond, where's Steven? Do you want me to call him?"

Diamond quickly shook her head no. Ms. Wallace asked, "Why? Don't you want to let him know what happened to you?"

There was so much she wanted to say, because at this moment she blamed her mother for all her pain, this crazy-ass man got her going insane, but now she's just looking at her mom in a daze, sort of crazy

3

and deranged, only wishing that she too could feel her pain. Diamond just cried. She no longer heard anything or saw anybody. She had cried herself to sleep, at least that's what Ms. Wallace thought. So, she grabbed the knitted blanket that laid across the back of the couch and put it on her little girl. She then kissed her on the hand, said, "I love you, baby," then went upstairs to her room.

So happy her mom was gone, Diamond had time to now think about herself for a minute. What she wanted to do with herself and her baby. The baby that she had been carrying for about two months. She dared not ask herself why he did it, why he beat her so bad. It wasn't the first time and she knew if she went back it wouldn't be the last time. As she thought about her unborn child she just became more depressed, then she began to cry with her favorite song on her mind. "I am a living testimony, I could have been dead and gone, but Lord you let me live on, I am a living testimony and I thank the Lord I'm still alive." For some reason, every time she was abused over the last six months, that song was always in her head.

As Ms. Wallace walked upstairs to her room, she was in a state of shock. Her beautiful baby. "Who would want to hurt my baby like that? Why didn't she want me to call Steven? He's such a good man, maybe I should call him. I know he will know what to do." What Ms. Wallace didn't know was that he was the reason why Diamond was in the state she was in right now.

Waking up the next day was something I wasn't looking forward to. I just wanted to sleep. I didn't want to talk about anything or see anybody. It was about 6 A.M. when I got up enough strength to make it up the stairs to my old room. When I did, I closed the door and locked it as if I were locking myself away from all my problems, my pain and my crazy-ass man. As I laid in my bed I just began to cry. I cried for my baby, because I knew sooner or later it would be gone. Either from me being stressed out or from him beating it out of me. After lying in the bed for a while I walked over to the mirror, very slowly. I knew my face was a mess. Even though I didn't want to see what I looked like, I needed to. As I looked out of my good eye, what I saw before me was so unpleasant and cruel. I just saw a lot of hate and wondered how something so right became so wrong. I know he loved me. Not just because his mouth said it, but because my heart felt it. What do I know about love right, I'm sitting here tore up and I still have every intention of going back to my man. I'll tell you this, if pain is love, I'm the most loved person in this world.

A black eye, half a swollen face, busted lip, three deep cuts on my face, one over my good eye, the other two on the left side of my face. Seeing this was enough to bring me back to tears. I went back to lay in the bed, then began having flashbacks about what happened the night before.

All weekend long I'd been asking Steven to take me out. He kept saying something about him having something to do. So just playing around I say, "You can hoe around some other time. You keep playing around and someone else will be getting your time." That nigga turned around so fast, grabbed me by the throat and said, "Bitch, I don't wanna hear shit out of your mouth about what I do, I'm out here busting my ass to take care of you and all you do is complain. What the hell you mean somebody will be getting my time. Bitch, if I even catch you looking at another nigga I will bust your mutha fucking head open." Then he pushed me to the bed. At this moment I'm just lying there trying to figure out what happened. His hard voice interrupted my thoughts. "Shut up, bitch, I'm going out and when I come back I want this place to look like something. Shit, cook, clean, do something. You always want to go out, but you don't do shit in. So, tell me why you deserve to go out?" He glared at me for a minute before walking to the door and slamming it behind him.

He was right. I didn't clean too often. I didn't know how to cook. But he knew that shit when he met me. So, what I didn't clean shit spotless, I made it look presentable in case anybody came by, which they never did. What more did he want. I wanted to go to work but he said, "No, you stay home, and I will take care of you." Later on I would come to find out that this was his way of controlling me. But me being young I didn't see that he wasn't really looking out for my best interest. At the age of twenty-four, I felt I had everything. I had a beautiful place to live, a man with a good job who took care of me. I mean I had any and everything as far as jewelry goes. Only thing I didn't have was a car. Steven said I didn't need one because anywhere I wanted to go he would take me. I would learn later that this too was another way of him controlling me.

Very early the next morning Steven had come home, and to my surprise he was drunk. It was a custom that after any arguing or fighting of any kind Steven would come home with a gift for me. He'd then apologize, we'd make love for hours and I would fall asleep in his arms. But for some reason tonight would change many things between us.

"Diamond, you up? Diamond, get up!" yelled Steven. That's not what woke me up. I was awakened by a hard object hitting me in the face. I woke up to see this nigga slapping me in the face with his dick. I said, "What the fuck...." Wham, right in the mouth. "Come suck my dick, bitch," he said as he was shoving his dick into my mouth. He got mad at me too. He was trying to fuck my face and he knows I can't deep throat. So, I wound up throwing up all over him. "You fucking nasty bitch" is what he said taking his dick out of my mouth. "Go get a towel and clean this shit up. And hurry up!" I'm kind of in a zone right now because a few minutes ago I was sleeping. Now this nigga is cursing and screaming at me for some shit that was his fault.

I come back in the room with a warm towel and he's lying in bed watching a porno. I went and wiped him down.

As soon as I was done he pulled me on top of him and started kissing me rough with his tongue quickly going in and out my mouth, while tightly holding the back of my head. As he continued kissing me he moved his hands down to my ass, squeezing tightly while grinding his hard penis against me. As his dick got harder he began to slap my ass real heard. Even though this was different from any other time we had sex, I was becoming aroused. Everything was twice as fast and twice as rough. He then reaching a full erection turned me on my back. He grabbed me by the neck as he began sucking on my breast very hard while roughly grabbing the other one. Then out of nowhere he sticks his dick in me, hard and fast. He then begins to fuck me. He kept going faster and faster and it felt like it was going deeper and deeper. I was confused. It felt good, but it also hurt, and I couldn't say anything because he was still choking me. After a few minutes of that I had to take his hand off my neck because I was about to pass out. That made him fiercer and controlling. He then slapped me, still fucking the shit out of me. "You don't touch me, bitch." Then he started to choke me again, now more violently then before. I hadn't realized the tears coming out of my eyes, but he did. When he saw that he damn near lost his mind. He let out a horrific laugh. "You fucking silly bitch. You wanna cry, you wanna fucking cry?" He then flipped me on my stomach, taking a good portion of my hair in his fist, he rammed his big dick in my asshole. I let out a scream again before my body went numb. He slapped me again and said, "Shut up, ain't this what you wanted?" That was the last thing I heard before everything faded to black.

Sunday afternoon I was awaken by the smell of breakfast; bacon, sausage, eggs and pancakes. When I looked on the nightstand next to me, there was a lovely platter prepared along with a glass of orange juice. After seeing I was up, Steven reached over and kissed me on my forehead, then my nose and then my lips. "Baby, I'm sorry about last night." Then he wrapped his strong arms around me and said, "I love you. I have a surprise for you." I said, "I see. What is this? Brunch?"

"This is not the surprise. This is the apology. Half of the surprise I will give you now and tonight you will get the other half." Forgetting about the unpleasant ordeal last night a big smile crossed my face as I began to think about what he could have gotten me. "What is it, baby?"

"Close your eyes and count to 3." So, I closed my eyes and began counting. "1, 2, 3." I opened my eyes to see a long black velvet jewelry box. When I opened it I damn near scared Steven from screaming so loud. "Thank you, baby! It's beautiful," I said while hugging him and kissing all over his face like a big kid. I then ran to the mirror, just now noticing a strange pain around my ass, too excited to pay it any mind, though. I held my two-carat tennis necklace against my neck, amazed by the diamonds and sapphires shining so bright. Out of all the gifts Steven has given me, nothing compared to this. After I put on my necklace I just stared at it in the mirror running my fingers across the diamonds. I saw him looking at me through the mirror, he was smiling, then he said, "I'm happy you like it, baby." He then got off the bed and began walking over to me. He turned me towards him and placed a kiss on my forehead before saying, "I love you, baby, and I would never do anything to hurt. I have to make a run, I will be back in a little while." Before heading out the door he said, "I spent time cooking that food for you, don't let it go to waste, beautiful." I looked at him and said, "Thanks, baby. I'm going to eat it."

So excited over my new best friend, I had to call somebody. Since I didn't really have any friends, I called my mom.

"Hello?"

"Hi, Mom, how are you?"

"I'm fine, baby. How are you?"

"I'm so happy, Mama. Steven just bought me a two-carat diamond necklace. It's so beautiful. You have got to see it."

"I know it's nice, baby. He's always buying you nice things. He's such a good man and he takes such good care of you."

"Yes, he does, Mama."

"Hold on a minute, somebody's on the other line…. Sis. Johnson is on my line; I'm going to call you later on. I love you."

"I love you too, Mom."

My mother was always happy to hear about something Steven did for me. She's the reason that we are together. She kept trying to get me to come to her church and meet this handsome man. She went on and on about him being a single architect with no children, and how we would be perfect for each other. I must admit when I saw him I couldn't take my eyes off of him. When I laid eyes on that six-foot chocolate brown man with curly hair, thick brows and a perfectly trimmed mustache, I was in love. I was twenty-three when I met him. He was thirty-seven and stable. He had a great career and drove a midnight blue JJaguar. He was any young girl's dream. Never did I imagine that this dream would sadly turn into a nightmare.

After I spoke to my mother on the phone, I ate my food before taking a nap. Still very excited about my necklace. I went to sleep thinking about what else he had in store for me.

I was awaken by the smell of Egyptian Musk mixed with Versace Blue Jean and a soft kiss on my forehead. "Wake up, baby girl." I rolled over smiling, "Hey, baby, you just got home."

"Yeah, wake up and get dressed."

"Where are we going?"

"It's a surprise. Can you get up and get dressed?"

"Well, how am I supposed to know what to wear?"

"Put on your white leather outfit, and wear your hair out."

"Okay. I will be ready in a minute." I went and got in the shower using my Vanilla Lace Victoria's Secret shower gel. When I got out, I dried off now applying the matching lotion and body spray. I figured we were going somewhere special since he wanted me to wear my white leather. It was a three-piece leather pantsuit. The top was a strapless midriff bustier, with three horizontal straps in the back holding it together. The pants were low-cut revealing the SND tattoo on my lower back and my dripping ice cream cone under my belly button, which said "Lick me" underneath the dripping cone. Then there was the jacket which also stopped at the middle of my back. It had my name written in rhinestones across the back. Of course, the outfit wouldn't have been complete without my white leather ankle stilettos. My mistake, my outfit wouldn't have been complete without my jewelry. I had a different kind of diamond ring on each finger of my right hand. On the left I wore my sapphire and diamond leopard on my pinky finger and my one and half carat diamond surrounded by sapphires on my ring finger. On my left arm I wore three tennis bracelets. Two, two-carat tennis bracelets and my xo sapphire/diamond bracelet which went perfectly with my new necklace. I wore my one and a quarter carat hoop earrings in my first whole and my two-carat diamond studs in my second hole. After getting dressed to impress, looking flawless in my best I went and did my hair. I unwrapped it unveiling my china cut bang from ear to ear as it fell down the back to my shoulders. I then bumped the ends, put on my eyeliner and some lip gloss and I was ready to go. One thing about being pretty, I never have to wear makeup to look good. Hell, for anybody to look at me they would need a pair of shades on. Diamonds are indeed my best friend.

Walking into the room, I see Steven in his off-white silk Versace outfit with matching Versace shoes. He looked at me and smiled, "Damn, baby, you look like you just robbed a jewelry store."

"Shut up, babe," I said laughing, before saying, "You don't look too bad yourself."

"I'm gonna have to carry my piece tonight," he said walking over to me.

"Why you fronting? You know you were going to bring it anyway"

"Bring your sexy ass over here, I think we got time for a quickie."

I looked at him and ran my hand across my hair, "Sorry, boo, you are not about to mess up my hair."

"Yeah, yeah, yeah, let's go," he said, slapping me on my ass and walking to the door. I then reached for my white Fendi bag and my white Fendi shades which had Diamond on the sides in diamonds. My baby always made sure I had the best. He even made sure I had a piece that fit right in my pocketbook. "Are you ready, superstar?" he asked.

"Yes, I am, handsome. Let's go."

Once we were in the car, I again asked where we were going.

"Baby, it's a surprise. I know I've been working a lot lately and not spending enough time with you. I just want to reassure you that you are still the most important thing in my life." Then he leaned over and gave me a kiss. I don't know why, but at that moment I felt special, desirable and very horny. So, I pulled up the armrest and unzipped his pants. "Baby, what are you...."

"Shhhh..." I then took out his dick and kissed the head. Then I took my tongue and twirled it around the head watching it grow from six to nine. I started giving him head while he was driving. It got so good he had to pull over. After a few minutes of being in my throat he said, "Shit, D, I'm about to cum." And indeed, he did. I know he's happy I didn't make a mess, he would've had to change. "Diamond, you gotta stop doing that shit. I ain't gonna ever let you go." He said while zipping up his pants.

"I know, babe, that's sort of the plan," I said while putting on some lip gloss. As he regained his composure he started driving again. I put in my ShaRae CD and turned to track nine. While listening to "All This Love," Steven asked me to roll up. He then got off the exit and went to the liquor store. He pulled up and asked, "What do you want to drink?"

"Umm, you can get me some chocolate Cask & Cream."

"Okay. Be back in a minute."

When Steven came back in the car he had this silly-ass grin on his face.

"Why you all hee-heeing with the bitch at the counter?"

"Diamond, don't start your shit."

"What shit? I seen you all flirty and shit with that bitch. You just better be lucky I didn't get out of the car."

"And do what? Make me have to check your silly ass?"

"Nigga, fuck you!"

"See, this right here is why we never go out, your ass is always overreacting."

"Fuck that, let you even see a nigga looking at me you be ready to fight."

"And, you're my property and shouldn't nobody be staring at you."

"But it's all good for you to be in the bitch face all smiley-smiley and shit, though. Let's go before you ruin my night."

"Why don't you light the blunt and shut the hell up, Diamond."

While driving to West Bubble Fuck, I backed the CD to track seven, before pouring myself a drink. The song playing is called "Hold On." The hook goes, "I'm tryna hold on to you, boy, but I feel I'm all alone/When it all comes down to it you're stressing me and I can't take no more/there is never an excuse but you find one for never picking up the phone when I call/and when you do pick up you don't even have the time to notice something's wrong in my voice." I usually play this after arguing with Steven's stupid ass. He always says I'm overreacting. He's fucking crazy and over possessive. But that was one of the things I used to like most about him. Shit, I guess I'm the crazy one.

We finally arrived to his big surprise. "Baby, where are we?" All I saw was a big warehouse on a block by itself. We pulled up to the back where all I saw was luxury cars. Looked like I was at a car show. The lot was gated and required an access code to enter. Once again, I asked Steven where we were. He looked at me and smiled. "Come on and see for yourself." There was this big black door. No handle, just a box with numbers on a wall to the left side of the door. After he put in a few numbers the door opened. At first I was kind of leery, very nervous I clutched my purse just to feel my piece. Then we came to another door. To my surprise it was a restaurant/lounge. As soon as we walked in Steven was greeted by two men who seemed to be very familiar with him. "Who's this pretty young lady by your side, man?"

"This is my wife, Diamond." I immediately smiled. Steven has never referred to me as his wife. "Tony, can you get us a booth?" This place was like nothing I've ever seen before. The place was dimly lit. Everything in sight being black and white. The carpet looked like a huge black and white checkerboard. There was a round bar in the middle of the floor. The bar was made of marble. There weren't any chairs. It was like a high ass plush couch separated to seat three people. It went like this around the whole bar; each one being black then white. There were only fifteen booths in the whole spot, each booth seating up to eight people. The seats were all black plush. They were very, very comfortable. The tables were round, white marble. Even the damn silverware had marble handles on them. There was nothing cheap about this place. I was enjoying every moment of this experience. Steven could tell I was happy by the look on my face. I looked at him again and asked, "Baby, where are we?" He simply replied, "We at The Spot."

After a few minutes a waitress comes over. She was a pretty girl; light-skinned with long black hair. She had big titties and a bigger ass which was very visible in the skin tight, short ass uniform she was wearing. "Can I get you two a drink?" she asked looking in my direction. "No thanks, I'm good."

"What about you, Steve? You want your regular?" she asked with a sly smile. "Yeah, Dawne, I'll have my regular," he said smiling back. Then he looked over at me and said, "Baby, you sure you don't want anything?"

"Yeah, matter of fact you can get me an apple martini, dry, make it two." The whole time I'm looking at Steven 'cause right now I'm feeling some type of way. Wishing I had taken more advantage of that spliff I left in the ashtray. I didn't want to start an argument, so I tried my best to keep my cool. When she walked away I said, "You and Dawne seem to be real cool."

"She's just a girl that works here. Don't start your shit, Diamond." I left it alone, having every intention on bringing it back up when we got home.

I tried to look past that. It's not like I'm insecure, so it definitely wasn't her appearance that bothered me. What bothered me was all the fucking eye contact, and this bitch calling him Steve like they all familiar and shit. But I'm a be cool. I sat back and sipped on my drink finishing both of them in less than ten minutes. Ready for a next one, my demeanor was changing very quickly. Then to make it worse, every bitch that came through the spot had to shout him out as well. Now I'm starting to boil, and I am so ready to go. Dawne comes by the table again to ask if everything is okay and if we were ready to order. Steven says, "Yes, we are ready," noticing the look on my face. "I will have a steak with shrimp alfredo and a water with lemon."

"And for you, miss?"

"I will have shrimp and chicken parmesan with linguine noodles and a Pepsi. You could also bring me another drink. Thanks."

"Okay, I will be back in a minute." Just then Steven says, "I'm going to the bathroom, be back in a minute." Then he leans over and kisses me on the lips. Steven knows I like when he shows affection toward me, especially since we spend majority of our time together arguing. "Okay, babe," I said while he walked to the rear of The Spot.

I was sitting by myself for a few minutes when I saw a familiar face appear through the door. He was light-skinned, about five feet nine inches, long wavy hair, about 170 pounds, looking just as good as he did last time I saw him. He was wearing my man's dress-up from head to toe. Except he had on black silk, with a black satin derby, with a white feather on the side. Alongside of him were four beautifully shaped women. I must admit they were something to look at. They were all dressed in white, in all shapes and sizes. The one on his left arm had on a white lace bra-top, which supported her double Ds sitting up high and perky. Along with a mini-skirt which revealed a nice pair of legs and some toe out stilettos, which strapped up to her knee. The lady next to her wore a white satin pantsuit. It swooped down low in the front, all the way to her navel, only covering her breast. The back was out completely, pants hugging tightly around her hips and her ass. The girl on his right arm had on a white skirt outfit. The top zipped up the front from her navel to right above her nipples, and a short mini skirt also revealing a tattoo of a sun around her bellybutton. She also had on a nice pair of clear stilettos. The girl next to her wore a white tube dress that was sheer around the belly area and bottomed out like a short pleaded skirt. All his bitches were fine. By looking at them none of them appeared to be over 20, but really who's counting.

They began walking, all moving at the same pace, same beat, same step. Then he spotted me. I swear his face lit up. As he walked my way so many ran things through my mind. I could definitely understand why he was so happy to see me. We had a beautiful relationship, but he just wanted something different in life. He wanted to become a pimp. I always told him fast money don't last, but it's been about seven years now and it looks like he is doing very well for himself. But now I'm fucked, I know Steven should be coming back any minute now and if he sees me talking to Kashmere he's gonna want to fuck me up. He walks his sexy ass up to me and says, "Hi, Diamond."

"Hello, Kashmere." I looked over to his girls and said, "I see you are doing well for yourself." He quickly responded, "Not as good as I could be with you on my arm."

"Let's not forget who I am, I knew you before the bitches, don't try to hit me with the game."

"Since you wanna be like that, I'd love to fuck you too. Now my question is, which one of these niggas got your pretty ass open to the game?"

"What are you talking about? I'm here having dinner with my husband." Just then Steven walks up. "Damn, nigga, you try to get at everything you see." Kashmere turned away from me to look at Steven, "My fault, my G. Hold up, Steve, that's you?" They greet each other with laughs and palms touching. "How you been, my G? Haven't seen you around in a while."

"I've been chilling, homey. Just trying to figure out why you trying to pick up my bitch."

"It ain't even like that, my man. Me and Diamond go way back. When I see one of my good girls here, I want to know who made her go bad."

"Slow down, homey, this is wifey right here. I just wanted to bring her somewhere nice."

"So, you bring her here. To 'The Spot'?" Then Steven puts his arm around Kashmere and says, "Come walk with me." Kashmere looked over to his girls and said, "K.B.'s come keep this young lady company." Then him and Steven walked off to the back. The first one to speak to me was the one with the bra-top on. "My name is Cookie. What's your name?"

"I'm Diamond."

"Your outfit is tight, Diamond."

"Well, thank you, Cookie."

"Since you're so cute, I will let you take a bite of this cookie for half price." I looked at her a little appalled and said, "Do you see me, sweetie? I wouldn't pay for pussy when I got my own. How would your daddy feel about you giving discounts on his shit?"

"The same way yours would," she said getting in my face. "Sorry, bitch, that's my husband. I don't suck dick for chips, whips or my crib." She backed up and said, "You do know your husband is a pimp, don't you?" I was a little thrown off, still not putting two and two together. "What the fuck are you talking about?" Just then the girl in the pantsuit started laughing. "Sweetie, your husband has fucked just about every girl in The Spot. I don't even know why he bring your square ass here where he work." Just then the waitress comes back and says, "Can I help you with anything, Diamond?"

"Yeah, you can find Steven and tell him to bring his ass over here." Dawne quickly walked away towards the back. "That was one of his hoes right there. He makes sure all his hoes work, 'cause he don't give them shit but dick," said the one in the pantsuit. "That's why I had to stop working for his ass," she added in. Then Cookie looked at me with a little sadness and says, "Before you leave here tonight, make sure you see Dream." Just then Steven and Kashmere come back. Kashmere looks at me with the same look as Cookie and says, "Diamond, it was nice to see you again." I managed to give him a smile. "K.B.'s, let's go." While walking away Cookie looked at me and winked her eye.

As soon as they walked away here comes Dawne with our food. She places the plates and drinks on the table. "I do hope you enjoy," she said smiling. Steven looked at my face and said, "Thanks, Dawne, it looks great," with a smile on his face. As soon as she walked away I went in. "Are you fucking serious, nigga? You a fucking pimp and this is how you want me to find out?"

"Damn, them hoes talk too much. Which one of them said something to you?"

"It don't fucking matter who said something, nigga. I'm fucking ready to go."

"Why don't you calm down, love. Give me a chance to explain," he said with the sincerest face, looking me right in my eyes. "Fuck you, Steven. I don't even fucking believe you trying to hit me with this bullshit right now."

"See, this is what I get for being nice to your ass. I take you out, try to show you a good time and this is how you respond to my kindness. Fuck you, Diamond." Then he motioned for Dawne to come while he walked off leaving me at the table like I'm the one who fucked up here.

I went to the bathroom for a second to clear my head. I didn't want to sit at the table looking helpless. I was pissed off, a little tipsy and ready to flip. Guess who walks in the bathroom; Dream's ass. I'm at the sink with a cold, wet paper towel wiping my face and in comes two bird bitches talking about Steven trifling ass. "Girl, I don't even know why you put up with that nigga. You have been his bottom bitch for the last eight years and you still ain't got shit."

"Shut up, Lex. I just love him so much and he keep telling me after the baby comes things are going to be different."

"Dream, you have got to stop falling for that shit. You see that bitch he came in here with all blinged out because of your pussy, that's who he trying to be with." Just then they came around the corner. They damn near jumped out their skin when they saw me standing there. "So, which one of you is Dream?"

"I'm Dream," said the light-skinned girl with a slight baby pouch showing. "You're the one I was told to see and now I see why." This bitch had the nerve to break fly on me and get loud like I wouldn't chop her ass in throat. She must've thought her home girl had her back. "I don't appreciate you walking up in here with my daddy like that, bitch."

"Excuse me. Look at me and look at you. Bitch, I'm Diamond who is flooded in diamonds. And you, you haven't even stepped your game up to white gold. Fuck out with your broke ass."

"Who the fuck you talking to, bitch. You popping on the account of my pussy. Steven told me about your broke ass. He just waiting to pimp you out." She should've never said that one. I punched that bitch dead in the face. She fell right to the floor and I kicked her ass in the stomach. Her punk ass friend ran out the bathroom screaming for help.

I ran out the bathroom heading for the door, just ready to go already. I make it to the exit door. As soon as I open the door who do I see? My nigga Kashmere, sitting out front in his Bentley coupe. "Hop in, Diamond, let me take you home." I jumped in the car and let him drive. I didn't say a word the whole way home and he let me be, in my silence. He obviously been to the crib before because he drove straight there.

While Diamond was running to the front, Steven was headed to the bathroom to see what was going on. He had wondered where Diamond disappeared to just that fast. He came in the bathroom to see Dream laying on the floor, holding her stomach, crying. "I'm going to kill that bitch of yours if I lose this baby."

"Stop being so dramatic, Dream. The quicker that baby is gone the quicker you can get your ass back to work."

"Steven, why are talking to me like this," she said still crying. "Dream, I'm your pimp, yeah, I give you dick, but I also sell you dreams. I'm still trying to figure out how I even got you pregnant. I never ran up in that without being strapped." She knew exactly how she ended up pregnant, by poking holes in the condom. "Steven, you don't mean that."

"Yes, I do, you cum bucket-ass bitch. I need to celebrate right now. She saved you a trip to the clinic." He laughed while walking out the bathroom. Lex began to help her friend up. "Why, you didn't do nothing, Lex. You just let her kick my ass."

"I did do something, I went to get you help. You know I'm not a fighter." Dream rolled her eyes as she went to the bathroom, feeling sharp pains in abdomen. "Lex, I'm fucking bleeding."

"Don't worry, girl, I'm going to call you an ambulance. Stay right here." Dream stayed in the bathroom. Right now, angry as hell about the events of the night. She was coming out to have a good night. Not only does she run into her daddy's wifey, but she kicks her ass causing her to lose her baby. All she could think about was revenge as the tears kept flowing.

After Steven left the ladies room laughing he felt like he needed some relaxation. He didn't see Diamond anywhere around and knew he had to prepare for the bullshit when he got home. He went to go find Dawne knowing she would help give him the attention he needed. He walked over to the bar where she was, as soon as she seen him she came his way. "How can I help you, Daddy?" she said in a sexy tone. "You can start with two shots of Henny, then you can meet me in the back room."

"Coming right up," she said with a smile. As soon she seen him walking towards the back room, she went and got someone to cover for her. When she got to the back room she saw Steven sitting there on the black leather couch, looking sexy as ever stroking his thick, chocolate cock, which was now at a full erection. "Come here, sexy." Dawne walked over to Steven taking out her bun, knowing how he likes to grab her hair when she sucks him off. "Get on your knees." She unbuttoned her uniform and got on her knees positioning herself right in front of him. "Kiss my dick.." She kissed the head and he let out a slight moan. "Kiss it all over.." She began placing soft kisses all over his hard dick feeling it harden even more while she kissed up and down his shaft. Then she licked it from the bottom of the shaft right up to the head. "That shit feel good, do it again.." She began licking all over his dick while he moaned and groaned, happy that her daddy chose her to please him tonight. "Suck my dick, bitch. I want you to put my big dick all the way down your throat." Dawne did exactly what her Daddy wanted. Steven became very excited watching his dick disappear in and out of her mouth while he ran his hands all through her hair, grabbing it, while his dick hardened from the moistness of her warm throat. It only took a couple of more minutes before he pulled her head away and bust all over her big tit-ties. He looked over at Dawne and said, "This is why you my number-one bitch. Now suck the rest of this cum out my dick." She did just that making Steven shutter a bit. She went over to the sink with a clean washcloth that was next to the couch, got it wet and soapy and washed down his penis. After she dried him off, he was ready to go home and face whatever bullshit awaited him. "It's been real, sweetie. Until next time." He said while winking and walking out the door. Dawne just smiled. She cleaned herself up and went back to work.

This nigga must take me for a mutha-fucking joke, thought Diamond sitting on the couch in the dark. Diamond has been home for almost two hours now and Steven still hadn't gotten there. After a blunt and half a bottle of Absolut she was fuming. "I got something for that ass. Nigga gonna try and play me for some bum-ass bitch. This nigga can't be serious, and he go and get the bitch pregnant. I got something for that ass." After an hour of vexing and still getting nowhere her anger took her to the edge. She rolled another blunt took out her gun and sat on the couch in the dark just letting her mind wander. After another hour she finally saw his headlights pull into the driveway. *Good, this bitch is sleep,* thought Steven pulling up to the dark house. *At least I don't have to go through the bullshit tonight.* He walked up to the front door expecting to go to bed and fall out. Unfortunately, an angry, scorned women had other things in mind. As soon as the Diamond heard the key in the door she went right over to it. The door opened and she gun-butted him. Not really knowing what's going on Steven turns around holding his head. He was surprised to see a crazed Diamond about to swing on him again with the gun in hand. "What the fuck is wrong with you, bitch?" he said while grabbing her arm in mid swing. "Fuck you, Steven," she screams. "You done fucked with the wrong bitch this time." He back-handed her making her fall to the floor. "You done lost your fucking mind. Who the hell you think you're talking to." So full of anger Diamond got up from the floor, tasting the blood trickle down her lip from Steven hitting her, with the look to kill in her eye. "Oh, you got balls now, what, you wanna fight, bitch?" Before Diamond's foot even made it to his dick, Steven jumped back now feeling threatened. He grabbed her by her arm twisting it behind her back and slammed her face twice into the glass mirror by the front door. Then he grabbed her by the throat and said, "I run this shit. If you ever again try to put your hands on me, you will not live to see the next day." He let go the grip on her neck and went upstairs. Maybe it was the shots of Henny, him getting gun-butted, or the fact that Diamond tried to kick him in the balls that put him in the rage he went into. Whatever it was, it left Diamond scared and feeling helpless. As she crouched in the floor crying, face burning from being cut by the glass, gasping for air from the grip he just had on her neck, she just cried thinking she had to get away from this nigga.

She finally got up enough strength to make it to the bathroom. She got some wet towels and tried to wipe her face. She felt her face beginning to swell, still feeling pieces of glass in it. She cried as she looked in the mirror trying to take the remaining glass out. Steven could hear her crying from upstairs and it made him feel a little bad. He made his way to the downstairs bathroom not really expecting to see the sight he saw. When he opened the door, he felt like he was looking at someone he didn't even know. He reached his arms out to her, feeling the lump in his throat preventing him from speaking. He had to gather his thoughts. He knew he didn't want her there looking the way she did, so he came up with the idea to send her to her mom's house. This way she could recover, and he could think of a way to make this one up to her. Deep down inside he really did love her and wanted to make her happy. He knew she would be upset about everything that happened, but he never thought she would take it to this extent. He actually blamed her for what happened to her. He walked her over to the couch laying her head on his shoulder.

"Diamond, I think you should stay at your mom's house for a couple of days." Diamond wasn't even upset about the gesture. She didn't really want to be around him anyway. Right now, she didn't know how to feel toward him. "You know I love you, right, D?" he asked, never looking at her face. She managed to let out a yes, just to answer him. "You can never tell anybody what happened tonight. I mean the entire night. I don't know what I was even thinking about bringing you to The Spot. I'm going to make this up to you, Diamond. I promise." All of this being said, never looking at her face. He just couldn't bring himself to see what he did to her. "I'm going to bed. Here's some money for a cab. I will call the cab for you. Just know that I love you and I never meant to hurt you." He stroked her hair and went upstairs to call the cab. Diamond knew why he didn't look at her. She also knew that he loved her, in his own way. She sat on the couch still sort of zoned out. There was a feeling of numbness that overcame her. As soon as she heard the horn blow, she got in the cab, not knowing if things would ever be the same between her and Steven again.

Chapter 2

It was about 9:30 the next morning when Ms. Wallace decided to call Steven. She figured that was the best thing to do at this moment. Hearing her daughter crying all morning and not knowing how to help, had her feeling helpless. Seeing her daughter last night made her remember when she was younger, and her mother cared for her after receiving a vicious beating from an old boyfriend. Never once did it cross her mind that Steven was the one who did this to her daughter. Ms. Wallace was much older now, and after finding the Lord she seemed to only see the good in everybody. Steven was so well respected in the church, everyone loved him. Then her mind began to think he must be worried sick about Diamond right now. Steven and Diamond haven't been apart since they moved in together a year ago. Ms. Wallace now felt an urgency to call him, completely forgetting that just hours before her daughter told her not to. She picked up her phone and called him, only to receive his voicemail. "You have reached the voicemail of Steven; please leave your message after the beep." "Hello, Steven, it's Ms. Wallace. I need you to call me right away. Something terrible has happened to my baby. Please, please call me back as soon as you get this message." Ms. Wallace hung up the phone knowing that Steven would soon call back. She decided to go downstairs and start making breakfast. She knew Diamond would be up soon and she wanted to make sure she had something good to eat.

Diamond woke up to a smell like no other. Some good old country ham and sage sausage. She really didn't want her mother to see how bad she looked in the daylight. Thank God most of the swelling went down, not much remaining besides the gashes from the glass cutting her face. She threw on her hooded robe that was in her old room and went downstairs. "Smells good down here, Mom," said Diamond coming into the kitchen. "Uh-uhhh. Go back upstairs. You ain't even brushed your teeth yet."

"Let me get a link, Ma."

"Here," said Ms. Wallace. "Now go upstairs and brush your teeth." "Okay," said Diamond as she went upstairs, happy that her mom didn't bug out over the sight of her face. Ms. Wallace was praying the whole time she was cooking to not see her daughter as she is but to see her how she remembers her. *Thank God for prayer,* she thought while squeezing some fresh orange juice.

Ms. Wallace outdid herself this morning preparing ham, sausage, bacon, eggs with cheese, grits with cheese, home fries and cheese toast. Even though Diamond's face was jacked up, her mouth was able to chew. She was starving right now, remembering how long it had been since she last ate. Diamond brushed her teeth quickly. Now she was in a hurry to get downstairs and devour the food her mom had prepared. She was so happy to be home right now. She sent up a quick prayer herself. "God, please don't let my mom give me third degree right now. I'm really not in the mood." She looked up to heaven, shot HIM a quick smile and proceeded to the kitchen. "Everything looks so good, Ma," said Diamond sitting at the table. "Now don't go making no huge plate. You know your eyes were always bigger than your stomach." They both laughed. "I'm happy you came here, Diamond. I'm not going to ask you again what happened, but I am happy you came home. You know I love you and I'm always here for you, baby."

"I know, Ma. Now let's eat. You know I don't like the mushy stuff." They both smiled as they filled up on that wonderfully prepared breakfast. Diamond didn't even complain about the pulp in her orange juice like she normally would have. She was just happy to be in a better place. She hadn't even thought about Steven until she heard the doorbell ring. "Who is that, Mom?"

"I don't know, baby, let me go check." As soon as the door opened she heard his deep voice. Diamond's first thought was *What the hell is he doing here?* Then she heard him talking to her mom about a message she left for him. It was now one in the afternoon and Steven comes to the house like he was Superman checking in because Lois had been hurt. Imagine that.

Steven came into the kitchen with tears in his eyes. Now seeing Diamond in the light made him even more remorseful about what had transpired only a few hours before. He pulled Diamond close to him and said, "I'm so sorry I let this happen to you. I should have been there to protect you." Diamond didn't know how to respond. Knowing this was more of a put-on for her mom than anything else. *He deserved an Oscar for this one right here,* she thought while the tears fell from his face. It felt so real to her, even though he was the one who did this to her. *Protect me, nigga, you did this to me* went through her mind, but she let his warm embrace engulf her, making her feel comforted, like here in his arms was the only place she wanted to be. Steven really did feel bad and the tears he shed were real. Diamond was his prize and for him to see her looking the way she did, it really messed him up inside. "Baby, let me take you home. Please?" Diamond looked at Steven then over at her mom who stood in the doorway smiling like she just seen a scene from *Romeo and Juliet* or something. Diamond walked over to her mom, gave her a hug and a kiss and thanked her for being who she was. Ms. Wallace wiped away her own tears looking at Steven, mouthing to him to take care of her baby. She made them wait a few extra minutes while she wrapped up the rest of the breakfast for them to take home. Diamond left the house still wearing the hooded robe. Walking to the car she wondered what was the next move in this game she played called LIFE.

Steven opened the door for her, something he has not done since they began dating. He placed the food in the backseat, got in and headed home. She was surprised that he had on her favorite ShaRae CD, playing a familiar song, "This Time." The hook goes, "This time I hope that we, can make this work out. The things that we been through, show what true love is all about." She knew he was back to the sweet sensitive man she fell in love with. But how long would that last? How long would it be until he turned into the beast she met last night. They rode in silence the whole way home. It wasn't until they got one block away from the house when he said, "I have a surprise for you." She didn't get excited like she normally would've. There was no gift she thought could make up for what he had done to her. As they pulled up to the driveway she noticed a baby blue JJaguar with a big white bow on it. Steven pulled up right behind it, looked at Diamond smiling and said, "It's all for you, baby." He looked at her with the sincerest eyes and said, "I promise last night will never happen again." He reached over to her and kissed her on the forehead. She managed to let out a thank you under very soft tones. "Come on, baby, let me show it to you." Diamond was very excited over the car. She just had too many things going through her mind right now to show the way she felt. "Maybe later, babe. The car is beautiful. I'm just not really up to it right now." Steven felt a little angry. He thought for sure this would be the perfect thing to woo her back over with. It was a brand-new Jag, sparkling from the glitter-coated paint job he had over the baby blue paint. How could she not get excited about seeing her name on the license plate of this car? He knew he couldn't show how he really felt so he acted understanding while he helped her out of the car.

Diamond didn't really know what the house was going to look like when she walked in. She expected to see blood and glass everywhere. To her surprise everything was back in place. You could tell he had the carpet cleaned. The carpet was off white without a spot on it. He had also replaced the mirror that was behind the door with a picture of him and her. Steven noticed her looking around and offered to run her a nice hot bubble bath. She was more than appreciative knowing this was just what she needed. Steven put the food in the kitchen, then went upstairs to prepare a nice hot bubble bath for the woman he loved.

Diamond didn't know how she should feel right now or what to think. It was Steven's idea to send her to her mom's house, which didn't bother her. So why did he come to get her so soon? She didn't want to get caught up with the special treatment that she was now receiving. She couldn't even get excited over the beautiful car that was in the driveway, the car of her dreams. She has noticed Steven's behavior changing over the last few months but didn't know what caused it. Now she wondered if it was the fact that he had a baby coming from one of his hoes. One of his hoes. That whole situation still didn't sit right with her. Her man was a pimp. This man from her mom's church, who was supposed to be an architect, her knight in shining armor, was nothing more than a pimp who got money from women who sold their body. She kept hearing Dream say, "He can't wait to put your ass on the track." Maybe that's what bothered her the most. But she just couldn't believe that. He just bought her a brand-new car. She already learned from the other hoes that he doesn't trick on workers. So, he must love her. He had to love her. She just felt so confused. She didn't know what to say to him or how she should say it. She didn't want to trigger anything that would bring that side of him back out. Her thoughts were interrupted by Steven calling her upstairs. She was surprised when she walked in and seen the candles lit up all around the dimly lit bathroom. She couldn't hide the smile that now covered her still bruised face as she smelled her Vanilla Victoria's Secret bubble bath.

"Come here, baby, so I can take off your clothes." Diamond walked over to Steven and let him undress her. She stepped in the warm tub which felt so good right now. She was surprised to see Steven get the hand sponge. He had never bathed her before. Steven knew he was up Shit's Creek and he had to make things right. He didn't care what he had to do to make it right. He just needed to get his lady back in his graces. Steven has always had some bad qualities about him, but things began to change when he met Diamond. He never had respect for women, that's why it was easy for him to choose the lifestyle he did. He noticed he had a way of making women do whatever it is that he wanted. All it took was a few kind words and of course his big dick. He would have them eating right out of his hand. Diamond was not that way at all. She wasn't quick to fall for his game and she didn't go nuts off the dick and that's why he chose her. She didn't know she had been chosen. But indeed, he did choose her. To be the mother of his children and possibly his wife somewhere down the line. He loved her for her strength, her knowledge and her ability to not fall for the bullshit. Everything was going good with the happy couple until Steven began to bring his work home. Like the other night when he came home and made her throw up. He was drunk and thought she was Dawne. He knows Diamond can't take all his dick down her throat. Then when he found out Dream was pregnant, it was like overkill. He was so happy Diamond kicked her ass last night and she lost the kid. That was like a big weight off of him. He had no intentions of letting Dream keep that baby. He was still trying to figure out how she got pregnant. Right now, none of that mattered anymore. Now all he could think about was making everything right with the woman he loved more than any other.

Diamond got in the tub enjoying the warmth of the water and the nice glow the candles set off in the bathroom. "How are you feeling, baby?" asked Steven while he placed the hand sponge in the water lathering it up with soap. "I don't know…there's so many things running through my mind right now."

"I told you I'm sorry, D," said Steven while washing Diamond's neck now sitting her up so he can wash her back. "I know I have been acting different lately, I've just been so stressed out with everything that's been going on." There were so many things Diamond wanted to say behind that, but she chose to stay silent. "I love you, Diamond. I promise what happened last night will never happen again."

"How do I know that, Steven? You are so unpredictable these days. How do I know you won't become the person that I met last night? You have become difficult to deal with this last few months. I don't even know who you are anymore. How long you been pimping?" Steven rinsed the soap off her back and looked her right in her eyes. "Diamond, I love you more than anything in the world. I promise, I will never again put my hands on you. I'm so sorry for the way I've been acting. You know me. You know me better than anyone else. I don't want to lose you. I can't lose you, Dee."

Just then Diamond felt a sharp pain in her stomach. She then began to see blood mix in with the bathwater. "Steven, call an ambulance."

"What's wrong, Diamond?"

"I don't know, just call an ambulance." Steven thought the red was from her period coming down. If he was paying attention to his woman for the last couple of months he would've noticed she hadn't been getting her period. "Hurry, Steven, it hurts," said Diamond now crying. "I'm calling now, baby." Now Steven was becoming nervous. He knew something was wrong. He helped Diamond out of the tub to get her dressed before the ambulance came. That's when he actually noticed how much blood was coming down. He sat her back in the tub because the blood was becoming too much for him to handle and he didn't want it to get all over the place. He went in the bedroom to get her clothes and some pads to put on. He could hear her screaming in pain while gathering everything together. He called 911 again asking where the ambulance was. He was now becoming frantic.

"Diamond, I'm here, baby. I'm gonna get you dressed and we're gonna go downstairs. The ambulance will be here any second, baby.

Everything is going to be okay." Diamond was bleeding profusely, and she was becoming very weak. Steven did manage to get her dressed and downstairs just in time to meet the ambulance at the door. They came in with the stretcher and laid Diamond upon it, then rolled her back out. Steven followed the ambulance in his car. He was so nervous right now, not knowing what was going on. When they got to the hospital they rushed Diamond straight upstairs where they began working on her. They advised Steven to stay downstairs. They were a little skeptical about the bruises on her face, but they didn't let him know that.

"Excuse me, miss, that's my fiancé up there and I need to know what's wrong with her."

"All we can tell you is that she had a miscarriage. She has lost a lot of blood and we have to get her back stabilized." The nurse changed her demeanor toward him when she saw his face almost hit the floor after notifying him of the miscarriage. "Are you okay, sir?" Steven looked at her with tear-filled eyes and said, "NO, are you telling me my lady was pregnant and she just lost the baby?" Now the tears were flowing nonstop. "Yes, sir, that's what I'm telling you. I take it you didn't know about the pregnancy?" Steven couldn't even speak. He shook his head no. "I am sorry for your loss. If you need to speak with someone we do have counselors here that can talk to you." Then she walked away. Steven was so upset right now. He didn't know what to do. He wondered why Diamond didn't tell him. Even though he didn't want a child for another year or two, it didn't change the way he felt about losing this one. He sat in a chair holding his head in his palms while the tears fell from his eyes, blaming himself for what had just happened. After an hour or two the nurse came back to let him know that he could go in and see her.

Steven walked in the room to see Diamond hooked up to an IV, looking much better than she did when the ambulance came. He walked over to her and kissed her on her forehead. "How are you feeling, baby?"

"I'm okay. Just in a little pain," said Diamond, managing to put a smile on her face. "I was thinking, maybe we can take a trip when I get you out of here. Maybe Mexico or Jamaica."

"That sounds nice, baby. I'm looking forward to it."

Just then a detective walks in the room and asks Steven if he could speak with him. "I will be right back, love. How can I help you, Mr.—"

"You can call me Detective Peterson. I was given a call by the hospital. First off, I would like to offer my condolences for the loss of your child, but of course that's not the reason for me being here. Your wife looks like she's been a victim of a terrible beating and you being her husband would of course be the first person we would question about this matter."

"You have got to be kidding me right now. Just so you know, Det. Peterson, me and my wife are very happy together. I got a call from her mother this morning saying something had happened to her. I know she went out last night. She was going to her mom's house because it was closer to where she was. When I got to her mom's house to pick her up this morning, this is what I saw. Apparently, she got into a fight with someone at the club or after the club. That's all she told me. She didn't want to talk about it, so I didn't want to push the issue. My wife is a beautiful woman. I could never, I would never do that to her. I don't believe you have the nerve to even come at me with this right now. My wife needs me and right now I need to be with her."

Detective Peterson looked at him suspiciously and said, "Just one question, Mr. Knight, why did she go to her mom's house and not come home to let you know what happened?"

"I'm not sure, Det. Peterson. When she feels better you will be more than welcome to come by the house and ask her yourself. Now excuse me, I need to be with my wife," said Steven while walking back into the room with Diamond.

"I don't believe these people here. Do you know they called the police to start a damn investigation? This just keeps getting better and better." Just then a nurse comes in the room with a beautiful flower arrangement. Both Diamond and Steven looked confused when they saw the flowers. "Excuse me, Nurse, who are these from?" asked Diamond, knowing that no one knew she was here. "I don't know, ma'am. She asked to be anonymous. There is a card inside, though," said the nurse while placing the card in Diamond's hand. By the look on her face Steven knew something was wrong. He took the card out of her hand to see, "How does it feel, bitch?" was written on the card. Steven immediately threw the card and flowers in the garbage. "Where did you get this from, Nurse?" From the tone of Steven's voice the nurse was scared to respond, thinking he might harm the sender. She wasn't aware of what the card said, but she knew it couldn't have been good. "A lady handed them to me. I was on my way to come check on Ms. Wallace and a young lady asked me to bring them inside." Steven knew exactly who was behind this. Diamond had no enemies, so it wasn't hard to narrow down who could've sent it. "Nurse, how soon can my lady be released? I don't want her here anymore."

"Just give me a couple of minutes so I can check with the doctor. I will be right back."

"How do you feel, baby? Do you feel well enough to get out of here?"

"I do, Steven, I don't want to be here anymore. Who do you think sent me those flowers?"

"I don't know, baby, but I will damn sure find out."

Just then the doctor comes in the room. "How are you feeling, Ms. Wallace?"

"I feel much better, Doc. I think I can manage."

"What about your face? Those scars look pretty fresh. I would've applied stitches, but it isn't bad enough."

"My face is fine, Doc. Got into a bar fight last night. That may be what got me here today," said Diamond with a smile. "In that case I will write up your discharge papers and you can be on your way. I do have a couple of prescriptions you need to get filled. One to prevent infection and the other will be to stop the pain."

"Thanks, Doctor…."

"Charles. The name is Dr. Charles."

"Well, thank you, Dr. Charles. You have been more than helpful."

"You are very welcome, Ms. Wallace. I do trust this man will take good care of you?" He said reaching a hand out to Steven. "I definitely will, sir," said Steven shaking the doctor's hand. "I will give you a few minutes to change and the nurse will be back with discharge papers for you to sign."

"Thanks again, Dr. Charles," said Diamond, now sitting up. "Before you go, Doc, can you take this IV out my arm?"

"Sure thing, I almost forgot."

"It's okay," said Diamond with a smile. After the doctor removed the IV he left the room. Diamond looked over at Steven and said, "My clothes should be in that clear plastic bag over there by the chair."

"Okay, babe." Steven went over to the chair to get Diamond's clothes and help her get dressed. "I hope you didn't call my mom."

"No, love, I haven't called anyone."

"Good. This would hurt her so much. She's been dropping hints about me being her only child and giving her some grandchildren."

"Don't worry, Diamond, you will make her a grandmother and I know you will make a wonderful mother as well," said Steven before kissing Diamond on the lips. This did make her smile. Despite the terrible events of the last couple of days, Diamond felt happy right now. In a way she felt free. She was also happy to be alive. When she laid in the tub earlier today, she thought she was going to die. Between the pain and the blood, she thought it was over.

The way Diamond was moving around surprised Steven. He remembered her being so weak before. He was happy to see her smiling and back to how he likes to see her. He made a mental note to get something to help her scars heal quicker while they were at the drug store. He really loved Diamond and promised to always show her. He just wanted everything to go back to how it was when they first met, although many things were now very different. He felt a vacation along with teaching her how to drive her new car, would help make things better. He just wanted to see her shine like the diamond he made her to be. After she finished dressing herself the nurse came back in the room with the discharge papers. She herself was surprised to see Diamond maneuvering around so well. "I see you are all ready to go, Ms. Wallace."

"Yes, ma'am. Never been one to like the hospital"

"Okay. Well, you can sign these papers for me and I will be out of your way." Diamond signed the release papers, got her prescriptions and was ready to go. No longer worried about the scars on her face, just happy to be going home.

As soon as they got in the car she asks, "You got any bud rolled up, babe?" Steven smiled at her and said, "Of course I do. Look in the center console." Diamond could smell the goodness as soon as she opened the armrest. To her it felt like she hadn't smoked in days. She lit the blunt and inhaled so deep it caused her to cough. "Take it easy, babe. It ain't going nowhere," said Steven while chuckling. "I know, babe," said Diamond still coughing. "I'm going to take you home, so you can get some rest while I go and get your prescription filled."

"That doesn't make any sense, Steven. We have to pass the drugstore on the way home."

"Diamond, you need to get some rest. These last two days have been hard on you and I want you to take it easy."

"Thanks for thinking of me, but I'm okay, really. I will stay in the car and you can run inside. You're still going to have to wait while the prescription gets filled."

"If you say so." Steven was very amazed at how well Diamond was handling the miscarriage. He thought she would be emotional behind it. Even after getting the flower delivery and reading that disturbing card, she seemed to be in bliss right now. He was happy about it but also a little concerned that she may be suppressing her feelings and might just explode. He wasn't going to question her though. He wanted her to stay this way as long as possible. "How about dinner and a movie tonight, love. I have a new recipe I've been dying to try out." Diamond bust out laughing, she looked at Steven and seen he was dead serious. "I'm sorry, baby, you want to cook for me?"

"Yes, I do. Is that so hard to believe?"

"Uh, yeah. I've never seen you make anything more than a sandwich. Wait, I forgot you did make me breakfast last week, I take that back."

"And it was good, wasn't it," he said smiling. "It was aight. I was just hungry," said Diamond laughing. "Whatever. That's why your plate was empty when you were done, right."

"You got that one, babe. Looking forward to dinner," said Diamond taking another pull of the blunt.

"Do you need anything else while I'm in the drugstore?"

"Yes. I need some pads. Make sure they are Always. Super. Overnight."

"Is that it, babe?"

"I want some ice cream. H agen-Dazs. I want Strawberry Cheesecake but if they don't have that you can get Cookies 'n Cream."

"Is that it, babe?"

"I want…I'm just playing. That's it, babe. Thanks."

"Okay. I will be right back."

"I will be right here waiting." Diamond was happy for things to be going so well right now with Steven. She knew he felt guilty for everything that happened and she planned on riding this out till the wheels fell off. She had no intentions on resting. She had a new outlook on life right now. First things first, she would began driving again and then she would begin to look for a job. She didn't know how Steven would feel about her working, but she didn't really care right now. All she knew was that this didn't kill her it just made her stronger and she was going to do all she could to make her life better. She had every reason to believe Dream sent her those flowers to the hospital, but she didn't want to say anything to Steven. She wanted to keep the mood light and calm, just like it was right now. If she had asked Steven to get her some pads a couple of weeks ago he would've spazzed on her. Now he's more than happy to do it. There was nothing else to do but take the good with the bad.

After twenty minutes Steven comes back to the car with the prescriptions, pads, ice cream and some cocoa butter sticks; which he was told by a lady in the store would help with the healing of Diamond's face. He was now all ready to go. He wanted to do something special for her, so he bought a copy of *The Notebook* while in the drugstore. He was now ready to get home to prepare the only dinner meal he knew how to cook, fried chicken and macaroni and cheese. He was going to stop by Popeye's and eliminate the hassle of cooking but knew Diamond would appreciate him cooking it more. "Did you think about me while I was gone?" said Steven looking at Diamond. "No," she responded with a smile. "Well, I guess I'm going to have to change that," he said before kissing her on the lips. "You will be happy to know they had your Strawberry Cheesecake ice cream." He looked over to see Diamond with a big smile on her face. "Good. I will be eating that after my lovely dinner you will prepare for me. What are you cooking anyway?"

"It's a surprise. You know how you love my surprises," he said with a smile. "Speaking of surprises, I was thinking that we can go driving tomorrow in my new car." Steven chuckled, "I thought you said you wasn't thinking of me. I just have a couple of things to do in the morning and I'm all yours."

"Thanks, baby," replied a happy Diamond. Steven was happy to hear Diamond mention the car. He was wondering how long it would take her to show him the reaction he wanted to see. They headed home with music playing, each thinking good thoughts with plans on enjoying the rest of the night.

They pulled up to the house and went inside. "I'm going to get in the shower, babe."

"Okay. Use the shower in the bedroom. I haven't had a chance to clean the bathroom yet."

"Okay." Diamond grabbed her pads while giving Steven a kiss. Then she went upstairs to enjoy a nice hot shower. Steven was downstairs all ready to prepare dinner. He had already cleaned and seasoned the chicken from earlier in the day. He had planned on the day going a little differently than it did. He was now happy that he made the preparations for the chicken sooner than later.

Diamond had got out the shower and the first thing she smelled was fried chicken in the air and boy, did it smell good. She threw on a t-shirt and some sweats before she went downstairs. "Damn, babe, that chicken smell good. Let me have a piece."

"I'm almost done, greedy," said Steven laughing. "Stop playing. Let me get that piece right there," said Diamond walking over to the bowl of chicken. "First you want to tell me I can't cook now you want to be eating my chicken before the meal is done. You funny, D."

"Whatever, nigga," said Diamond breaking a piece of the chicken cutlet. "This shit is good, babe. Why you don't cook more often?"

"Because I only cook chicken." They looked at each other and started laughing. "Is the food almost done?"

"Yes, Diamond. I'm just boiling some corn on the cob. When it's done we can eat."

"You're taking too long," said Diamond whining. "Stop acting like a baby. Do you want to watch the movie while we eat or after we eat?"

"We can watch it after. While we are eating you can tell me why you love me and why you're being so nice to me," said Diamond while walking out of the kitchen. Steven had been prepared for all of this. He knew he would have to do anything possible to get Diamond's forgiveness, he was just happy that she was no longer upset with him which would make this a lot easier. Diamond went to the car to get the other half of the blunt she left in the ashtray. She came back in the house and turned on the radio while she smoked, and

Steven finished preparing the food. He walked into the living room and said, "You greedy and stingy. You're not going to share? That's messed up."

"Shut up, babe, all you had to do was say pass that. Don't start bitching up on me because you in the kitchen." He walked over to her and took the blunt. "You're right. I'm letting this kitchen shit get the best of me," he said while shaking his head. "It's okay, babe. I was just playing with you."

"I know," he said with a smile. Then he passed her back the blunt while he went to go prepare the table.

"Did you take your meds, D?"

"Yes, Dr. Thompson. I am medicated and ready to eat. Please tell me the food is done."

"Come in the kitchen, big head." Diamond walked in the kitchen to see dinner on the table along with candles and dim lights. "Looks like you went all out. Aren't candles usually for steak and lobster," said Diamond sarcastically. "Not tonight, darling. Tonight, it is strictly for chicken, macaroni and cheese and corn." They shared a laugh while Steven went and got the champagne out the freezer. "This right here is for me. No bubbly while you're on meds."

"So, what am I supposed to drink?"

"You have a choice of some nice ice-cold water or some even colder carbonated soda. Any soda of your choice."

"Oh, you got jokes tonight."

"No, love. I'm just trying to service you."

"In that case I guess I will have a nice cold Sprite. I will also take a foot rub during the movie."

"Anything you want, baby." Steven got up to get a can of Sprite out the fridge along with a glass to pour it in. "Is there anything else I can get for you while I'm up?"

"No. It looks like you have taken care of everything." They began eating. *I have to get him to cook more often,* she thought to herself.

"So, Mr. Thompson, tell me why you love me." Steven looked her right in the eyes and said, "Because you are Beautiful, Intelligent, Thoughtful, Charming and Honest."

"Hmmm. Let's try that again. When I put together the first letter of each word, it spelled out bitch. Now really. Why do you love me?" Steven laughed. He knew she would see through the acronym he has used so many times before. "Because of that very reason. You were always able to see through my bullshit. You never let nothing I say go straight to your head without you analyzing it and really thinking it through. I always had to be real with you and that's why I respect you like no other. I was really hurt today when I found out that you lost my baby. You are the only woman I could ever see having my child. That's why I've always given you everything and treated you the way I have. Up until these last couple of months at least. You're my life and one day I promise to make you my wife." Diamond felt a tear come from her eye and quickly wiped it hoping Steven didn't see it through the candle light. He then reached out to her taking both her hands in his. "I know I'm a piece of shit. I guess the real reason I even took you to The Spot was because I was tired of living a lie and I just didn't know how else to tell you. I didn't think the night would end the way it did. But I am happy you know now."

"If everything you say is true, then I am here, and I won't leave you. If you ever put your hands on me again, I'm gone. If I ever find out you're fucking anyone else, I'm gone. And if you ever lie to me again, no car, no jewelry or meal will be able to win me over."

"I respect it, Diamond. Just give me a chance to make it up to you."

"You got it, babe."

They ended the night falling asleep in each other's arms on the couch watching *The Notebook*.

Chapter 3

The next couple of weeks seemed to fly by. Steven made sure to be on his best behavior, spending more time at home and being a better man to his lady. He knew it would be a long time before he could make this right, but he would do his best to try. Diamond's face was starting to heal but some of those scars she would carry until the day she died. Even though Diamond loved Steven and appreciated all the efforts he was making, she was still hurt. She didn't know if the monster she had seen would come back. Every time she looked in the mirror it was a reminder of that horrible night. Although, she did wonder how he was doing sexually since they hadn't had sex since before she had the miscarriage. As much as she wanted to know, she didn't really want to know. Especially now since she knows what he actually does for a living. A part of her didn't even want to have sex with him anymore knowing that he got that girl pregnant. The thought of her man running up in a whore with no protection really got to her. This was definitely something she wanted to talk about, but how? How do you bring up a conversation like this without things going left? Things were getting back to normal or at least their normal.

Steven knew that he messed up this time. He knew that if he didn't get it together Diamond would leave him. Despite what he'd done, he really did love her and hoped that one day she would be his wife. Steven had a very hard life growing up. The fact that he watched his dad shoot his mom and then turn around and kill himself really left him in a bad way. He didn't know it at the time, but his parents had been caught in a love triangle. His mom was tired of the life her husband gave her and she decided she was ready to leave. Mr. Hunter wasn't happy with her decision and that was the outcome. He tolerated his wife's cheating for years because he too had someone on the side but when she told him she wanted to leave, that changed everything. At the age of thirteen Steven became a ward of the state. Luckily enough for him he was placed in good home with foster parents who actually cared about him. It didn't take him to long to adjust because of the love that surrounded him.

Mr. and Mrs. Thompson couldn't have the one thing that they longed for, children of their own. After many tries and a lot of money wasted, they decided to adopt. They adopted two children, a brother and sister, Calvin and Aleese. Calvin and Aleese were also victims of a Domestic Violence situation. Calvin watched his dad abuse his mom for years. He came home from school one day and found his mom laying in a bed with her wrist slit and his three-year-old baby sister crying in her playpen. He immediately called nine-one-one. The officers came, and they took him and his sister into the system. He never knew what happened to his dad and he really didn't care. He knew anywhere he went would be better than where he was. In one week they had a new home with the Thompson family. Mr. and Mrs. Thompson were in their late thirties when they adopted the two children. They were happy to finally have what they had been missing. Mrs. Thompson even took a leave from work, so she could spend time with the kids and get to know them better. With her knowing that Calvin found his mom dead, she made sure to have him see a therapist twice a week. She thought herself very lucky to get these children that were so well mannered and behaved given their current situation. She adored Aleese as well. She had the prettiest brown eyes and curly hair. Mrs. Thompson was happy that the little girl was too small to remember what happened to her mom. Within months the children had adjusted, and they were all one big happy family.

The Thompsons took good care of the children and loved them as their own. They were happy with their family. It wasn't until five years later when Steven came along. The family was watching the news one night when they seen the story come up about a husband killing his wife and then turning the gun on himself, leaving behind a thirteen-year-old son. Mrs. Thompson immediately looked at her husband and grabbed his hand. At that moment, he knew that now orphaned teenager would soon be in his home. Within a week, Steven became a new member of the family. Just like she did with the others, Mrs. Thompson took a leave from work. Since Steven's situation was more traumatic and he was older, she wanted to fill him with nothing but love. She would have conversations with him about his mom, what he remembered about her, what he missed about her, how he felt about what happened, how he felt about his dad, about what he did. She was surprised to find out that Mr. Hunter was actually a good guy and he did what he did out of emotion. She was more surprised to see how quickly Steven adjusted to his new home. He was happy to be in a stable environment. Being with his new family gave him something he never experienced. Family. Even though there was enough room for Steven to get his own room, they thought it would be a good idea for him and Calvin to share a room. The two guys became best friends as well as brothers and kept this relationship until they were grown men. Amongst other things, church was now a part of the family life. Every Sunday morning Mrs. Thompson had the children ready for Sunday school. This was something new for Steven, just as it had been for Calvin and Aleese when they first arrived. Just like them, he was just happy to be a part of a family.

As the years went by everyone got older. The boys were getting ready to graduate high school and Aleese was now a teenager. As much as the Thompson's wanted all of their children to go to college,

Steven made it clear that he wasn't headed in that direction. Even though he was one of the smartest kids in the class, he just couldn't see himself doing another four years in school. While Calvin went away for school, Steven stayed home. He helped his parents out around the house and with Aleese. Over the years Aleese and Steven's relationship grew closer. He would threaten any boy who even looked at his little sister, she felt so safe with him. She loved when he would take her to school and have her friends swoon over him. She loved him just as much as she loved Calvin and she was happy that she had him since Calvin had gone away to school.

One day Mr. Thompson came home from work and had a talk with Steven about what he planned to do now that he wasn't going to college. He told him he would give him a couple of months to figure it out, but he had to do something. He could take some local classes, or he would have to get a job, but he wouldn't be in the house all day and running the street at night. Steven knew Mr. Thompson meant well and took everything he said to heart. He knew he couldn't just be a slouch, but he didn't know what he wanted to do. What he did know was that he didn't want to work for anyone. It wasn't long before Steven started selling drugs. It wasn't until five years later when he met Kat, the prostitute that changed his life forever.

Kat was a short, thick, white girl, with green eyes and long black hair. She never had a chance to do anything more than lay on her back. At the age of twelve her Dad started having sex with her. When him and her mom didn't have money for drugs, they decided to use their daughter to support their habits. By the age of fifteen she had gotten snatched by a pimp. It's sad to say but this was the best thing that happened to her. At least now she wouldn't have to worry about having to her father inside of her while her mom nodded off enjoying her high. Mike had been in the life for over fifteen years when he met Kat. He had heard about her from one of his boys who served her parents a couple of times. Even though she was fifteen her mind and her body were far more mature. He knew with the right guidance he had a money maker on his hands. Kat was used to strangers doing whatever they wanted to her since this had been her life for the last three years. Since her parents got high all the time, they needed her home all the time. She never got past the seventh grade. The only thing her parents left her with was a bad coke habit. You would think her having a pimp would be a bad thing, but it wasn't. Not only did she now eat regularly she also had a clean place to sleep. Over the next ten years Mike taught Kat a lot about the game. Every thousand she made him he gave her a hundred. Since she never had money, this seemed like a lot to her. He took care of her living arrangements, brought her clothes and fed her. So, the money she made she would save. Since she was white, young and down for anything, she was getting anywhere from five hundred to eight hundred per date. After ten years she had almost fifty thousand saved up that only she knew about. Mike made a lot of money off Kat over the years. After ten years Mike felt that she needed a break, so at the age of twenty-five he retired her and had her training the new girls and picking up his money. Kat looked at him as a father figure since he was the only man who took care of her and never had sex with her.

One day while Kat was out doing some shopping she seen Mike with a lady and two young boys. She had the biggest smile as she walked over to him. He seen her coming, but he was with his family and his wife knew nothing about what he really did for money. She crossed the street, walked up to him and said, "Hey, Mike." He looked at her with a confused look on his face, "I'm sorry, do I know you?" Immediately it hit her, *This must be his family,* she thought. She replied back, "I guess not. Sorry." Then he walked away joking about the incident with his wife. Kat was hurt. She didn't know if it was the fact that after knowing this man for ten years she never knew he had a family, him acting like he didn't know her or the fact that he laughed and made a joke about her. At that moment she decided that she would never again let anyone make her think they cared about her. She would show him that he really didn't know her.

Before she did her pick-ups for the night, she packed a bag with all the money she saved and everything she didn't want to leave behind. You would think that Mike would've told her not to work that night but in his mind he had Kat's loyalty and he knew that she would never betray him. Kat left the state that night with close too eighty thousand dollars. The fifty thousand she had saved up and twenty-five thousand dollars that she collected that night. After her last pickup she headed to New York and didn't look back. She didn't know anyone out there, but she knew with that kind of money she was off to a good start. *He tried to play me, I'll show his fat ass,* she thought while driving down the highway with her music blasting and her blunt blowing in the wind.

Five years had now passed and at the age of twenty-three Steven was still on the corner hustling and living home with his parents. He wasn't really saving any money, spending everything that came his way. Kat had been in New York for about a month before she first spotted Steven on the corner with the rest of the corner boys. She had been watching him for a couple of weeks before she chose him. It's usually the other way around but Kat heard about pimps from New York. She thought it would be best to choose than to be chosen. Kat didn't know what it was but there was definitely something that drew her to Steven. One day she walks up to him and says, "I can change your life." He started laughing when he heard that. He heard about what freaks white girls are, but he never had the chance to experience one. "How do you plan on doing that...,," he looked at her waiting for her to give him her name. "Kat. My name is Kat. Take a ride with me and say good bye to this corner life." Since he didn't have anything to lose, he told his boys he would see them later and walked back to the car with Kat. "What's your name, handsome?"

"Steven."

"Do you drive, Steven?"

"Of course I do, my car is over there," he said pointing to a Honda Civic across the street. "Nah, Daddy, this is you right here," she said tossing him the keys to her white Audi A6. He looked across the street at his boys and yelled, "Y'all wish y'all was me right now." He laughed, got in the car and drove off.

"So, what's up with you, Kat? You roll up on a nigga, talk about changing my life and tell me your whip is now mine. What do I have to do for this?"

"Let's go to my crib and we will talk about it then."

"Cool, just tell me where I'm going." Steven was a handsome dude, chicks were constantly throwing themselves at him so pussy was never a problem. He didn't know what he was in for, but it wasn't what he expected. During the ride they had small talk. They pulled up to a building about twenty minutes away from where she met him at. They got out the car and went upstairs to her place. She had a studio apartment which she didn't plan on being in for long. She had money for a bigger place, but she didn't want to spend money she was trying to make money. When they got inside she turned the TV on while Steven sat on the couch. "You want a drink?" she asked. "Yeah, what you got?"

"Hennessy."

"I'm good with that, Ma."

"You want something with that?"

"Nah. I'm good with it straight."

"Oh, okay. That's a good thing. I like you already."

"Lol. You ain't seen nothing yet, shorty."

"Neither have you, Daddy." They sat on the couch and started talking while Steven rolled a blunt. "I hope you don't mind," said Kat as she pulled out a mirror from the drawer under the coffee table that had some coke on it. "Nah, shorty, do what you do." Since Steven sold drugs, he was no stranger to some blow. He partook occasionally, never making a habit out of it. She did some lines before putting some on the tip of a card and giving him a bump. "Where you get that from?" Steven was very impressed with the quality of the product. "I got a connect. It's fire, ain't it?"

"You already know it is. Let me get another bump." She hit him again. "You not done rolling that weed up yet?"

"I would've been if you weren't distracting me." They laughed while Steven took a lighter out his pocket and lit the blunt. He had copped an ounce of some Blue Dream from his boy earlier that morning. He couldn't wait to fire it up.

"Come here," said Steven tapping his lap. They were only halfway through the blunt but the Henny and coke had him feeling right. Kat came over and sat on his lap. "Little lady, how you going to change my life." Kat kissed Steven on the lips then on his face as she slipped his shirt over his head. The tattoos on his chest were really turning her on. She hadn't realized it, but this was the first time she actually chose the person she was going to sleep with. She had a chance to get away and start a whole new life and all she was looking for was another daddy. That's all she knew. As she kissed Steven on his chest he started taking loose his belt and unzipping his pants. His dick was hard as a rock right now. She took her jeans and her panties off and straddled him. She started grinding her hips on him as she felt herself getting wet. "Do you have a condom?" she asked. "Yeah, let me get it out my pocket." He put the condom on and she got on top and started riding him. He loved how she took all of him. He usually had a problem getting a girl to ride because of his size. He grabbed her fat ass as she went up and down, cumming over and over again all over his condom. Then he told her to turn around while he was still inside of her. The sight of her ass bouncing up and down turned him on more. He stood up, still inside of her and he bent her over on the couch and grabbed her by her neck while he hit it from the back. After she came a few more times, she told him to put it in her butt. He never had anal sex before, but he wasn't about to question her now. He took his dick out of her pussy and put two fingers inside of her getting them wet. He then took one of the fingers and put it in her ass, then he slid the other one inside. Watching her bounce her ass with his fingers inside of her was turning him on in the worse way. He changed his condom before he eased his rod in her ass. He didn't think she was going to take all of him, but she did. He had to stroke it slow because it felt too good and he wasn't ready to cum yet. But Kat took over and started backing that ass up. It was over after that. Steven came within a matter of minutes and Kat came right along with him. That was the best nut he ever had although he would never tell her that. He took the condom off and threw it on the floor as he laid across the couch. He slapped her ass as she walked to the bathroom to clean herself up. She came back with a hot washcloth and wiped him down. He was surprised at how good that felt too. Maybe it was the cocaine in his system, but he was still horny. He took another bump and relit the blunt while Kat went and made more drinks. When she came back to the couch she seen Steven sitting there with the blunt in one hand and his dick in the other. "You want some more, Daddy?"

"Nah, I'm trying to see what that mouth do."

"You sure you ready for that? I don't want you falling in love or nothing."

"Bitch, I know you a hoe. Only hoes can take my dick like you just did."

"Let me be your hoe, Daddy," said Kat walking over to Steven. "Shut up and put this dick in your mouth, bitch."

Steven stood up while Kat got her on her knees. He grabbed her hair in his hand as he stroked her mouth. Her mouth was hot and wet. She began to moan while he slid all of his dick in and out her mouth. She had never been aroused by giving oral sex. It was one of the things she did the least but Steven had her bobbing like she was bobbing for apples and she was loving it. Her pussy began to pulsate with every stroke he took. Like he was fucking her pussy and not her mouth. Steven was loving every minute of it. "Suck Daddy big dick. You like how that big, hard dick feel going in and out your mouth? Yeah. You sucking it like you like it. Get that mouth wet for Daddy. Get that mouth fucked," he said while his dick hit the back of her throat. "Where you want this cum at, hoe? You want it down your throat, you nasty bitch?" he said fucking her mouth harder now. "Yes, Daddy," she tried to get out while his dick was quickly going in and out her mouth. The vibrations on his dick made him cum so hard. He had to sit down immediately. "Come suck the rest of this cum out my dick, nasty." Kat still on her knees, crawled over to the couch and sucked the rest of the cum out of his dick. Right then Steven realized what she wanted. He knew a few people who was about that life and he seen the kind of bread they were making. *She is about to change my life,* he thought while looking at her mouth on his dick. "Clean my dick off." Kat got up, went to the bathroom and got a rag nice and hot for him. Watching her fat ass walk away, all Steven thought about was how rich this bitch was about to make him. She came back in the living room to see Steven smiling at her. "What you smiling at, Daddy?" she asked while washing his dick and balls with the hot rag. "I was sitting here thinking about how you going to change my life."

"Does that mean you in? You going to be my daddy?"

"Kat, I'm not even going to hold you, Ma, I've never done that before."

"I know, Daddy. That's why I chose you. I'm going to teach you everything I know. Just make me one promise."

"What's that?"

"You have to always keep me first. I don't care how many bitches come after me, I have to be number one."

"You got it, love. Now kiss my dick." After she kissed his dick, she was ready for round three.

Kat went to the kitchen for more drinks. This time she just brought the bottle back with her. She put it on the table in front of the couch then walked over to the dresser by the bed and got some massage oil. Steven was laying on the couch rolling another blunt up, watching Kat walking back and forth. *Why this white girl got so much ass?* he thought to himself. "Wait, don't roll that up yet. Let's add this White Widow to it."

"Bring your ass then." Steven already knew what that White Widow was hitting for. He knew they was about to be fucked up. Five hours had already passed and Steven had no intentions on leaving any time soon. This was all in Kat's plan. She knew she would have to get this nigga open off of her and make him know why she would be his bottom bitch. She did a few more lines while she poured them both more drinks. The drugs and the alcohol had him feeling some way but he knew better than to put his mouth on this bitch. He almost called his homegirl over but that thought quickly went away when he remembered the bigger picture. Getting this paper. He took a couple of bumps before taking a swig of his drink. "Why don't you put something sexy on and dance for Daddy," said Steven while he lit the blunt. He took two pulls before passing. "Yo, this shit right here, though." Kat took a pull and started coughing, then they both laughed. She passed Steven back the blunt, kissed him on the cheek then walked over to her closet to see what she was about to put on for him.

Steven took some more bumps while he watched her look at outfit after outfit. Then she went in her top drawer and pulled out something black. That's all he could see from where he was sitting on the couch. Kat was looking for the perfect outfit to put on. Everything in her closet had too much material for what she was trying to do right now. She went in her top drawer and pulled out her black fishnet bodysuit. It looked more like a fishnet bikini with material down the front and back to make it a one-piece outfit. Steven's rod started to rise looking at her get all that ass in that outfit. Then when she put on the toe-out lace-up pumps, he was at full attention. She walked around the apartment turning on all the lamps. Two of the lamps were illuminating blue fluorescent lighting and the other two with purple lights. She then walked over by the front door and turned off the lights. She walked over to the stereo and put on her Adina Howard CD. It wasn't long before T-shirt and panties began to blare from her speakers. She walked over to Steven and downed the rest of the liquor she had in her glass. Took a couple of bumps and a few pulls and began to dance for him. She moved her body from side to side while she began touching on herself. The loud music and the lights had Steven feeling like he was really in the strip club right now. The only thing that was missing was the pole. Kat sat on the table in front of Steven and opened her legs wide. She then lifted one leg up on the table and arched her back. She took two fingers from her right hand and put them in and out her mouth before rubbing them over clit. While she did that she rubbed and grabbed her nipples with her left hand. Steven started stroking his now fully erect penis watching Kat make herself cum. He had never been with a woman like this before. For a quick second he remembered just being on the corner with his boys and now he was in a sexual fantasy that seemed never-ending. After watching her cum for the second time he walked over to her on the table. He stood in between her legs and rubbed the head of his dick up and down her clit until she came again. After she came, he walked over to her face and started hitting her in the face with his big, hard dick. "You like that, don't you, bitch. You like this big cock all over your body. Put this dick in your mouth now." Kat opened wide while Steven stood over her dipping his rod in and out of her mouth. She loved how his balls kept rubbing against her nose every time he came down. After a few minutes of that he took her hand and walked her over to the couch. He sat up but Kat told him to lay back. She went and got the coke and put some on his dick and on his balls. She licked all the coke off his dick before she began sucking it off his balls. Once it was all off, she lifted up his balls and slid her tongue from the area under his balls to the crack of his ass. Normally Steven wouldn't have let this happen but right now, it just felt to good. Before he knew it, Kats tongue was going in and out his ass and he was about to cum. He grabbed her head up and shot his cum all over her face. He beat her face with his dick until all his cum was out. Then she kissed his dick before getting up and going to the bathroom. *I could definitely get used to this,* she thought as she walked to the bathroom. Steven sat on the couch, fucked up, not thinking about anything right now. He was faded.

While Steven played around on his phone, Kat cleaned up. When she looked at her clock it was three in the morning. It was way too late to order take out, so she made some sandwiches. "Daddy. You want ham or turkey?"

"Give me ham."

"You eat lettuce and tomatoes?"

"No tomatoes. Put some mustard and mayonnaise on it."

"I got you, Daddy." The first thing Steven did when he picked up his phone was text his mom. He knew she worried about him, so he made it his business to keep her from worrying. He didn't believe how late it was. It was about three or four when Kat pulled him away from the store and now his clock is reading three twenty-two. *Damn, today was a good day,* he thought to himself while Kat was asking him what he wanted on his sandwich. She thought this would be the perfect time to have her conversation with him. She served him his sandwich on a plate along with a nice glass of ice water. She figured after all the drinks and drugs they had earlier, he could use some water. Steven knew he would get used to this lifestyle quickly. He quickly had a vision of many hoes at his beckon call. He ate his sandwich and listened to Kat talk. The next day he moved out of his parents' house and in with Kat. That's when his new life began.

Over the next year Kat taught Steven everything she knew. She had also gotten new prospects. Among the first of the girls to come was Dream. So, it was only right that she thought she would have Steven's heart once Kat was gone. After Dream came Light, Flawless, Casey, Karen and Dawne. Over the next ten years this team had become a family. Especially when Kat died two years ago from an overdose. Steven seen her getting out of control, so he took her off the street and put her back in the studio apartment he met her in. Even though they had moved out of there years ago, he didn't want to get rid of the place where it all started. That day Kat told him she would change his life he had no idea of all the money he was about to see. Because she was a white girl she was catching a rack from one date.

Some nights double or triple that depending on the appetite of the patron. The first week Steven left home he counted ten thousand dollars. That was after the splurge. Once he got used to the income, he stopped spending so much of it on bullshit. Kat also would bring the other girls on her dates. She had no problem sharing, that meant less work for her. She got all the girls her same deal, for every thousand they made they kept a hundred. Since all of these girls, all except Dream, came from pimps who didn't give them shit, they were cool with this arrangement. This was Dream's first time on the stroll. Kat met her at club one night. She knew she was young as hell, but her body was saying something else. At the tender age of sixteen Dream became the first of many. Since she was the baby of the group everyone looked out for her. Steven made sure he had a go at her before she got turned over to the wolves. Dream would be the only girl besides Kat who he would fuck. He would get head from any of them on any given day but he made it his business to not have them open off him. He took everything that Kat taught him and combined it with his entrepreneur skills. Within ten years Steven was a very successful business owner. He used the money that Kat had saved up and him and his brother Calvin went into business together and opened up 'The Spot.'

'The Spot' started off as an exclusive place where only the high rollers would come to. You paid for your stay by the hour and every plate was a hundred dollars, regardless of what was on it. Steven knew the perfect people to hire, his girls. Now that he employed them in the daytime he defaulted on their original agreement of a hundred off every thousand, now he took it all. There were many back rooms in 'The Spot,' which were also rented by the hour. One day Calvin brought the idea up to open the basement up and make it a strip club. Steven gave it the green light as long as Calvin managed it. Steven was making more money in a night than he could've ever imagined. He had the girls staying at loft in Brooklyn and he brought a house in long island. He wanted to get away from the city life. After going into his second prominent year as a business owner he now wanted someone he could share his money with. He was ready for a family.

Steven always kept in touch with his family. Him and his mom had a bond that would never be broken. Although, he always wondered how his birth Mom would've reacted to his success, his mom never fell short in letting him know that she was proud of him and how she knew that he would get himself together and do something with his life. One day his mom called him, inviting him to church as she would do. He told her the same thing he always did, that he would try and make it. Mrs. Thompson made it her business to check on all of her children at least once a week. She and her husband were very proud of the children they raised. A year after Steven and Calvin opened up 'The Spot,' they decided on buying their parents a new house, but the Thompsons didn't want that. That's when the two sons decided to build them a third floor which now housed two rooms. One room had a gym for Mom and the other room had a hot tub for Dad. They also remodeled the original two floors. With brand-new paint to the whole house, new carpeting and new furniture. That was enough to make both parents very happy.

Mrs. Thompson couldn't have been more proud of her boys. She just wished she could get them to come to church more often. Aleese was the only one who still went regularly. At the age of twenty-nine, she still lived at home with her parents. After getting a degree in criminal justice, her mom got her a job at the firm she would soon retire from. During the remodeling of the house, Aleese had her brothers remodel the second floor. They took away the third and fourth bedrooms. Which now gave Aleese and her parents bigger bedrooms. The rooms were now connected by an adjoining bathroom which Aleese designed herself. Since her parents already had a bathroom in their room this would pretty much be her bathroom and she made sure it was as luxurious as it could be. Her brothers made sure to always keep her focused in school and away from their extracurricular activities. They were very proud of her accomplishments and even more proud that she didn't end up like a lot of the girls she went to school with. The fact that Aleese seen so many of her friends pregnant before they finished high school made her more determined to succeed for them. She wanted to be their example. She didn't have any intentions on ever having children. She liked being selfish. Not having to look after anybody, just being free to pick up and go whenever she wanted to. She was doing better financially than most people her age. She had a great salary and no rent to pay, now that she had her room remodeled, she really wasn't planning on leaving home.

Knowing how much the boys would listen to their little sister, Mrs. Thompson figured she could get Aleese to get them to come to church. She had Aleese call them and tell them that the church was honoring their Mom on the following Sunday and how surprised she would be if they came. It worked like a charm. The next Sunday Mrs. Thompson was the happiest she had been in a long time. When she seen both her boys walk in looking like they stepped out of a magazine she poked her chest out. She seen all the young ladies looking at them as they took their seat next to her. She had some handsome boys and she knew it. Yes, even though they were now thirty-four, they were still and would always be her boys. While church was going on Steven and Calvin were surprised to see a couple of faces that they seen in their club. While they were pointing people out, that's when Steven seen her. The woman that he would make his wife. She was the most beautiful person he had ever laid his eyes on. He knew he had to have her. As soon as church was over he went looking for her, but he couldn't find her. He didn't mean to be rude to the people who were trying to talk to him, but he was only interested in finding this mystery lady. One thing was for sure, he would be coming back to church until he found out who she was.

The family went back to the house for Sunday dinner. Mrs. Thompson knew they would be ready to eat so she started preparing dinner the night before. She made some BBQ ribs, baked ham, macaroni and cheese, sweet potatoes, collard greens, cornbread and some chocolate cake, which was Calvin's favorite. Mrs. Thompson couldn't believe she finally had her family together around the table. It felt just like old times. These were the moments she looked forward to now. "So, when one of y'all children going to give your mama some grand-babies?" They all started laughing. Aleese was the first one to respond, "Don't look over here, Mama."

"Aleese, do you even like mens? I don't think I've ever seen you with a man." Steven and Calvin bust out laughing while pointing to Aleese like two little school children. "Mama, how you going to ask me that? You know I was going out with Shaun in college."

"Aleese, you haven't been in college in five years. I haven't seen you with anybody since you been home, baby."

"I've been dating, Ma. Just haven't met anyone worth bringing home to meet you."

"Okay, baby. Y'all two over there laughing. I haven't seen y'all bring anybody home yet either." Steven replies, "Well, Ma, I may be bringing someone home soon. I seen somebody at church today that I would like to get to know."

"Well, look at God," said Mrs. Thompson. "See what happens when you come to church." Aleese interjects, "I gotta hear this. Who was you looking at, Mr. Thompson?"

"I don't know what her name was. She had on the black skirt with a black and white shirt and her butt was like, pow." Aleese started laughing. "You know how many people had on white and black today with a butt like pow?"

"You gotta do better than that, bro."

"I will be back next Sunday. I will have her name and her number this time next week. I got this, little sis," said Steven while rubbing his hand in Aleese's hair. She pushed his hand away. "Get outta her messing up my hair. Better yet, you should give your little sister some money so I can get my hair done."

"You spoiled, you know that," said Steven, while throwing a hun-dred-dollar bill at his sister. "Thanks, big bro," said Aleese sliding the money in her top. "You mighty quiet over there, Calvin. I know you don't think I forgot about you."

"No, Ma. I didn't think that. I was just chopping it up with Pops for a minute. How you been enjoying your workout room, Mama?"

"I love the workout room, son. Me and your father spend more time in the hot tub than anywhere else." Everyone started laughing. "That's too much information, Ma."

"Well, we older. We not dead. We still like to get nasty."

"NOOOO!!!! Make it stop," said Aleese. "Yeah, so I'm about to go now," said Steven. "Oh, so now you want to leave when your parents are talking about being freaks, right?"

"Yep. I'm out of here. Mama, this is for you," said Steven putting an envelope in her hand and giving her a kiss before making him a plate to take home.

Mrs. Thompson had become used to Steven coming and giving her money. What he didn't know was that she saved everything that he has given her over the years. She called it her rainy day stash. Let's just say if it did rain, Mama would be okay for a few years. She walked into the kitchen. "Go in there and talk to your father while I make this plate for you." Steven picked up a piece of ham out of the pan, said, "Thank you, Mama," then went to join his father and brother on the couch who were now watching a football game. "Who's playing, Pop?"

"Jets and the Colts."

"This should be a good game," said Calvin. "Yes, it should. So why y'all don't come by and visit your old man more?" Steven replies, "First of all, you ain't old, Pops. From the sound of it, you and Mama be pretty busy." They all started laughing. "Well, you know, that's one of the best things about having the house to ourselves. Well, the third floor at least," replied Mr. Thompson while raising his Heineken in the air. "You know your sister ain't never leaving." Calvin replied, "I'm kind of happy she here with you two. That's why I don't come around so much. I hit up Aleese every day and check on y'all. Don't ever think we not checking, Pops." Mr. Thompson had no idea his boys did that. It touched him right in his heart. "Well, just come by more often and see your mama. And please, one of you, give her some grandkids already!!" Just then Mrs. Thompson came in the living room with Steven's plate. "Here you go, son. You have enough food for two days. I know you don't have anyone cooking for you, so you're welcome to come by here anytime and get you a homecooked meal. You know I still cook every day."

"I will keep that in mind, Mama. I love you," he said before giving his mom a kiss. "I will check you later, Pops," he said before kissing his dad on the forehead. "Alright, son. Don't forget what I said." Calvin stood up to give him a hug, "Alright, bro, see you tonight at work."

"Lata, Steve."

Chapter 4

Five months had now gone by since the dreadful night and Steven was ready to have sex with his lady. Of course, he's been having sex, he was just tired of wearing a condom. He had been trying to wait for Diamond to let him know that she was ready, but it didn't look like it was happening. So, Steven decided to plan a special night for his lady. Since he wanted everything to be perfect he decided to do everything at home. He figured if it was just the two of them alone, there would be no way he could mess the night up. Since Diamond has been driving, she has been spending a lot of time outside of the house. Which gave Steven time to get things together. He even called Ms. Wallace the day of his special night so she could keep Diamond held up for a while. Ms. Wallace could see that something was going on between her happy couple, but she couldn't put her finger on it. She was more than happy to see that her favorite guy was once again doing something special for her daughter. It was her who got the couple together. She had such high hopes for the two. She too was waiting for some grandkids. Diamond was now twenty-five and not getting any younger.

Ms. Wallace still remembered the day she saw Steven and his brother walk into the church to sit with their mother. She couldn't wait until church was over so she could go and play matchmaker. She was one of the first ones who came to greet Mrs. Thompson when church was over. "Hey, Diane. How are you on this blessed day?" she asked while giving her a hug. "I'm doing just fine, Ms. Julie. What have you been up to?" asked Mrs. Thompson returning the hug. "Well, you know I'm not one to beat around the bush. Your son. Is he single?" Mrs. Thompson started blushing. "Well, Julia, I do hope you aren't having any freaky thoughts about my baby." The two ladies started laughing. "Diane, you know you play too much. Once Mr. Wallace went home to be with the Lord, that was it for me. Now my beautiful daughter Diamond would be perfect for him."

"I thought she was still with that guy."

"No. They been broken up for months now. I'm trying to get her back out there. I haven't seen your boys in years. They sure grew up to be some handsome men."

"Thanks, Julia. Steven is single. I will put in a good word for her."

"I do appreciate it. I tried to be the first one to get to you," said Ms. Wallace as Sis. Glenn started walking in their direction. The two ladies shared a laugh before kissing each other and going their separate directions.

That day after church Diamond and her mother went home and had dinner like they have every Sunday since Diamond broke up with Charlie. Ms. Wallace had made some baked turkey wings, white rice, string beans, yams and cornbread. Diamond sat at the table while her mom put the food out. While going from the kitchen to the dining room she started a conversation. "So, Diamond, did you see Mrs. Thompsons son come in the church today?"

"Yes, Ma. There were two of them."

"Well, I'm talking about the tall, dark and handsome son."

"I saw him."

"And, what did you think, baby?"

"He was okay, Ma."

"He was okay! Girl, is something wrong with your eyes? That man was more than okay." Diamond laughed. "Okay. He was a handsome man."

"Now that sounds more like it. I spoke to Diane about getting y'all together."

"Mommy, I know you didn't do that."

"Yes, little girl, I did. Did you see that man? He is tall, black and handsome and he got himself together. That man looks like money."

"And what have you always told me? His money is not my money."

"Yes, baby. I did tell you that. All I meant was that he looks like he will be a great provider for you. I wouldn't have to worry about you. That's all I want is for you to meet a nice guy who will treat you like your daddy used to treat me."

"Aww, Ma. I don't know if I will ever find what you and Daddy had. I don't think they make men anymore like Daddy."

"Now that's a lie. Steven's dad, Joe, he is a good man. I'm sure the apple doesn't fall far from the tree." Diamond was now ready to eat and was getting very tired with this conversation.

"You're at the table now. Can we eat?"

"Yes, greedy. Since you're in such a rush to eat, you say grace." Diamond closed her eyes and began to pray. "Lord, we thank you for this food you have provided us with. Bless this food and the hands that prepared it. Amen."

"Girl, your prayers are getting shorter by the day."

"Ma, you know I just broke up with Charlie. Why are you rushing me to be with someone else?"

"You and Charlie broke up six months ago, Diamond. How long do you plan on moping around this house? That man is out living his life and you sitting here miserable. You have to get it together. You are way too beautiful to keep spending weekends at home in your room. Get it together, Dee-Dee." Diamond despised these conversations with her mother. Charlie really hurt her, and she couldn't understand why her mom didn't see that. A new man is the last thing on her mind right now. After what happened with her and Charlie, she didn't know if she would ever date again. "I hear you, Ma. I'm just not ready yet. Do you mind if I excuse myself," said Diamond as she left the table. Ms. Wallace couldn't wait for her daughter to get over this guy. She told Diamond when she first met him that he wasn't the right one. She couldn't help it that she was right.

Diamond went upstairs and laid across her bed. She turned the radio up loud so her mother wouldn't hear her crying. She had been trying to get over Charlie, but it's been hard. Her and Charlie were together for three years. She thought he would be the person she spent the rest of her life with. To her, they had the perfect relationship. They had met one day at her job. She was working at Victoria's Secret at the time. At first, she thought he just like to buy his lady nice things from the store, but when she saw he was showing up twice a week she figured it had to be more than that. One day he finally asked her out and the two were inseparable ever since. Over the last six months of their relationship Diamond started to feel something changing. All of a sudden Charlie was always busy and no longer had time for her. After two weekends of trying to get in touch with Charlie, she decided to go to his place.

She used her key that she was given years ago. She immediately heard sexual noise coming from his bedroom. She went back outside while she got her mind together and decided what she was about to do. She was hurt and couldn't stop the tears from coming down her eyes, but she wanted answers. She couldn't just let this go. She went back in the house and walked straight to his bedroom and opened the door. "So, this how you going to treat me after all these years? Who the hell is this, Charlie?" Charlie couldn't believe this was happening. He knew once Pam came into town he should've gotten that key back from Diamond. Pam was now putting clothes on while yelling at Charlie. "Who the fuck is this busting in our house, Charles?"

"Charles? Your house? Charlie, you better say something now," said Diamond. "Charles, what's going on?"

"Everybody just relax," said Charlie. "You been acting strange for months now and I come here to find this woman in your bed. You have two seconds to start talking." Pam looked at Diamond and said, "This woman is his wife. Now who the hell are you?"

"Wife?"

"Yes. His wife that has his two children who will be here at the end of summer." Charlie putting his clothes on said, "Diamond, I'm sorry. I wanted to tell you. I just couldn't find the words. She just popped up."

"She just popped up. You have a whole wife, Charlie. Three years, Charlie. Three fucking years I gave you. I don't ever want to see you again," said Diamond as she threw his key at him and left the house. She didn't want to give him the satisfaction of seeing her crying, so she left the house as fast as she could.

Diamond got in her car and pulled off as fast as she could while the tears flowed from her eyes. *How could I be so stupid?* she thought to herself. She pulled up on the next corner because she could no longer see from all the crying she was doing. Just a few months ago they were talking about marriage and having a kid of their own and today she meets his wife who already has his children. How could this happen to her? She didn't know who she could call since she didn't have friends. This was something she definitely didn't want to talk about with her mother, but it looks like she didn't have a choice.

"So, this is what you came to New York for? To hook up with some girl while I stayed down South taking care of your children. I knew your ass was trifling. That's why I was sleeping with Tony and Kevin and your boy Chuckie. Poor little girl. Trusting your lying ass." Charles flew across the room. "What your hoe ass just say?" he asked with his hand around her throat. "What you just say to me?" Pam wanted to talk, but his grip was too tight. All she could do was gag. "I just lost the best thing that happened to me because of your ass. If

I wasn't married to you I would've been married that poor little girl," said Charlie before letting her neck go. "I fucking hate you. Get out of my house."

"Charles, where am I supposed to go?"

"Take your hoe ass back down South. Matter fact, I'm going to be down there in a couple of weeks. I want a paternity test and a divorce."

"Ain't this some bullshit. It was all good for you to do me dirty, but you don't like it done to you. I'm out of here." Pam knew her husband. She knew that she overstepped, but she was hurt too. She came to see her man, who she hadn't seen in years and this happens. Here she is in the bed with her husband and some girl comes in with a key and she's the one who is now in the dog house and getting kicked out.

Charlie was so upset right now. He really did love Diamond. He wanted to tell her about Pam and the kids, but he didn't want to hurt her. Diamond really was the best thing that ever happened to him. She gave him a whole new outlook on life. She made him want more and strive to get more. When he met Diamond, it was at a bad time in his life. He had originally moved to New York because his dad was sick, and he wanted to be with him in his last days. His Dad left him the house that he now lived in. Pam had tried to come with him when he left, but he never really wanted her. At fifteen Pam got pregnant. Since Charles' mom was such a pillar in the community, she couldn't dare let her son get someone pregnant and not make an honest woman out of them. So, she made him marry her before the baby was born. Pam moved in with Charles and his mom after they were married. His mother wanted to make sure that they both finished school and she didn't dare trust anyone else with her new grandbaby. Three years later Pam was pregnant again. Charles was a handsome, intelligent, young man who was no stranger to the ladies. Two years after being married, he wasn't even interested in Pam anymore. He remained a good father, but he stopped having sex with her regularly.

So, when she got pregnant the second time, he questioned it and questioned her. When the baby came out he definitely became skeptical. He knew that wasn't his kid, but his mother wasn't trying to hear it. After Charles graduated, he moved out, leaving Pam and the kids with his mom. He would come by to see them on the weekends but that was all.

After a couple of years Charles decided to try and make it work with his wife. They stayed in his place for a couple of years before his dad got sick. Once his dad got sick, Charles came straight to New York. For four years Charles blew Pam off every time she asked when he was coming back. Last year he finally told her he was moving to New York. She took that as her and the kids were also moving to New York since they were living together when he left. So, when she called him from the airport to tell him to come get her, what could he really do. He walked back towards the room where he heard Pam going off. "Yo, you don't have your stuff together yet? All you came here with is a bag."

"Why are you doing this to us, Charles? You know me and your kids love you."

"It's just not what I want, Pam. I never loved you. I tried to make it work, but that was really for my mom. You know I would've never married you if I had a choice. When I get dressed, be ready to go. Be happy I'm not ready to go to jail behind that slick shit you said earlier."

"I didn't mean it, Charles. I was just angry."

"Nah, B, you meant that. Knowing I already thought little C wasn't mine. Is that Chuck's kid? Don't start looking sad now."

"Whatever, Charles. You don't have to take me anywhere and no. Little C isn't yours." Why did she say that, next thing she knew she was getting up off the floor. "Go wipe the blood off your face and get out my house. You will never see me again." Pam walked to the bathroom. She cleaned herself up, Googled a cab number and headed back to the airport knowing her and Charles were really done this time.

The first thing Charles did when Pam left was roll up a spliff. He was so disappointed in himself for letting Pam get him so angry. Pam was the only girl he ever had to put his hands on. He hated how she was just so disrespectful out of her mouth. *Did she really think she could just say whatever she wanted to say to me and I would just take it,* thought Charlie. Right now, all he wanted was to have Diamond back. He thought of what he should've done and how things may have been different right now if he had done them. He didn't know why he didn't just tell Pam about Diamond. Why did he feel the need to lie and lead this double life, when he knew he had found the woman who should've been his wife and the mother of his children? *How could I be so stupid?* While smoking, he kept trying to call Diamond.

An hour had passed since Diamond left his house and he couldn't imagine what she was dealing with right now. After calling her for thirty minutes straight, he decided to have a couple of drinks. It was a little after twelve in the afternoon and he was now twisted. That's when the voicemails started. "You reached Diamond. If you're listening to this, I'm probably busy right now. Leave a message and I might get back to you. Lata." Beep. "Hey, D, I just want you to know how sorry I am. Call me back."

"Hey, baby. You know I love you, right? You are the most important person in my life and I would never want to hurt you. Please call me back."

"Diamond. My world revolves around you. I can't breathe without you. I certainly don't want to live without you. Can you please just call me back so I can explain what happened? I don't love her, D. It's only you I want. Baby, just call me back."

"Are you okay, baby? Please, just call me back so I know that you are okay. I'm worried about you." The last message he left was their favorite song off the ShaRae album, "Love at First Sight." "Baby, you know it's been about us since we met. I never knew love until I met you. I never wanted to be with someone as much as you. I fucked up,

D, and I'm sorry about that. I need you in my life, baby. You made me a better man. Nobody else but you. Please let me make this up to you. Call me back, love." After about an hour Charlie got in the shower and decided he was going to find his woman. He knew a couple of spots that Diamond liked to go to. He was hoping he would find her there. He had to get her back.

Diamond sat on that corner for what felt like hours. She always thought of herself as a strongminded female who was able to sift through deception. How could she be so wrong? She knew this man loved her. From the way he held her, the way touched her, the way he did little things to make her feel special. Every Sunday they would spend the day together. When the weather was nice, he would take her on a picnic at various parks. They would take trips to the botanical gardens, admiring the different flowers and enjoying the beautiful scenery. He wrote her poetry and cooked her dinner. He gave her massages and rubbed her feet. Nothing compared to when he would hold her from behind and talk about their future together. Just thinking about all of this made her angry. She smoked the blunt she had planned on smoking with him when she got to the house. She knew this would be the only way she could calm herself down. *How could I be so naïve?* she thought to herself. She reached for her pocketbook and was very surprised to see so many missed calls and voicemails from Charlie. At first, she threw the phone because she was still emotional. Then she became curious about what he had to say.

After listening to the last message, she was more confused than ever. *So, I wasn't bugging, he really does love me. What do I do? Do I take him back? Do I let him explain? What am I talking about. I just caught him in bed with another woman. I think I should let him explain.* Her thoughts were interrupted by the phone vibrating in her hand. It was Charlie calling again. "Hi, Charlie," she managed to get out. "Diamond, I've been so worried about you. Where are you, babe? I need to tell you what happened." As happy as Diamond was right now, she was also sad and so very confused. "Diamond, are you there?"

"I'm here, Charlie. I'm only a couple of blocks away from you. I just needed a minute to get my mind right."

"Come back to me, baby. I need you."

"I'm on my way, Charlie." *What am I doing?* thought Diamond as she made a U-turn and headed back to his house.

Charlie had just gotten out of the shower and got dressed when he called Diamond. He had every intention in going to find her. To his surprise he didn't have to try as hard as he thought. He called Diamond again, looking forward to hearing her voice again on the answering machine. The joy that filled his heart when she picked up the phone. He could tell immediately that she had been crying from her voice. Once she said she was on her way, he started rolling up. He knew weed wouldn't change what had happened, but it would make the environment serene. Right now, he just needed things to be as peaceful as possible. The fact that she was even willing to talk to him made him feel hopeful about the upcoming moments. He had no idea how to start this conversation. He just wanted to remain hopeful that he still had a chance to get her back. *I can tell her how much I love her. No. I can ask her to marry to me. No, too soon for that. I guess I could.* His thoughts were interrupted by the doorbell. That's when he remembered she through her key back at him.

He ran to the door to let Diamond inside. As soon as he closed the door, he fell to his knees in front of her and started crying. "Baby, I'm so sorry. I never meant for this to happen. I've never loved anyone like I love you. I can't live without you. Please don't make me live without you." Charlie was now on his knees holding on to Diamond by the waist. Diamond just looked down on him as the tears fell out of her eyes. "Get up, Charlie."

"Dee, I'm sorry."

"You are a sorry-ass nigga, Charlie. I agreed to hear you out, so get up and let's talk." Charlie wasn't used to Diamond being cold to him. He knew she was hurt and he had to make it up to her. He knew there was one thing he could do that she couldn't resist. He started to undo her belt. "Charlie, I didn't come here for this," said Diamond. When he seen she didn't pull away he turned her around so her back was against the back of the couch and pulled her pants all the way down. "Charlie, what are you doing?" said Diamond, only talking, not resisting. "I'm saying sorry, baby," said Charlie while spreading her legs apart now kissing on her second set of lips. Diamond knew she was in a compromised position. Nobody ate pussy like he did, and she was not about to stop him. As she looked down on him, she grabbed his head while his tongue rubbed across her clit in between him kissing and sucking on her lips. "Fuck my face, baby." Diamond loved when Charlie rubbed his face in her pussy. It was something about his nose bone hitting her clit that made her cum every time. Charlie loved how Diamond didn't have an odor. He could and has eaten her out for hours. He loved to please her, and he loved it even more how she responded to him pleasing her. It had only been about twenty minutes when he felt her legs shaking while experiencing her third orgasm. He was going in for the kill, not planning on stopping until she told him to. "Wrap your legs around my neck, baby." Diamond had no idea what he was about to do, but right now she didn't really care. Charlie was doing what he does best. Before she knew it, he was standing up, now walking to his second bedroom, never missing a beat as he was still making her cum.

Charlie knew better than to take her to his room after everything that happened earlier. "How you doing up there?" asked Charlie, never taking his mouth off of her. The vibration from his voice felt good on her. "Make me cum, Charlie." That's all he needed to hear. He got back on his knees and laid her on the edge of the bed and spread her legs apart while he let his long, thick tongue go in and out her Pleasure Palace. Just as she was about to cum, he stroked her placing two fingers inside of her while he sucked on her clit. Diamond tapped out after that one. Charlie knew she was done when he stopped, and she was still shaking. There were only two other times he had her like this. He began to kiss on her lips again, watching her body shake with every kiss. He wanted to hear her say stop. Instead she said, "Did you eat your wife's pussy like that this morning?" He couldn't believe she just asked him that. "Diamond, you are the only woman I have ever put my mouth on. If you're ready to listen, I'm ready to talk." The fact that Charlie didn't know what he was doing the first time he gave her oral sex, made her remember that she had to teach him what to do. "Not now. Let me take a nap first." This was the first time Diamond had been in his house and not in his room, but after what happened, she didn't know if she would ever go back in there again. Charlie got up, picked her up, pulled the covers back, then laid her in the bed. "Charlie, where are you going?" asked Diamond when he didn't get in the bed with her. "I'm going to wash my face, babe. I know you got me looking like a glazed doughnut right now. I'll be right back, my love," he said, before kissing her on the forehead.

Charlie went in the bathroom and turned on the hot water. He looked in the mirror and laughed, looking at his ladies cum all over his face. He really did look like a glazed doughnut. While looking in the mirror he also seen that his lip was busted. *Damn. She fucked my mouth so hard she bust my lip,* he thought. He didn't care. The only thing that mattered to him was that she was there. He still had his first love. He knew he would have to do more than give her special attention to make things right and he planned on doing that. He wanted to make her a nice dinner and tell her the absolute truth about Pam. In three years this was the first time he messed up. If she loved him like she said she did, there is no way she wouldn't take him back. This is what he told himself. After washing his face, he went in the room to check on Diamond. She was knocked out and snoring. He felt accomplished while he took out his phone and recorded her. "This is the love of my life who swears she doesn't snore," he laughed while recording her sleeping then gave her a kiss before he hit the stop button. He thought this would make her smile tonight during dinner.

What a day this has been, thought Charlie as he took a seat on the couch. He turned on the cooking channel while he sparked up his spliff. "What's cooking today, Chef?" he said, talking to the TV. The chef had a seafood special going on. Shrimp, lobsters, and crabs. It looked great but after a day like today he didn't really feel like cooking. So, he thought it would be best to just order some take out. He would've just taken her out it this was a regular day, but today was far from a regular day. Since he wasn't going to cook anymore, he decided to go lay down with his baby. He finished his spliff and walked to the bedroom. When he got inside, he just looked at Diamond for a minute before getting in the bed with her. He thought about how beautiful she looked sleeping and how stupid he was for what he did. He pulled the covers back and got in the bed, holding her from behind. He held her tighter than he ever did before. He whispered in her ear, "I love you, Dee," and fell asleep.

Diamond woke up to Charlie staring at her. "You know I'm still mad at you, right? Don't think just because you put me to sleep means that I'm just supposed to forget today."

"Give me a kiss, beautiful."

"Nope. I'm not kissing you," Diamond said with a smile. "You going to make me beg for it, babe?"

"Yep."

"I'm ready to talk, if you ready to listen."

"I'm here, right? That means against my better judgement, I thought it would only be right to hear what you had to say." Charlie went on to explain the whole story to Diamond. From when he first got Pam pregnant, to the marriage, to what happened today. Even though none of it condoned what happened this morning, she didn't feel as betrayed. "You know you could've just told me this a long time ago. Since you didn't, and you decided to bring her here and sleep with her, what do you think I should do? There has to be some type of recourse."

"Babe, I didn't bring her here."

"But you did know that she was coming."

"Yes, I knew she was coming."

"And instead of you telling me the situation, you decide to start ignoring my calls and let her ass come anyway."

"You are absolutely right, Diamond. I should've told you and I'm sorry I didn't. I never loved her. I don't know what I was doing, but I promise you she will never be back here. I made it very clear that I will be going down there to get a divorce and a paternity test for our second child."

"Is that right?"

"Yes, Diamond. I want to marry you. I want you to be my wife and the mother of my children."

"You see, Charlie, the thing right now that's stopping me from being happy about this moment, is that I no longer trust you. I would've understood. I could've dealt with the truth, but you didn't want to tell me the truth. I had to walk in on it and find out for myself. What would've happened if I didn't come through the door? You would've kept lying to me?"

"Diamond, what I did was selfish and inconsiderate. It doesn't change how I feel about you. If you didn't walk through the door, Pam would still be here right now," he said with his head hung low. "At least you're being honest now. I don't know if I can get past this. You know how I feel about honesty. I told you when we met that there were three things I required of you. Your love, your time and your honesty. Without trust, there is no us." Diamond laid her head back on the pillow as she felt the tears begin to come. "Why you had to fuck her, Charlie?" Charlie pulled Diamond to him, so her head was in his chest. "I'm so sorry, Diamond. If I could take it back I would." Diamond just cried. She didn't know if she would be able to get past this. Charlie was now crying silently, holding Diamond. He now feared that this might be the last time he had the opportunity.

In Charlie's mind, this whole scenario played out differently. He thought once he told Diamond the truth all would be forgiven, and they would just move on. He thought she would see how much he loved her and everything would go back to the way it was before. Charlie didn't have much experience in the relationship department. Besides Pam, this was the only relationship he ever had. He had a lot of sex, but not a lot of relationships. This was one of the reasons why Diamond was the first girl he ever put his mouth on. He just knew for sure once she came over they would be able to work everything out. As he held her to him and cried, he knew that if she left him, he would never again find what he had with her. He's met many women in his lifetime, and none were worth more than what he gave them. Diamond was different. She didn't stress him out about where he is and what he's doing. If he was going out with his friends, she wasn't constantly hitting him up to check on him. She respected his time which made him appreciate her time with him even more. He had a friend with Diamond. They did everything together and could talk about anything. Well almost anything.

"Diamond. I know I messed up, but if you give me another chance I promise to do right by you. Baby, I promise."

"I don't think I can do that. After tonight I don't know if I can see you again." Charlie cried some more as he held her closer. "I don't know if I can live without you, Dee. I don't want to imagine life without you." There were many things that came to Diamond's mind at that moment, but she decided to keep quiet. She didn't believe in second chances. She refused to be like people she knew who had been cheated on. The one thing she learned from them, was that once a cheater, always a cheater. Maybe Charlie could be the exception to the rule, but she wasn't ready to find out. Diamond pulled back from Charlie so she could look him in his eyes. As she looked at his red, teary eyes, she just wanted to tell him everything would be okay, but she couldn't. "Let's just make tonight beautiful. In the morning I'm leaving you. I don't know what may happen in the future, but right now, I just can't do this. So, we are both going to get up out of this bed. I'm hungry, I need to smoke, and I want you to fuck me sleep. I love you, Charlie. More than you know, but the way you had me feeling today, I just can't get past that. Not today at least." Diamond kissed him on the lips and got out of the bed. "I'm about to get in the shower, what's for dinner?" Charlie looked at Diamond and said, "You can have whatever you like." He was heartbroken, but what could he do? It was his own fault.

"Diamond, you okay in there?" asked Ms. Wallace through the door. When Diamond didn't respond, she opened the door to check on her. When she seen Diamond appeared to be sleep, she turned her radio down and went back to what she was doing. Diamond was up, she just didn't feel like talking to her mom. It had been six months since she walked out on Charlie. She left while he was sleep so she wouldn't have to see him cry again. As much as she loved him, she had to let him go. It took a month for him to finally stop calling her every day. He knew Ms. Wallace didn't care to much for him so he didn't go to her house. He didn't know what Diamond had told her and he didn't want to make things worse. Every now and then he would still call, and Diamond would look at the phone and get sad. She didn't just lose her man, she lost a friend, but she knew she was doing the right thing. And now her mom is in her ear talking about another man. That was the last thing she was interested in right now. Yes, Steven was a handsome man, but to her, he was too handsome. Too handsome meant too many women in her eyes. So, she decided at that moment, while lying in the bed that she would not be going to church next Sunday just in case he showed up. She did not appreciate her mom trying to hook her up with this stranger. Yes, he was a sexy stranger, but he was still unknown.

A week had now passed, and Sunday was here again. Knock, knock. "You can come in, Mommy."

"And why are you not up, getting ready for church?"

"I'm not going today, Ma. I don't feel good."

"Oh, you don't feel good. Well, what if God told you he didn't feel good today. That he didn't feel like waking you up today still in your right mind."

"Ma, I'm not up for the sermon today. Just let me know how church goes."

"So, this is what you want to do with your life? You just going to sit around moping over some man like he's the last man alive? Girl, you better get up and get it together. There are more fish in the sea." That was the last thing Ms. Wallace said before walking out of Diamond's room.

Ms. Wallace headed to church prepared to enjoy another wonderful service. She had all intentions on speaking to Diane again today about her son. She had to get her daughter back to the world. Diamond never gave her details on why her and Charlie broke up, but she seen the affect it had on her daughter and she was starting to worry about her. Ms. Wallace was a praying woman, and she believed Steven was the answer to her prayer for her daughter. When Ms. Wallace saw Steven come in today, looking as good as he did last Sunday, she knew she was going to get him. What she didn't know was that Steven was already interested in her daughter. Steven had stopped by his mom's house during the week to get a plate. That's when his mom told her about the conversation she had with Ms. Wallace after church the previous Sunday. Of course Steven asked what did the daughter look like. Once he heard the description, he immediately smiled and said, "Ma, that sounds like the girl I was looking for. You have to introduce me on Sunday."

When church was over, Mrs. Thompson showed Steven who Ms. Wallace was since she didn't see Diamond in church that day. Steven made an introduction on his own. He walked over to Ms. Wallace and said, "How are you on this beautiful day?"

"I'm doing just fine, son. How are you?"

"To be honest, I'm a little sad today. I was expecting to see this beautiful young lady I saw on Sunday, but she's not here. When my mother told me the woman who created my future wife was here, I said all hope isn't lost." Ms. Wallace began blushing. "No, son. All hope isn't lost. My daughter, Diamond, wasn't feeling good today."

"Diamond. A beautiful name for a beautiful girl. I need you to do me a favor, Ms. Wallace. Here's my business card. There are three different numbers for your daughter to reach me on. Tell her I would love to take her out one day. Just as friends, no strings attached." With the biggest smile on her face Ms. Wallace said, "She will definitely be calling you." Steven leaned in to give Ms. Wallace a kiss. "You better be happy I'm not into younger men," she said playfully. Steven smiled back at her and said, "Enjoy the rest of your day. I look forward to hearing from Diamond soon." Then he walked away.

Ms. Wallace couldn't wait to get home to tell Diamond about everything that had happened at church. When she got in, she was happy to see that Diamond was up and moving around. She even had heated up the dinner Ms. Wallace prepared the night before. Ms. Wallace had made a meatloaf, BBQed a pork shoulder, made some mashed potatoes, yellow rice and broccoli with cheese. Since she was home, she took it upon herself to make some cornbread. Diamond knew what time to expect her mother home. Her Sundays were like clockwork. "Well, look at you up and about," said Ms. Wallace after coming inside the house. "Hello to you too, Ma. How was church today?" Ms. Wallace walked in the kitchen and kissed her daughter on the cheek. "Since you in the kitchen, why don't you get the table together. I will change my clothes and we can talk about it while we eat." Ms. Wallace went to change her clothes. By the time she came back Diamond had the table ready. "Since you didn't go to church today, I think it's only right you say the blessings over the food."

"Okay, Ma. Dear God, we would like to thank you for allowing us to have food to eat. We ask you to bless those who are less fortunate, that they too will be blessed with a hot meal. Thank you for allowing us to see another day, as there were some who weren't given that same opportunity. Thank you for my mother, who prepared this meal and bless me, the partaker of this meal. Amen!"

"Look at you, Dee-Dee. That was much better than last Sunday." They both laughed while they began putting food on their plates. "So, how was church today?"

"Church was amazing. Pastor Jenkins preached to us about second chances. I wish you were there to hear it."

"Oh, okay. What else happened? I know there's more."

"Well, baby girl, you won't believe what happened today. It seems like you have an admirer."

"Who is it this time, Ma? It better not be Sis. Johnson son with that big ole' water head." They laughed. "No, baby. It's that handsome, chocolate man I told you about last Sunday."

"Is that right. What exactly did he say?"

"He said he wants to marry you, but he will settle for a friendly date right now." Diamond laughed, thinking her mom was overexaggerating. "You laughing, but I'm serious. Here's his card. He said there are three numbers on here for you to reach him on. He also said he is looking forward to hearing from you very soon." Diamond took the card and looked it over. It was a thick, black card with gold writing on it. She smiled at her mother and said, "Maybe I will call him."

"Yes, Dee-Dee. That's what I'm talking about."

"Ma, you know I have to get back home. Why you ask me to come over today when I told you I was coming tomorrow?"

"I just wanted to see you, baby. I don't see you as much as I used to."

"Mmmm-hmmm. I heard Steven talking to you this morning. What are you two up to?"

"Me, and Steven, up to something? Why would you say a thing like that?"

"Spill it or I'm leaving."

"You always have to ruin the surprise. He's at home planning a special night for the two of you."

"That's all you had to say," said Diamond now taking a seat on the couch. "How is everything going between you two? You don't call me every day like you used to. You don't come to church anymore. You got a job and a car, and you don't know how to act. And why are you working when you have a man with a good job taking care of you?"

"Ma, you know Steven isn't an architect, right?"

"Diamond, of course I know. I knew him and his brother owned a restaurant/lounge."

"So, why you didn't tell me that when you were busy trying to get us together? You told me he was an architect."

"When you looked at the business card what did it say?"

"It said Thompson and Thompson Architects and Designers."

"There you have it. I figured he didn't want you to judge him and think he would be around women all day at work."

"Oh. That's what it was."

"Yes, baby, that's what it was."

"Okay, Ma. How long are you supposed to keep me here?"

"Until he calls me and says to release you."

"You two are a trip, boy." Steven called about an hour later. Diamond gave her mom a kiss. Promised she would come by more often and headed home.

Chapter 5

Diamond was excited when she pulled up to the house. She had no idea what Steven had planned, but she knew he never did anything half assed. She was surprised to see all the lights out through the window. When she unlocked the door and opened it, all she saw was candles lit in a pathway heading to the dining room. She took her shoes off at the door and put on her slippers. It was so quiet. She was wondering where Steven was and what he was up to. "Steven. Where are you?" she said following the trail of candles. "I'm right here, baby." When she got to the dining room there were two vases filled with long white and blue stemmed roses. There were red rose petals all over the floor. He even had her vanilla-scented candles burning. He came over to her and gave her the tightest hug. While holding her he says, "Baby, I know things that I have done haven't been right, but you are my life and I want to make you my wife." At that moment he let her go, dropped down on one knee, reached in his pocket and pulled out a velvet ring box. As soon as Diamond saw him get on one knee she immediately had butterflies in her stomach. She put her hands over her mouth when he opened the box, revealing a Diamond and Sapphire two-carat ring. "Diamond, you are a special lady and I would be a fool not to make you mine. I know things haven't been perfect, but you see I've been making the effort to do better. I spent my whole life looking for you and I never want to be without you." He took the ring out the box, placed it on her finger and said, "Diamond Anyiis Wallace, will you give me the honor of being your husband?" Diamond was crying once he opened the box and she saw the size of that ring. "Yes, Steven. Yes, I will marry you." Steven stood up, picked Diamond up, and spun her around while kissing her. "I'm going to make you the happiest woman in the world."

He put her down and pulled out her chair from the table. "Have a seat, my damey." She smiled, knowing that he got that from one of her favorite movies, *Pootie Tang*. "For dinner I will be serving you, salmon and steak with some wild rice. Would you like to eat now or should I spark this blunt up first?"

"Since you already have it rolled up, let's get lit, Daddy." Now that is the response Steven was looking for. He gets called Daddy on the regular, but it's only special coming from one person. Hearing Daddy let him know he was getting some play tonight. Steven and Diamond walked over to the couch. He turned the TV on and told her to sit back and put her feet in his lap. He lit the blunt and passed it to her. He reached under the coffee table and pulled out the massage oil. He began to rub her feet while he told her how much he missed her. "Baby, I've really been missing you. I've missed your kisses. I've missed the way you used to hold me and rub my head. I've missed how your hot, tight, wet box wraps around my rod squeezing it with every stroke. I've missed putting my face in your pleasure palace making you cum, over and over, and over again. I miss your tongue on my rod, licking me all around as I rise with every touch. I miss how you play with my balls taking them in and out your mouth like this." At that moment, he took her big toe and started sucking it. Taking it in and out his mouth before putting the other four toes in his mouth all at once.

Diamond was dripping at this point. Her and Steven hadn't had sex in six months and she was long overdue. She took her foot out of his mouth and gave him the blunt. "What you doing, babe?"

"Shhhh," said Diamond as she took her pants off and stood in front of him, exposing her beautiful pleasure palace that he was dying to be in again. "You want me, Daddy?" Steven was already hard. He put the blunt down and pulled her up on the couch. Now she was standing over him with her pleasure palace in his mouth. She began to ride his face, rubbing her wetness all over him. He let her cum over, and over, and over again until he couldn't take it anymore. He pulled his rod out and sat her right on it, and oh, did she feel so good. He stroked her long and deep while he sucked on her breast. He had one hand choking her and the other hand on her ass. The sound of her cumming and the way her box clung to him, had him cumming way sooner than he anticipated. He held her on him tightly while he came inside of her. He was definitely trying to get her pregnant. This time, on purpose. She went to move, but he held her there. She felt so good on him, he didn't want her to get up. And she stayed right there while he held her tight. Oh, how she loved this man. He lifted her head up and kissed her on the lips. "I never meant for you to find out about my lifestyle the way you did, and I'm really sorry how everything turned out that night. I can't imagine my life without you in it. I want you to be my wife, and I want us to have some babies running around here. From this day forth, I promise to always put you first and to always make sure you're straight. You will never worry or need for anything as long as you with me." Then he kissed her on her lips. He held her close as he leaned forward to get the half smoked blunt. He was soft now, but he was still inside of her and wasn't ready to let go.

"You know we can't stay like this forever, right?"

"Why can't we, Mami?" said Steven, kissing Diamond on her lips and her face before lighting up. "I'm getting up, baby. Don't think I don't know what you just tried to do," said Diamond, looking at Steven with the side eye. Steven laughed, "I was just sitting here trying to kick it with you. I was about to feed you, but you wanted to smoke. All I did was rub your feet. The next thing I knew, you was walking up to me putting your precious parts in my mouth," said Steven, pulling Diamond close to him again. "You are absolutely right, Steven. You were about to feed me. I'm hungry, Daddy. I'm going upstairs to wash up and put on an outfit for you. Thank you for making the night special for me, babe," said Diamond before heading upstairs. Steven looked down at his manhood rising. He knew by proposing he would definitely be having sex, finally, but he had no idea he would be getting an outfit tonight. It's been a while since Diamond had dressed up for him. She used to do it for him all the time when they first got together. Sexy outfit, wig, and heels. He made it a requirement and she was more than happy to comply. Steven went to the bathroom off the kitchen, wet a rag and washed his half-erect penis off before putting on his silk pajama pants he got from inside the linen closet. He left the food sitting in the oven, so it would stay warm. He figured they wouldn't be eating right away, but he wasn't expecting the delay to be too long.

He was almost finished setting the table when he saw Diamond coming from the living room in a long, silver, silk gown. It had plunging v-lines in the back to her voluptuous apple bottom, and down the front to her belly button. And a long split that went up the front of the dress. She had on a short, black wig and some four-inch, rhinestone stilettos, with a single strap going across the toes. When Diamond saw him stop and stare, she knew she accomplished her goal. "Damn, baby. You looking real good right now. I'm ready to skip this meal and go straight to dessert," said Steven, now walking Diamond from the living room to her seat at the table. Diamond smiled, noticing how hard he was in his silk pants. "I'm sorry, baby. That's just what you do to me." Steven had every intention of making up for all the months Diamond had him waiting. He knew he was making a baby tonight.

Steven remained a gentleman all night. He served Diamond like she was the Queen of England. They ate, drank, told jokes, and enjoyed each other's company. This was something that they both needed to do as a couple. They needed to get that old thing back.

Steven cleared the table while Diamond walked over to the couch. She poured a glass of white wine before sitting down. She made sure to cross her legs, so when Steven walked in, he would see nothing but thighs. She turned the radio on, which now had the quiet storm playing. The living room was still dark, only being lit from the candles that led the way to the dining room. Steven put all the dishes in the dishwasher then came into the living room. The first thing he noticed was Diamond's thighs. "You know you was looking real good tonight, love," said Steven as he walked into the living room. "Well, thank you, Steven," said Diamond taking a sip of her wine. He sat on the couch and lifted up Diamond's left leg, so that he is laying in between her legs. His head is laying on the right leg, with her left thigh at his lips. He ran his fingertips up and down her leg while kissing on her thigh. "I don't remember this dress, love. How long have you had it?"

"I got it a couple of months ago when I was out shopping," said Diamond. Diamond was aroused right now. She rubbed Steven's waves as he continued stroking her leg and kissing her thigh in between conversation. He knew he was getting to her, he just wanted to see how long she could go before she couldn't take it anymore. When he felt her begin to squirm, he knew it was almost time. He took her left hand and placed it in his silk pants. As she began to stroke his big, hard, rod, he began to bite on her thigh. "I want you to put him in your mouth, baby," said Steven. Before she knew it, she was in the sixty-nine position. The way he was sucking the cum out of her pussy while he stroked her mouth, had Diamond in a state of erotic bliss. "Cum in mouth, Diamond," said Steven, while using his tongue to explore the insides of her pleasure palace. "I'm cumming, Daddy," said Diamond with his dick still in her mouth. He loved when she talked with his dick her mouth. Getting head was one of Steven's favorite things sexually and Diamond knew that. She knew what to do, how to do it, and when to do it. When she started beating his rod with her two-hand twister move, she knew it would be moments before he was covering her with his love. "I'm cumming, baby, Dee, I'm cumming," said Steven as he came, burying his face in her pleasure palace, while doing so. Diamond sucked the remaining cum out of his penis and just laid there. Steven swung one of her legs over, so now he was able to lay comfortably on her thigh. As Diamond laid there on his rod, kissing it, while his cum dripped down her face, Steven asked, "So, what are we going to name her?" Diamond smiled and said, "Who said it's going to be a girl?"

Everything was now back to normal since Steven was now getting pleasured regularly at home. Work was good, money was great, and home was even better. Steven was just waiting for his good news to come. He couldn't wait to tell his mom that he was going to give her a grandchild. Then it happened. Steven had been home because he hadn't been feeling good. He thought it was a stomach virus, so he took a few days off of work. By the third day, Diamond had also taken off since she was now throwing up. She thought she just caught whatever he had. Now they are both laying in the bed with their buckets next to them. "Diamond. How you feeling, baby?"

"I was just fine until I started taking care of you. Now you got me sick."

"Come over here, baby," said Steven, tapping the empty space next to him. Diamond came over and laid her head on his lap. "I sorry I got you sick, baby," said Steven playfully, bending down, kissing Diamond on her cheek. Steven started stroking her hair, "When's the last time you had your period, baby?"

"I don't know. I just had it, though."

"No, you didn't, babe. The last time you had your period was two weeks before I proposed to you."

"No." Diamond started to think about it. Steven was right. She hadn't had her period in over two months. Diamond jumped up and looked at Steven. "Steven. No. I can't be." Steven got out of the bed, walked over to Diamond's side of the bed, then walked her over to the bathroom. He opened the medicine cabinet and pulled out a pregnancy test. "Since when do we have pregnancy tests laying around the house, Steven?"

"Since I told you I was going to give you my baby. Now go pee on the stick," said Steven after opening the box, now passing her the test.

Steven sat on the side of the tub while Diamond took the test. "How long is it going to take you to pee?"

"I'm nervous, I can't pee right now."

"Turn the water on."

"What?"

"Turn the water on. I heard that running water is supposed to make you pee."

"Really, Steven?"

"Really, Diamond. Now turn the damn water on."

"Okay, okay." After a few seconds Diamond started peeing. "Pee on the stick, Dee. It looks like you missing it."

"So, now I can't see the stick?"

"I'm just saying, it looks like you missing it from right here."

"So, you want to hold the stick, Steven?"

"What you bugging for? I was just making an observation."

"Observe this then." Diamond gave Steven the pregnancy test, wiped herself, flushed the toilet, washed her hands, then left the bathroom. Steven didn't even care that she called herself having an attitude, he was just waiting for the plus sign to show. And it did. As soon as Diamond heard Steven jumping around, making a whole lot of noise, she knew it positive.

Diamond had gotten back in the bed. Things were just getting back on track with her and Steven, she didn't know if having a child right now would hurt or help their relationship. Steven ran in the room jumping around. "I'm going to be a daddy. I'm going to be a daddy." Looking at him so happy made Diamond feel a little better about the situation. He laid on the bed and turned over to Diamond. "I love you, baby. You just made me the happiest man ever." He kissed her on the lips then kissed her belly. "Hey, little girl. This is your daddy talking to you. I love you already, beautiful, and I'm going to spoil you something terrible." Then he kissed her belly again, he laid down and pulled Diamond on top of him. She laughed and said, "I'm still sick. I thought you were too."

"You're not sick, baby. You're just pregnant. We have to celebrate. I have to call my mom. You have to call your mom. I have to call Calvin. I love you, baby." Steven jumped out of the bed, threw on his pajama pants and headed downstairs. As Diamond leaned back over the side of the bed to throw up, her smile quickly disappeared. *I hope I don't have to deal with this for the rest of my pregnancy,* thought Diamond. Then she immediately thought about something she could do about that. Diamond wiped her mouth off with the towel that was on her nightstand and went back to sleep thinking about this new news.

When Diamond woke up, she was surprised to see her mom sitting in a chair sleep herself. "Mom? What are you doing here?" Immediately Ms. Wallace smiled. "Hi, baby. Once Steven told me you were having a baby, I had to come right over. Last time I saw you, you said I would see you more often. Guess what, baby?"

"What's that, Mama?" asked Diamond, full of sarcasm. "It's been almost three months, that's what. Now let me see that ring."

"It's over there on the dresser, Ma."

"Why is it not on your finger, baby?"

"Because I've been sick, Ma, so I took it off." Ms. Wallace walked over to the dresser and took the ring off the mannequin hands ring finger. "This is beautiful, baby girl. Wait till I tell Diane about this ring."

"Thanks, Ma."

"So, now you can tell me why I'm the last one to find out that my own daughter is having a baby."

"Because, Steven has a big mouth."

"That's what you want to say right now?"

"Yes, Ma. I would've called you, but as you can see, I've been sick."

"I see that. That's the reason I'm here. Steven wants me to be here to take care of you. He doesn't want you to go back to work."

"Ma, I'm going back to work as soon as I get over this bug."

"Why you have to be so stubborn, Diamond? If this man wants to take care of you while you carry his child, why can't you just be still and let him?"

"Because, Ma, I just started doing stuff on my own. I like my job. Do you even care that I just got a promotion?"

"Maybe I would care if I knew. You don't call me anymore to tell me anything. So, if this is the only way I can spend time with you then so be it. You better call your job and tell them that your husband said you are going on maternity leave." Then Ms. Wallace left the room.

This was probably the second time Ms. Wallace had been at her daughter and Steven's home since Diamond moved in two years ago. The home was more beautiful than she remembered. Steven showed her the room she will be staying in while she stayed there. It looked like one of the hotel rooms she once frequented. She definitely knew she could get used to this. When she got the call from Steven, that her baby was having a baby, she couldn't have been more excited. She didn't know when her and her daughter had become so distant. Diamond used to call her mom for everything and tell her everything. Somewhere along the way that ended. She sincerely hoped that by her spending this time with her daughter, it would get them close like they used to be. Steven never wanted Diamond to start working, so he was more than happy to have a reason to make Diamond stop. He didn't like the fact that he now had to share her with people. He liked being the only person in her life beside her mom. Steven thought by having her mom come stay there she could help Diamond get ready for motherhood. He knew Diamond wasn't ready and Ms. Wallace would be the perfect person to get her there. And he also knew that as long as Ms. Wallace was there, he wouldn't have to be there as much, and he would come home to a clean house and dinner cooked.

As soon as Ms. Wallace left the room Diamond called Steven. The phone rang three times before a familiar voice picked up. "Hey, sis. Congratulations."

"Thanks, Calvin. I see Steven has told everyone the new news."

"Yes, he did. The family is very excited, sis. You know we going to be putting in some extra hours. We have to get everything ready for this wedding and this baby."

"Thanks for the heads-up. Where's your brother?"

"He's in a meeting right now. We had to get some replacements and he's been doing some hiring and firing all day."

"Okay. When he gets done, tell him to call me. I really need to talk to him."

"I got you, sis. He should be wrapping it up in an hour or two. Let me be the first to say it, welcome to the family, Dee. You already know we love you, right?"

"Yes, I know, Calvin."

"You know if I would've seen you first you would've been having my baby, right?" Laughing Diamond said, "Of course I do. I love you too, Calvin."

"Lata, Dee."

"Lata."

Calvin looked over at Steven who was getting head from a new prospect named Jade. "Yo, call your lady when you done."

"Aight, bro. Good looking out on that call."

"No doubt. What shorty hitting for?"

"I'm about to let you see for yourself. I still got three more to try out." He looked down at Jade and said, "Go let my brother see what that mouth do, while I see how that pussy feel. Nah, don't walk over to him. Crawl." Steven slapped her ass while she crawled toward Calvin. "Now get on that chair, right on your knees." Calvin walked over and stood in front of the chair, so Jade could have full access to his rod while Steven slid on a condom and took her from behind. Nobody had better pussy to him than Diamond, but he still had to check out his product before he put it out for distribution. He wasn't ready to waste his nut on her, so he called in the next one while Calvin took his place now fucking Jade from behind. His dick was bigger than Steven's, so he never mind going after his brother. This is typically what the guys did during the day at work. The real work didn't begin until the night time. With this good news Steven just got, he knew he would be needing more money, which meant that he needed more pussy working for him. All he was focused on now, was his baby girl. He wanted to be able to give her the world. These hoes would be the ones who would help with that.

He sat on the love seat that was on the opposite side of where Calvin was, picked up his phone and had his secretary call in the next two ladies. Treasure and Strawberry. When he saw them walk in the room, he knew he was in for a treat. "So, Treasure and Strawberry, I'm sitting here with a stiff dick and I need some attention. I just finished fucking Jade, and I need to be cleaned." Strawberry went to the sink, wet a washcloth and lathered it up, then walked back over to Steven. While she did that, Treasure took off his shoes and his pants. Folding his pants along the crease, before placing them on a hanger. While Strawberry washed Steven's rod, Treasure went to go look for a towel. Treasure winked at Calvin as she looked at him finishing up with Jade. Nothing turned her on more than a big, black, stick. She came over just in time to dry Steven off. "Get on your knees and put my dick in your mouth," Steven said to Treasure. "Mmmm. You like how this dick feel in your mouth? I seen you looking at my brother dick like it was his dick you wanted. You. Come here and suck my balls," he said to Strawberry. He had his hand on each one of they head, while they kneeled side by side, pleasing him. He had his dick in the back of Treasure throat. He was just waiting for her to gag on it before he slid her over to his brother. Steven was also jealous. He couldn't fuck her mouth the way he wanted to because Strawberry's mouth felt to good on his balls and he couldn't dare make her stop just to violate her homegirl. "I'm done with you. Go to him. Crawl to him." As soon as she was dismissed, Strawberry quickly took her place on his rod. She put his hands in her hair, as she tried to get his attention. His eyes were currently fixated on Treasure's big ass, swallowing that thong she had on. "Fuck my mouth, Daddy," said Strawberry, now licking up and down the shaft of Steven's hard cock. Steven did just what she asked him to do. He stood up in her mouth as he grabbed her hair is in hands. "This what you want, bitch? You want to get that mouth fucked. You like how that feel?" asked Steven, stroking her mouth faster and faster. Calvin found his brother entertaining the way he talked to this hoes. Calvin was more of the silent type. He let his wood do the talking for him. While Steven was getting ready to blow Strawberry head off, Calvin was smoking a blunt watching Treasure bounce her ass up and down on his dick, while Jade was making her booty clap in his face. He was definitely an ass man, and right now he was as happy as he could be. He slapped Treasure's ass as he felt her pussy tighten up on his dick. He then told her to sit up while he flipped her over the arm of the chair and started fucking her from behind. Grabbing her waist with his left hand, while choking her with right. She sounded so sexy when she came, thought Steven. It almost reminded him of when Diamond came. "Go heat this rag up. Come back and take care of me." Strawberry ran her tongue across the head of his dick before she got up to lather the hot rag. "I will be right back, Daddy." He couldn't care less what a bitch thought. All Steven saw was money. After Strawberry washed and dried him off, he pointed at his pants. She went to get them along with his shoes. "Go look in the drawer over there under the TV and get me a t-shirt." He loved how hoes followed directions. After getting dressed, he looked over at Calvin who was now sitting up in the chair. Jade was dancing in front of him with Strawberry while Treasure rubbed his back. "I'm about to head to the house for a minute, C. Don't forget there's one more out there. All of y'all bitches is working tonight, so I better see y'all when I get back. "Okay, Daddy," they said collectively. Steven smiled as he walked out of the door.

Steven really didn't think he was doing anything wrong. As he headed downstairs he saw Dawne at the bar, so he stopped by for a drink. "Hey, Daddy."

"What's up, D?" he said while Dawne kissed him on his cheek. "I thought you was off today?" Steven asked. "I'm just trying to get my money up. I saw this nice Jaguar I'm about to stunt in."

"Oh, okay. You should've just told me. I would've helped you out with that."

"Okay, Daddy. I'm telling you now. How are you going to help me?"

"Pour me a shot of Henny while I tell you." Dawne poured the shot and gave it to him. He looks her in the face and says, "For the next week, instead of giving me all of your money, give me half. I know what type of money y'all make. So, all you need is a week. Keep taking these extra shifts and you work hard at night, you'll be right where you trying to be. And your ass better not pull up in the same Jag my lady got."

"Were you about to go home, Daddy?"

"Yes, I was, Dawne. What's up?"

"You smell like a female. Not like pussy, but like perfume."

"So, you going to let Daddy go home and I'm not smelling right?"

"No, Daddy. You know I would never do you like that. You want to go back to your office?" He quickly said no, since he knew Calvin had the four girls in there. "Let's go to office in the basement. Bring the bottle with you." Dawne grabbed the bottle of Henny and followed Steven downstairs. Out of all his girls, Dawne was his go-to girl. She was the only one of his girls who knew what he liked without him ever having to tell her. He knew it was because she paid attention to what Kat did and the way she did it. Dawne was the only one of his original girls that were still with him. After Dream dropped those flowers off at the hospital when Diamond was in there, Steven had to do something to make sure that never happened again.

Steven opened the office downstairs and turned the light on. Steven sat down on the black leather couch while Dawne poured him another drink. She then went to the bathroom which had a shower big enough for about ten people. She got the water temperature right and placed a towel on the flower outside of the shower. She took off all her clothes, then took the pin out of her hair, as she shook her head from left to right. Steven loved when she did that. She bent down on her knees to take off Steven's shoes. Then she sat up and loosened his buckle. Steven stood up and began unbuttoning his shirt as she took his pants off one leg at a time. She then took his socks off and his boxers off. She took a washcloth and a towel from the linen closet before they both walked into the black marble shower. Steven sat on the bench that sat in the middle of the shower. This made it easier for Dawne to bathe him. She washed him from his head to his toes. Once she was done, she dried him off. She rolled him a blunt while she went to the closet to find him a suit closest to the one he just had on. Dawne put lotion all over Steven's body. When she was on her knees, putting lotion on his legs, he said, "Give Daddy what he like." Dawne immediately placed him in her mouth. Steven moaned a little. To him, Dawne's mouth was magical. He knew he wouldn't be able to keep standing much longer either. Dawne didn't just suck his dick, she made love to his dick. If he could ever marry a tongue, this would be the tongue he would have for life. Just walk around with it in his pocket, touch it and get happy thinking about the pleasures it will bring to him once he had it alone. Dawne was his real-life super head. Dawne laid across the couch to make it easier for him. He laid on top of her with his dick in her mouth, now hitting her tonsils. He loved when she let him fuck her mouth. He grabbed her hair as he stroked her mouth, every stroke feeling as good as the last. "I'm cumming, Diamond. I'm about to cum, baby." He laid there for a second shooting all his cum down Dawne's throat. He turned to the side, so she could turn to her side and get some air. She knew better than to take her mouth off of Steven until he told her she could do so. "You got all the cum out of my dick?" Dawne sucked it one more time, sucking on the head to make sure she got it all out. "Yes, Daddy. It's all out." She got up to get a washcloth to wash his dick back off. After she dried him, he slapped her on her ass and said, "Get Daddy dressed." He looked at his watch, which now said three-thirty. *Damn, the time fly when you getting good head,* he thought to himself. "You know Kashmere been in here twice asking for Diamond. I told him she don't be in here like that. He even had Cookie ask me about her."

"That nigga shouldn't even be talking to you. Next time he brings up my wife, tell that nigga to come see me." Steven didn't like the fact that Kash knew his wife. Not just knew her but been up in her. "I'm out. See you tonight, Dee." Then Steven headed home.

Now Steven had an attitude. He had tried to get it out of his mind before he got home but he couldn't. He called Diamond on his way to the house. He knew her mom was there and he needed to have this conversation outside of the house. Diamond picked up on the second ring. "How nice of you to return my call."

"Don't be a smart ass, Diamond. Get dressed. I will be at the house in twenty minutes. Be ready." Diamond could already sense that something was wrong. Steven didn't sound like he did this morning when he was calling the world and giving his new news. She was already prepared to hear some shit. She had a trick for his ass. She put on a pair of her tightest jeans, a pair of red stilettos and her red Gucci shirt, and let's not forget her short black wig. She got dressed and stood outside so he wouldn't even have to call her. She was posted up against her car when he pulled up. She was looking so good Steven had to get out of the car when he got there. He walked up to her smiling, "You did this for Daddy?"

"Yes, I did, baby," she said, while taking off her sunglasses. "Let's go inside so I can taste you."

"Nope. You said you wanted to talk. You said to be ready when you got here. So, I'm ready. Let's talk."

"Baby, we can talk later. Matter of fact we can talk now. Come get in my car for a minute." Steven got in the car and opened Diamond's door from the inside. "I'm not getting in the car."

"What you talking about? Stop playing and get in, Diamond."

"Nope. That is not your let's talk face. You think I don't know you by now?"

"Dee, get your ass in the car and stop playing with me. I said we going to talk." Diamond got in the car and closed the door.

"Why you so fucking sexy, yo?"

"Here you go," said Diamond getting ready to open the door. "No, baby, wait. I really did want to talk to you," said Steven rubbing his fingertips up and down her arm. "Why is Kashmere going around asking about?"

"Because that's my homie. Me and Kash knew each other since junior high school."

"Well, we ain't in junior high school no more, and I don't want him checking for you." Diamond heard the sincerity in Steven's voice. She knew she had to be careful with the next words that came out of her mouth. She wanted to say, "Who you think you talking to? I will talk to whoever I damn well please." What she said was, "Don't worry about it, babe. I will take care of it."

"Nah, Dee. I don't think you're listening to me. I don't want you to even look in his direction if you see him headed to it."

"Okay, Steven." Diamond knew that Steven wasn't going to let up. That whatever power kick he was on right now wasn't about to be over anytime soon. She leaned into him and kissed him on the lips. "You see, Daddy, you focused on the wrong thing right now." She sat back in the seat and let the back recline all the way back. She put her right foot on his dashboard and said, "I'm looking this good, and you sitting here thinking about that nigga. You didn't miss me today, baby?" After that night at the club, Diamond linked up with Kashmere a few times. Of course her and Kash both agreed it was something that should stay between the two of them. She couldn't understand why she was hearing that he was asking about her, but she was sure going to find out. There was a time when she thought her and Kash would've spent their lives together, but he had other things in mind for his life.

Steven was looking at Diamond like she was a whole snack. Those shoes were driving him crazy. She was right, he was worried about the wrong thing right now. He picked up his phone and made a call. "Hi, Ms. Wallace...I'm about to take Diamond out, you need anything while we gone?... Okay. See you tonight." Diamond immediately started laughing while she let her seat come back up. "Are you kidding me right now?"

"What you talking about, Dee?"

"And the son of the year award goes to, Mr. Thompson, ladies and gentlemen." Steven started laughing. "Don't be mad because your mama love me. Oh, before we pull off, go in the garage and get that new silk sheet set you brought last month." Diamond made the, how do you know that, face. Steven looked back at her and said, "This is my house. I know everything." He slapped Diamond's butt as she got out of the car. She came back inside the car with a confused look on her face. "What's wrong, babe?" Steven knew she probably discovered that the ten-thousand-dollar watch she had brought Steven for his birthday was now missing. "Did you move anything in the garage?"

"What are you talking about, Diamond?" Diamond knew it had to be him. They weren't the type of people to have company over and if they did, they wouldn't be in the garage. So, she decided to play with him. "There was something in there that I brought for a friend. Guess I will just have to replace it." Steven knew what she was doing. He was not going to bite. "Oh, okay. It must be a pretty special friend."

"It's just an old friend. I guess you could say he is special." Steven was beginning to get mad. He had to remember that it was him, she was referring to and this was all a game.

"So, when you start buying stuff and hiding it in the garage?"

"When you started clocking what I bring in and out the house."

"You started tripping, Dee. I'm the one who gets the credit card bill. It's like you started working and you started spending more money."

"That's because I work near stores I can shop at. So, now you have a problem with me spending money?"

"That's not what I said, baby. You can buy the mall if it will make you happy. I just want you to stay focused on what's important here. I'm trying to get us to the place where we can always be comfortable. I don't just want to be rich, baby, I want to be wealthy. I want our kids and our grandkids and they grandkids to be good. Me and Calvin been thinking about expanding the business. We talking about opening up a restaurant only. I was thinking about letting you run it, but you about to have your hands full with my little princess. So, I'm thinking about letting our parents run it. They can take turns in between helping out with the baby. That's just the beginning, babe. The world is going to know that we were here. So, my beautiful lady, my future wife, what are you going to do to help make money?"

"I don't know, babe."

"Oh, by the way, I took the watch. It looked good with this suit I wore to my meeting a couple of weeks ago." Diamond smiled and playfully hit Steven. "I knew you had it." He lifted his arm to dodge her hit. "You mad, babe? You big mad or little mad?" said Steven while laughing.

"Steven, you been driving for a while now. Where are we going?"

"Why you so nosey? You always gotta know something."

"At least tell me where the weed at. I know you have something rolled up in here somewhere."

"You know I do, baby. Just got some of that Christmas Tree from my nigga Chris."

"Why your boy always have some product with a crazy name?"

"I don't know, but it be good as hell."

"That AK-47, tho."

"I know, baby. Me and C was lit at work one night."

"One night. You mean every night." Diamond got serious for a minute and said, "Those five months when I wasn't haven't sex with you, were you having sex with someone else?"

"You really want to know, Diamond? You know there's no coming back from this answer."

"Just tell me, Steven. I'm sure I already know."

"You ask if I was fucking someone. No, I wasn't. There is no one person who can come close to giving me what you do. You forgot already how I was all up in that thing when you finally gave her back to me?" Diamond smiled as she remembered what happened that night. She wanted to believe Steven, but she knew better. Since they lived together, they never went longer than three days without being active sexually. Steven knew that Diamond probably didn't believe him, but he wasn't going to let anything interfere with the plans he had right now. And technically, he didn't lie. There was not one person who he let give him head, there were multiple women. She asked if it were someone, so he focused on the one when he gave his answer. Now sex on the other hand, he only had sex with a few of the multitude and it was only for work purposes only. So, that was more of a business transaction. With the straightest face he said, "I couldn't wait to bury my face in your pleasure palace. Just like I'm about to do right now." Then he took his right hand and stroked Diamond through her jeans. Diamond arched her back in response to his touch. She looked at him and bit her bottom lip before passing him the blunt. "Where are we going, Daddy?"

"We are almost there, baby." Next thing Diamond knew, they were pulling up in front of the Radisson Martinique. Diamond looked over at Steven and said, "You give me a speech about wasting money and you go and get a hotel room?"

"When I'm doing it for you, baby, it's never a waste of money. Everything I do, I do it for you, and don't you ever forget it," said Steven before kissing her on the lips. "Grab the bag in the trunk and don't forget to put the sheets in there."

Steven went in to pay for the room while Diamond was getting everything together outside. He stayed with a getaway bag packed just in case. Today happened to be one of those just in case days. It had really been a long day for Steven. He really didn't have all of this planned, especially since he had to go back to work tonight. When he saw Diamond come out the house looking like a joint, everything changed. That was one of the best things about him going into business with his brother, he knew if he didn't make it everything was covered.

It was a little after eight when they got into their room. The first thing Steven had Diamond do was change the sheets on the bed. He had a thing about comfort. Yes, the hotel had great sheets, they just weren't his silk sheets. While she did that, he called Calvin. Steven never wanted Diamond to be suspicious of what he did, so he always made sure to have conversations in front of her. The only person who had the number to the phone he carried regularly was his family, so he could never get caught out there anyway. "Yo…yeah, bro, I'm not making it tonight…. Nah, I'm with Diamond. Still celebrating my new news…. Thanks, man. How did everything work out with the new employees?... Yeah, I could tell… Okay. Looks like you got everything covered. Meet up with you in the morning…. Cool." Next call Steven made was to room service. He ordered Diamond a filet mignon with red potatoes and asparagus. He wasn't really hungry, all he wanted to do right now was get some sleep, but he knew that wasn't about to happen. He also ordered some strawberries and champagne. He knew that along with what he had packed in his bag for Diamond to wear would definitely put him in the right mindset. After Diamond made the bed up she walked over to the couch to undo the straps on her shoes, to take them off. "What you doing, baby?" asked Steven. "I'm trying to get comfortable. These shoes are coming off."

"You can take them off and put them right back on. I did have something for you to put on, but I think you can just take those jeans off and let me see you walk around in those shoes." Diamond loved when her man looked at her like sex. After she found out what he did for a living, she began to feel insecure. Her man being around women who have sex for money, got to her a bit. But Diamond had her own way to deal with that. She took her shoes off, so she could take her jeans off. Steven loved the black thong she wore. They had an open pair of red lips right above her clit. "Come here and let me kiss those lips, baby."

"Nope. You're going to have to wait for it."

Just then the waiter was knocking on the door with room service. Steven opened the door for him, allowing him only to push the food cart through the door, gave him a tip and sent him on his way. "You know I'm hungry. I need to eat, babe."

"Put those shoes back on and come get it." Steven saw that Diamond was up for games tonight. He was going to make her beg him to give it to her now. "Before you come over here, walk over there to the bag and hand me my pouch." Diamond knew what that meant. Steven's pouch was guaranteed to have pre-rolled blunts and his nose candy. Steven admired Diamond's body as she walked to the bag. He loved her legs, her thighs and her ass. For a quick second he wondered if her body would still look like this after the baby. That thought quickly vanished as she squatted down to look in the bag. Diamond didn't have the fattest ass he had seen, but it damn sure felt like the most perfect ass he had ever seen. He loved that Diamond's skin was so smooth. She had no bumps or blemishes, and most of all, she had no body odor. "You dancing for me tonight, Dee." She smiled as she walked over to Steven. She knew that was a request and not a question. "I guess you're going to have to order me some red wine then, Daddy." And immediately Steven made the call.

The hotel room looked more like a studio apartment than just a room. As Diamond walked over to Steven at the table he sat at, he tapped his leg so she could have a seat on it. "You know I love your sexy ass, right," said Steven before kissing Diamond on her lips. He then took one of the strawberries in his hand. He traced it on her lips slowly before telling her to take a bite. After she bit it, he kissed her, putting his tongue in her mouth and using it to take the strawberry from her. "You said you were going to make me wait for it, I can hold out way longer than you can, love." Steven turned Diamond to him, grabbing her ass and placing her on his erect penis. He ran his tongue up and down the side of her neck before sucking on it softly. Diamond was turned on right now but she was not going to break. "I thought you wanted me to dance for you, Daddy."

"You don't have to move to dance for me. You can dance right here. Right here on this big dick I got waiting for you." Steven grabbed Diamond by the waist as he moved his hips allowing her to feel his manhood underneath her, in between her legs. He grabbed her head and whispered, "I'm going to make you beg me for it." Diamond wanted him right now. Steven knew all of Diamond's weaknesses, and he was attacking them one by one. So Diamond decided to play along. She just realized that he had to want her as bad as she wanted him.

She began to kiss him soft and sensually on his lips and face, as she unbuttoned his shirt. She got back on top of him, grinding her pleasure palace all over his rock-hard stick. She began to kiss up and down his chest while grinding herself on him in a circular motion. Then all of a sudden she heard music, she heard a loud, muffled version of "Somebody's Gotta Be on Top" coming from the bag. Steven had turned the music on while Diamond was trying to arouse him. He did like the game, and she was definitely about to win. So, Steven decided to change the game. He lifted her up off of him, stood up and said, "Nice try," before kissing her.

His timing couldn't have been better. As soon as he stood up there was a knock at the door. It was the red wine Diamond had ordered. Although Diamond did continue to smoke weed throughout her pregnancy, she refused to drink anything other than wine as well as partake in any other drugs. "Looks like you had great timing, babe. Can you pass me a glass?" Steven went to give her a glass before getting the speaker out of the bag. He poured himself some champagne as he took a couple of bumps and lit his blunt. He scrolled through his playlist looking for the right song. Then he pressed play. All Diamond heard from the speakers was "Dive In" by Trey Songz. He then walked over to Diamond. He picked her up and carried her over to the king-sized bed. He pulled her to the edge of the bed, spread her legs apart, and he began his show.

As Steven put on a show for Diamond like only he could, Diamond did what she did best. Got high, sipped on her wine, and enjoyed the show. This was the first time since they been together, that Steven did anything like this. As a matter of fact, he told Diamond that she was going to be doing the dancing tonight. She definitely wasn't mad about the change in plans. As Steven took off his clothes, he moved his body the way he would if they were fucking. And after he took off his pants, he stood in front of her, grabber her face and rubbed her face all over his silk boxers, which was the only thing that stood between her and his penis. She loved when Steven was aggressive. Their rough sex was one of the things she fell in love with first. "Tell me you want it, Dee," said Steven, who now had his dick out. He was rubbing the head on Diamond's face and across her lips. Taunting her, telling her to tell him how much she wanted it. Diamond pulled her thong off and threw it on his face. She then sat back on the and used her finger to motion Steven to come to her. "Tell me you want it first."

"I want it, Daddy. Come here." Steven took the thongs off his face and smelled them before throwing them on the side of the bed. As soon as he got close to her, she opened her legs and he buried his face in her pussy. After about an hour, he finally came up for air. He took a couple of bumps, some more sips of champagne, then took some coke and put it on Diamond's hot box. He had Diamond begging him to stop. Two hours later he finally listened. Diamond was now sleep and Steven was still horny. He laid Diamond on her stomach and fucked her until he came. He loved how Diamond pussy still got wet for him. Half asleep or not.

Chapter 6

Diamond was awakened the next morning with kisses on the back of her neck. "Good morning, baby," said Steven. "Good morning, baby," replied Diamond, as she turned her head in his direction, so she could give him a kiss. "I love you even with your stinky, morning breath. Give me another one." Diamond smiled as she gave him another kiss. "You know, baby, I've been thinking a lot about our future. I really want to make some changes in my life."

"What kind of changes are you talking about, babe?"

"You know me, and Calvin got the club. I know we haven't really spoken about the other situation, me and the girls."

"You mean your hoes?" says Diamond.

"If that's what you want to say, then yes, my hoes."

"Just tell me one thing, Steven. Are you fucking them hoes?" Looking in her eyes he says, "Diamond, believe me when I tell you. It's only you I want. I would never jeopardize either one of our lives by having sex with those girls." Diamond knew Steven was lying. "So, if you weren't willing to jeopardize our lives, how did Dream get pregnant?"

"Look, D, I made a mistake. I knew Dream before I met you. I guess you can say me and her had history. I promise you I never went inside of her without protection, so I can't tell you how she pregnant. Look, baby, I'm trying to tell you I don't want that life anymore. I'm really trying to do right by you," then he rubbed her belly and said, "for our baby." Diamond sits up in the bed and says, "Since we're being honest right now, I guess this is the best time to tell you. I had sex with Kashmere and this might be his baby." Steven grabbed Diamond by the neck, "What the fuck you just say?"

"Diamond. Diamond. Wake up, babe," said Steven after Diamond woke him up, screaming in her sleep. "What's wrong with you, babe?" Diamond woke up and jumped straight up with sweat all over her face. "I guess it was just a bad dream." Steven pulled her to him and laid her head on his chest. "I don't ever want to lose you, Steven."

"Baby, I'm not going anywhere. There is nothing you could do to make me leave you," he said before kissing her on her forehead. "Now that you're up, there is something I would like to talk to you about." Diamond jumped out the bed and ran to the bathroom. Steven was going to go after her until he heard her throwing up. Steven loved his girl, but not enough to watch her throw up. When he heard her stop and the water running, he said, "Don't forget to brush your teeth."

"Shut up, Steven," said Diamond laughing. Diamond wasn't nauseous. She made herself throw up. She felt her dream about to come a reality. What did she do? She had to find a way out of this situation. As the water ran, she sat on the side of the tub deep in thought.

Diamond's phone rang, she looked at it and hesitated to answer since she didn't know the number. "Hey, baby girl, how you been?"

"Kash, is that you?"

"Yes, it's me. I went through a lot to get this number, you know. I just wanted to check on you."

"That's sweet of you," she thought as she began smiling. "I never got to tell you thank you for getting me home that night. It was just so much going on."

"You don't have to thank me, baby. I was just happy to be there for you, like you have always been there for me. I'm about to be at your house in a few minutes. I want to see you. Ever since that night, I haven't been able to stop thinking about you."

"Kash, I don't think that's a good idea."

"It's cool. Your man is at the club. Trust me, he's not coming home anytime soon."

"Okay then. But you can't stay that long."

"See you soon, baby girl. Daddy is coming for you." Diamond smiled as she hung up the phone.

It had been three months since the incident at the club and Diamond had been in the house for the most part. Even though she was driving now, she was still adjusting to her appearance. She always kept a long bang now, and always kept on shades. She did appreciate how kind and attentive Steven had been after everything, but a part of her wanted him to feel what she felt. She was very surprised to hear from Kashmere, and she wondered how he got her number. She made a note to ask him that when she sees him. Diamond got in the shower and threw on some jeans and a shirt. As soon as she got dressed her phone started ringing. "I'm outside."

"I'm coming out now," she said before hanging up the phone.

Diamond didn't pay attention to Kashmere's car that night. She was definitely feeling his deep burgundy Tesla. He opened the car door from the inside and she got in. He immediately leaned in to give her a hug. He may have held on to long as he buried his face in her neck, inhaling her vanilla aroma. "I see you still wearing that Victoria's Secret Vanilla." She smiled feeling his breath by her ear and said, "You always did pay attention." Then he let her go and sat back against the door. He went to take her shades off before she stopped him. He stroked the side of her face and asked, "Why you got them shades on? Let me see you, beautiful." Diamond took off her shades and put her head down. "Diamond, I already know what happened. That's why it took me so long to reach out to you. I heard you were better now, so I wanted to make sure for myself." Kash took his hand and lifted up Diamond's head and turned it facing him. "You were always the most beautiful girl in the world. I was a fool to choose my lifestyle over you. You were there for me when nobody else was. Hell, you dressed my first hoe and did her hair. That's when I knew that you really loved me you know."

"Kashmere, tell me what's up? Why are you really here?"

"I just wanted to see you. I told you that you have been on my mind crazy. I feel like you shouldn't be with Steven, you should be with me. You know I would never put my hands on you. Your man Steven, he's a bugout. After Dream sent you those flowers in the hospital, he went to go pay her a visit. Nobody has seen her since. If he ever does anything to hurt you again, I'm going to kill him, D. Look at your face," said Kash, after moving her bang out of her face.

"It's really not that bad. He already knows that if he puts his hands on me again I'm leaving."

"No, you not. If you stayed after this, you will stay after anything else. Why you didn't go back to your mom's crib?"

"Because I didn't want to. Me and Steven are together."

"Fuck that dumb shit you talking, D. I didn't leave that night I dropped you off. I stayed around, parked a few houses down from you. Something just didn't feel right. I seen you get in the cab that night. I followed the cab and seen you go to your mother's house. Why didn't you stay there?" Diamond put her head back down. She was not expecting all these questions. She didn't know how to respond. She didn't know how to feel about him following her and watching her. "Diamond, I've known you since junior high school. You know I would do anything for you. I'm sorry if you feel like I'm pressing you right now, I'm just trying to understand why you came back to him."

"Because he loves me, Kash. He came to get me the next day, and we been good ever since."

"I see your Jag over there. That's what you mean by being good? What happened to you, D? The girl I knew, who I fell in love with all those years ago, would never allow any man to put his hands on her."

"Obviously, I'm not that girl anymore," said Diamond, with her head still looking down.

"I want to take you out next week. We can go anywhere you want to go. I just want to spend some time with you and make you smile again." At that moment Kashmere's phone started ringing. He silenced the phone and continued his conversation. "I gotta make moves, but you got my number now. Just think about whatever it is that will put a smile on your face and I will make it happen." Kashmere's phone started ringing again. "I have to take this, babe."

"Go ahead, I will give you a call."

"Can I get a kiss, baby girl?" Diamond leaned over to him, giving him her cheek to kiss. "I will take that, beautiful. I will be waiting for your call." Diamond winked at him then put her glasses on before getting out of the car.

Diamond went inside the house and sat on the couch. She lit a blunt as she thought about the conversation her and Kash just spoke about. He asked a lot of legitimate questions that she should have had answers for. What happened to the person she used to be? She used to be so strong and focused. Now she was just complacent. Halfway through the blunt, she began to think about where she wanted to go. Lamar, also known as Kashmere, was at one time the love of Diamond's life. He was her high school sweetheart all the way till the twelfth grade when he dropped out and decided he wanted to be a pimp. It didn't surprise her since he was the only boy in a family full of hoes. She loved him enough to dress his first hoe and then let him go. Then it hit her. Kashmere was going to be her revenge on Steven. At that moment she knew where she wanted to go and she knew what she wanted.

Over the next week Diamond began to get out the house more. That's when she started working. She knew that if she was going to get back to being herself, she had to start becoming independent again. Steven was not feeling the fact that she wanted to work. Especially since he could give her any and everything she wanted. He knew he was still in the dog house, so he couldn't tell her no. He was also on edge since she wasn't doing her womanly duties. Since he was the cause of her miscarriage, there wasn't anything he could say about that. Diamond was putting her plan together, and everything was falling into place. Now that she was out of the house more, she was able to speak to Kash as much as she wanted. He even asked her to call him by his given name. She had already saved his name as Lamar incase Steven was around when he hit her up. Over the next few weeks, Diamond and Lamar would meet in the city for lunch, shopping, dinner, movies, whatever she felt like doing at the moment, Lamar would make it happen. Diamond would always hit Steven up before she would see Lamar to avoid him interrupting her time out. Then the day finally came.

Diamond called Kash one day on her lunch break and said, "I want you to make love to me, Lamar." Kash had been waiting to hear those words for weeks now. Diamond told him that she hadn't had sex since she lost the baby, so he knew he could do whatever he wanted to do and not think about Steven. "When do you want me, baby girl?"

"Tonight. All night." She knew Steven wouldn't be back home till about five or six in the morning. She was ready. She knew Kashmere's favorite color was burgundy, so she found this sexy, lace, wine-colored lingerie. She planned on wearing it with these silver stilettos Kashmere had brought her when they went shopping a couple of weeks ago. It had now been a month since they reconnected and she was ready, but so was he. He knew that Diamond's favorite sexual pleasure was oral sex. Since he only fucked his hoes, that was one thing he hadn't been able to do in a long time. He was looking forward to giving her that work.

Diamond had packed her bag the night before and put it in her trunk. She was off work the next day and she didn't want to be doing too much. She didn't want Steven to become suspicious. Steven left the house around 6 like he always does. She had plans to meet Kash in the city by 9. The more time she spent with Kashmere, the more she began feeling like her old self again. The fact that he never approached her about having sex, made her want to give it to him more. It has now been four months since she had sex and she was so ready to give it up. Not to her man, but to the man who made her feel whole again. She was pulling up to the hotel when her phone started ringing.

"Hey, D, where are you right now?"

"I'm pulling into the parking lot. What's up?"

"Something came up. I'm not going to make it."

"Lamar, you gotta be kidding me right now."

"I'm sorry I couldn't reach you earlier to tell you. I just got caught up in something."

"Whatever. I'm out," said an angry Diamond hanging up the phone.

She sat in her seat angry, with tears coming out of her eyes. She was so unfocused, she jumped when she heard the knock on her window. She smiled as she seen Kashmere's face. He opened her door for her. "Come here, sexy lady," he said taking her hand as she got out of the car. "I know you didn't think I was going to miss this night with you. I been waiting for this since the night I seen you at 'The Spot.'" He wiped the tears from Diamond's face before kissing her on the lips. "You have anything you need me to carry?"

"Yes. My bag is in the trunk."

"I see you got on that outfit I bought you," said Kash, admiring the pink and gray romper he had got for her one day while they were out. "I hope you ready for Big Daddy," said Kash. "I hope you ready to be fed," replied Diamond. He took her hand as they headed to the entrance of the hotel. Kash had already gotten the room. He had arrived an hour early to make preparations. He wanted this to be a night that Diamond would never forget.

The two made small talk as they walked to the elevator. "What floor are we on, Lamar?"

"We are going to the fifth floor, love. Room five-twenty." They got off the elevator and walked to the room. Kash opened the door, allowing Diamond to enter first. He wished he could've taken a picture of her face when she walked in. "Oh my god. You did all of this for me?" she said, turning around to give him a hug. "You're worth it, baby girl." The first thing Diamond did was walk over to the table where there stood a huge gold vase, with three dozen blue long-stemmed roses. She took one out and smelled it as she looked around the room. The floor and the round, rotating bed were both covered with rose petals. Kash walked over to put Diamond's bag on the bed. He then walked over to her, took her hand and led her to the red leather sofa that sat in front of the TV. Looking into her eyes he said, "I told you I was going to make tonight beautiful, babe. I love you, Diamond, and I always have." Diamond leaned in and kissed him. He held the back of her neck as he returned a passionate kiss. She began reaching for his pants when he said, "Slow down, baby. We have all night."

"Lamar, I want you right now. Right here, on this couch."

"Your wish is my command, baby. Sit down." Diamond sat on the couch wondering why he hadn't bent her over by now.

He walked over and dimmed the lights. He turned on the TV which showed a fireplace, with wood burning. You could even hear the crackle of the flames. He began taking his clothes off while he walked back in her direction. He pulled off his shirt first, as Diamond stared at him wondering if he was about to do what she thought he was about to do. Then he took off his wife beater and threw it at her. She caught it and smiled, as she put it up to her nose to smell it. She loved his scent. Then he unbuckled his belt and pulled it out of his pants slowly. He then unbuttoned his pants, then unzipped them before taking them off. Diamond is now biting her lip in anticipation. Her pleasure palace was now wet and throbbing. She wanted him so bad, but she didn't want to stop his show. He walked over to her and sat down on his knees in front of her. "Give me your foot." She raised her left foot for him. He undid the strap on her shoe before taking it off. Then she gave him the other one and he did the same. "Now stand up." She stood up as he undressed her. Leaving her wearing only the lace, wine, thong and bra set. She wanted to be prepared in case she didn't get to put the lingerie on. He picked her up and she wrapped her legs around his waist and they began kissing again as he laid her on the bed filled with rose petals. "You are so beautiful, baby," he said as his tongue began to make its way down south. He began sucking on her neck as he tried to undo her bra strap. "It's in the front, babe," said Diamond, as she felt his hands on her back. Kash, never missing a beat undid her bra before placing her breast in his mouth. Diamond moaned as his tongue ran across her nipples before he began sucking them. "Let me feed you, Daddy," said Diamond. He knew exactly what she wanted, and he was ready to feast. He kissed his way down to her pleasure palace, where he planned to be for a while.

He grabbed her thong with his teeth, using his mouth to remove them from her body. He spread her legs apart and kissed her on her clit. He kissed her multiple times before placing her clit in his mouth. Within minutes Diamond was cumming. When he felt her getting ready to cum for a second time, he put his finger inside of her. He was eating her pleasure palace like it was his last supper as he moved his finger in and out of her at a fast pace. That's when she had her first orgasm for the night. The faster that finger went, the quicker the next orgasm came. Her wetness felt so good on him, he had to feel her. He got off the bed, flipped her over, pulled her down to the edge of the bed, lifted up her ass, arched her back, then slid inside of her fast. She moaned so exotically as he filled her up with all of him. She just kept cumming back to back and before he knew it he was cumming too.

He didn't tell her, and he didn't stop. He grabbed her hair and went harder until she tapped out. When she finally gave him the signal, he stopped, but he never pulled out. He stayed inside of her as he rolled over, so they were now on their sides.

They were both sweating and panting by now. Almost two hours had went by and they didn't even realize it. He kissed her on the back of her neck and said, "I love you, D. You're going to have my baby too." Diamond smiled, not realizing that he came inside of her. "I love you too, Lamar."

The loud knock on the door brought Diamond back to reality. "Diamond, what's up with you? I been calling you for a minute now. You okay, babe?" She threw some cold water on her face and said, "I'm sorry, baby. I must have zoned out, I'm okay. I think your baby is getting the best of me," said Diamond now standing up from the sitting on the side of the tub. She walked out the bathroom where Steven stood waiting for her. Steven bent down and kissed her belly. "That's right. That's Daddy's little princess in there," he said before kissing her belly again. "Your little princess is hungry."

"Just tell me what you want, baby. I got you," said Steven before kissing Diamond on the lips. "I want some French toast and bacon. Ask for extra bacon, babe. And where's the blunt at? I smell it burning."

"Well, my beautiful one, that's why I was calling you. It's in the ashtray." Steven slapped Diamond on the butt as she went over to sit on the couch. She took the blunt out the ashtray and lit it. Steven walked over to the couch and sat next to her. "You sure you okay, babe? You been bugging since you woke up screaming. What was you dreaming about?"

"I don't think you really want to know, babe."

"If I'm asking you, that means I want to know, Diamond." Diamond looked at Steven and said, "I dreamt I was at your funeral." She didn't know what else to say. What she did know is if she told the truth, she would probably be at her own funeral. Steven didn't know what to say behind that one. That was the furthest thing from his mind. "Come here, baby," said Steven as he pulled her to him. "I'm going to be just fine. I've been doing a lot thinking, and babe, I think I'm ready to be the man you need me to be. I want to be here for you and the baby. I've been thinking about becoming legit. I told you about the restaurant, but there are a few more things I have in mind. I've really been considering giving up a percentage of the club. When the baby gets here, I don't want to have to be rushing to work every night. I want to be home with you. Waking up in the middle of the night, changing diapers, all that stuff that fathers do." Diamond just sat there in his arms, smiling and confused.

"When you say give up a percentage, what percentage are you referring to?"

"I'm turning the girls over to Calvin. I'm ready to give up that part of my life for you. I don't want to marry you and not give you all of me."

"When you say, the girls, are you referring to your hoes?"

"If that's what you want to say, then yes, Diamond. I'm giving all my hoes to my brother. The only money I will be collecting will be from the restaurant."

"How many of your hoes have you slept with, Steven? Don't lie to me."

"Diamond, believe me when I tell you. It's only you I want. I would never jeopardize either one of our lives by having sex with those girls." Diamond knew Steven was lying. "So, if you weren't willing to jeopardize our lives, how did Dream get pregnant?"

"Look, D, I made a mistake. I knew Dream before I met you. I guess you can say me and her had history. I promise you I never went inside of her without protection, so I can't tell you how she pregnant.

Look, baby, I'm trying to tell you I don't want that life anymore. I'm really trying to do the right by you, for our baby."

"Steven, what happened to Dream? Does she still work for you?"

"No, she does not still work for me. She won't be working for nobody." Diamond sat back and said, "What the hell does that even mean?" Steven kissed Diamond on the lips. "Let me order your food so you can eat and we can leave. I need to check in with Calvin and see how it went last night. I told you we got some new workers."

"New hoes you mean?"

"I'm not in the mood for this right now, D. You eating or nah?"

"I can wait till I get home. I'm ready to go."

Steven seeing that Diamond now had an attitude, was ready to leave. After that last conversation the two didn't have too much to say to each other. They got dressed, packed up their things and headed back to the island. The car ride was very dry. Steven's phone was blowing up. He knew it had to be Calvin. Diamond got tired of hearing it vibrate, so she answered it. "Hey, Calvin, what's so important that you keep calling back to back?"

"Hey, sis, put Steven on. It's important." She put him on speaker phone. "Yo, C, talk to me, man."

"Bro, you have to get back here as soon as possible. We got a situation."

"I'm on the highway. There's a little traffic right now. I just need to drop off Diamond and I will be right there."

"Aight, bro, see you soon." Calvin knew he was on speaker phone, so he couldn't say what the problem was. Steven knew it had to do with the girls because bro is the code word for the hoes. Steven meant to say something to Diamond about answering his phone, but he was just trying to get to 'The Spot' right now. He pulled up to the house, gave Diamond a kiss and headed to work. Steven had no idea what could be going wrong. 'The Spot' had been open for a few years now, and there has never been an issue there. Steven pulled in the driveway and headed straight to the office. To his surprise, Calvin was in there with four chicks he never seen before. "Bro, you finally made it," he said while giving Steven a half a hug. "I thought it was an emergency, man."

"It is, man. You don't see these fine-ass women in here?" The two of them started laughing. "So, Steve, I would like you to meet Vanilla Skye, Cinnamon, Fiah and Mariah."

"I see you trying to get a mixed vibe in here. You know I haven't dealt with no white girls since Kat."

"I know, man. I'm trying to see what that white money do. I've been thinking about opening up another location. Since you trying to be a family man now, I didn't know if you would go in with me, or if I had to do it on my own."

"You doing too much talking right now in front of these hoes. There's a time and a place for everything," said Steven looking at the women in front of him.

Cinnamon was the only black girl in the room. Vanilla Skye and Mariah were both white girls. Fiah was a sexy Dominican girl with the prettiest ass Steven had seen in a while. "Right now, I think it's time for my dick to be in somebody mouth. He went and took Vanilla Skye and Fiah out of the room. He hadn't showered this morning, and he was so vain when it came to him having the cleanest, meanest, penis. "I'm headed downstairs, bro. Thanks for the call."

"No doubt," said Calvin as he poured drinks for Cinnamon and Mariah. The two ladies followed him down the stairs to the restaurant where Steven took two bottles from the bar. Then they went down another flight of stairs to get to the shower. "Exactly how old are you, ladies? I mean your bodies look grown, but your faces don't." Fiah answered first, "I'm twenty-six, Papi, but I can be younger if you want me to be." Then Vanilla answered, "I'm only nineteen. I hope that won't be a problem, Daddy."

"Not at all. Just want to make sure y'all are legal. You would never have a reason to be down here unless you work for my brother. I got the hoes upstairs, he got the dancers down here. There is no doing both. If you work for me, all you will be collecting is your paycheck. My hoes are my employees. They run the bar, they host and serve. Any money you make from my pussy that's between your legs, that's all mine. So, the choice is yours. I had a long night and a longer morning. I need a shower and I need to release some tension." This was Steven's speech as he passed the strippers' stage and made his way to the bathroom. This bathroom required a key card that only he and Calvin possessed. There was another, regular bathroom that they had for the dancers which was on the other side of the room.

When he walked in the bathroom he immediately smiled thinking of the last time he was in there with Dawne. "Over here is the linen closet where the washcloths and towels are kept. Now undress me, so we can get started." Vanilla was on her knees taking off his shoes and his pants, while Fiah was unbuttoning his shirt and taking off his t-shirt. He knew he just told Diamond he don't fuck these hoes, but he already knew Fiah was getting tossed up before he got out of the shower. He just didn't know how to go about doing it without Vanilla being there. The ladies continued to undress him as he smiled, forgetting about the conversation him and his fiancé just had. He went to turn on the shower and have a seat inside while the ladies undressed themselves. Vanilla took out her compact mirror, which contained coke and her tiny straw. She took a couple of lines while she watched Fiah roll a blunt. She had been crushing on her since she first seen her upstairs with Calvin. When Steven picked the two of them, she felt lucky that she would be able to have the boss and the baddest bitch, both at the same damn time. Steven opened the door and said, "Vanilla, come bring me that white girl along with a bottle of Henny." She stood up from the sofa and poured the drink and said, "I'm coming, Daddy."

She stepped in the shower with the bottle and the mirror. He took both from her as he called for Fiah to come and join them. He did a couple of lines before taking the bottle to the head. He seen that she had just finished rolling her blunt. "I'm coming, Papi," she responded. He told her to grab the lighter that was sitting on a ledge in the back of the shower. Once she gave it to him, he lit the blunt before taking another drink to the head. He commanded them both to stand under the water so he could watch Vanilla bathe Fiah. He seen the way Vanilla was looking at her and he was prepared to see a show. He only had the water coming out the front shower head, so he was able to enjoy the show without the water affecting his session. He went to get the mirror to take more lines as he watched Vanilla take a bar of soap and begin washing Fiah's body.

He felt his manhood rise as he watched Vanilla wash her neck, then her arms and underarms, then move to her breast. *Her breasts are sitting so perfect right now,* he thought as he began to stroke himself. As Vanilla got to Fiah's legs, she got on her knees, washing her ever so sensually. Fiah enjoyed feeling this woman's hands on her. She could tell this wasn't the first time she had done this. When she felt the soap make its way between her legs, she held her head back. Steven was enjoying the view of the water running down her body while Vanilla tried to replace the bar of soap with her tongue. Steven took another drink and hit the blunt some more before placing them both on the ledge. He held on to the coke tho. "Vanilla, come to me." Vanilla stopped kissing on Fiah's thighs and crawled over to Steven. He placed some coke on his dick and told her to make it disappear.

As she began licking his stiff rod from the base to the head, he began to moan. Fiah feeling left out walked over the bench he was sitting on. As Vanilla made the coke on his dick disappear he had Fiah standing in front of her playing with herself. As he guided Vanilla's head up and down his dick with one hand, he sucked on Fiah's titties and grabbed her ass with his other hand. After he seen Fiah make herself cum again he told her to get on her knees and join Vanilla. As Vanilla sucked his dicked, Fiah sucked his balls. This continued until he was ready to cum. He told them both to stop and sit up in front of him as his cum shot all over both of their faces. He then made them lick the cum off of each other before he walked over to the shower and had them bath him.

It was moments like this that Steven loved his life. As these two women wash him thoroughly with a cloth, he felt like a king. He got out and let them dry him off as he sat on the couch and told Fiah to bring him the bottle, the blunt and the coke. Vanilla finished drying his feet as Fiah came with what he asked for. He lit the blunt then handed it to Fiah. He took a couple of more lines before handing the mirror to Vanilla. "Vanilla, I want you two to get back in the shower. Finish Fiah off." Vanilla smiled, knowing that what she wanted, she was about to get. Fiah was happy too. She already knew she was about to be in for a treat. The both took a shot from the bottle before heading back in the shower. Steven sat on the couch and watched the two kiss and touch before Vanilla sat Fiah on the same bench and got on her knees in front of her. Fiah grabbed her breast as Vanilla's tongue made love to her hot box. Steven sat up in anticipation as he wished at that moment it was his tongue making love to Fiah. He felt himself begin to rise again as he heard Fiah cumming over and over again. He knew he had to have to her before the night was over. Right now it was almost time for work and he was faded. "Alright, y'all. Now it's time to tell me what you want to do. Y'all with me or with Calvin? They both chose him. "Okay, so y'all know the rules. I'm about to get dressed. So y'all take a shower and get Daddy his money." He took another swig before getting dressed. By the time he was done, so were they. The restaurant was already open by the time they got back upstairs. He introduced both of the new girls to Dawne and told her to show them the ropes. Then he headed upstairs to see what Calvin was up to.

He wasn't surprised when he seen Calvin hitting Mariah from the back while she was eating Cinnamon's box. If he knew his brother, he knew he had already had both of these women multiple times. "Yo, C, you ain't done yet?"

"Nigga, what it look like?"

"It look like it's time for these hoes to get to work, nigga." They both laughed. Calvin took his wood out of Mariah and stood up. The two women both got up and begin giving him head. He just stood there with his hands on both of their heads putting his dick in one mouth and out of the other. Then Mariah dipped under and ran her tongue from his balls to his ass. It felt good, so he didn't stop her. He grabbed Cinnamons head and held it on his dick as he bust the only nut right down her throat. Steven watched, as he thought about trying that same position later on tonight with Fiah and Vanilla.

Diamond couldn't believe she had been in the house all day and hadn't heard from Steven since he dropped her off. Of course she had to deal with her mom asking a million and one questions. So, she just stayed in her room talking to Kashmere. She loved that he always made time in his day to talk to her and tell her how special she was to him. He had been trying to see her again since their first night together. She did feel a bit of deception when he told her that he came inside of her. She didn't think he would do that to her knowing that her man was crazy. She had no clue who this kid belonged to and she didn't want to think about all the worse scenarios at this time.

Diamond laid in her bed and her phone rang.

"Hello?"

"What's up, beautiful? Is it a bad time?"

"No. What's up, Kash?"

"Baby, why do you sound like that?"

"Kash, what happened to Dream?"

"Yo, D. I don't even want to get into that. I only know what I heard."

"So, tell me what you heard then."

"I'm not even going to do that. If you want to know, you have to ask your man."

"I did ask him and he didn't tell me."

"D, you know I love you to death. All I can tell you is that I wish you would leave him and come with me. Your man is different kind of crazy. I'm just telling you, if he ever puts his hands on you again, I'm going to kill him."

"I can't leave him right now. He's changing. He loves me."

"Diamond, I love you. I love you more than he will ever be able to. Just promise me that if it gets crazy, you will walk away."

"He's not going to put his hands on me anymore, Kash. But, if he does, I promise that I will walk away."

"Yo, D?"

"Yes, baby."

"I'm not going to share you forever."

"I know you're not, babe. Just give me some time."

"Diamond, you don't hear me calling you?"

"I have to go, Kash. My mom is being annoying again. I can't wait until she goes back home. I'm on the phone, Ma. Be down in a minute."

"Don't trip, baby. You know if she wasn't there I'd be exploring your pleasure palace right? I miss you cumming in my mouth, baby."

"I miss your mouth making me cum, Daddy. Uggghh."

"What's wrong, Mami?"

"You're making me want you and I can't have you."

"I will have you soon enough, love. Go see what your mom wants, beautiful."

"Okay. I will talk to you later."

"I love you, D."

"I love you too, Kash."

Diamond hung up the phone then went to see what her mom wanted. Ms. Wallace was in the kitchen frying some chicken. "What's up, Ma?"

"Nothing, baby. I haven't seen you since you got in the house hours ago. You and Steven left yesterday and you come back home alone. Are you always here alone?"

"When I'm not at work, yes, I am."

"How is your job going?"

"It's cool. It gives me something to do. After sitting in this house for months, I just want to be outside. Now Steven is talking about me quitting because of the baby."

"Well, is that what you want to do?"

"Eventually I will when I start getting big. But that's not a thought right now." Ms. Wallace took chicken out the skillet and placed it on a plate before putting some more in. "I know you're hungry. I'm going to fix your plate now. Should I put a plate up for Steven?"

"If you want to. By the time he gets in the house, he usually gets right in the bed." Ms. Wallace could tell by her daughter's tone that Diamond wasn't as happy as her mom thought. "Baby, is there anything going on that you want to tell me about? I don't see that glow in your eyes that used to be there. Is everything okay with you two?"

"Yes, Ma. Everything is fine. It's just this baby. Things are about to change. I'm about to be a mother. I don't know if I'm ready for this, Ma. And so soon after I just lost a baby."

Ms. Wallace stopped what she was doing. "What are you talking about, Diamond?" Then Diamond felt stupid because she didn't tell her mom about the miscarriage. "Me and Steven didn't want anyone to be worried. The reason I went to the hospital the day after I left your house wasn't to get checked out. I went because I had a miscarriage." Ms. Wallace walked over to her daughter with tears in her eyes and placed her arms around her. "Baby, I'm so sorry. Why didn't you tell me? You didn't have to go through that alone."

"Mom, I'm okay. Really. Steven was right by my side through the whole thing." Ms. Wallace stood back and looked at her daughter. "Diamond, I find that hard to believe when the man is never home."

"That's why he asked you to come stay, Mama. So, he can spend more time in the office." Ms. Wallace went back to fixing her daughters plate. "Girl, please, he asked me to come over here to teach your butt to cook. You didn't have hardly anything in your fridge. Do you ever cook?" Diamond laughed, "For what? He works in a restaurant, he can eat whenever he wants to." Ms. Wallace passed Diamond her plate and said, "Look a here, you better feed your husband, so you know exactly what he's eating. You hear me now."

"I hear you, Ma. Now make your plate so we can watch a movie together." Diamond went to the living room and sat on the couch. She knew where the conversation was going with her mom and she was not in the mood for it. How can she have a conversation about him possibly cheating when she didn't even know if she was carrying his child. Oh, how her Christian mother would have a field day with that one. Ms. Wallace came and joined her daughter on the couch. They watched Lean on Me as they ate their food. Julie had the biggest crush on Morgan Freeman. "You know, Diamond, Morgan was almost your daddy." Diamond laughed, "Mommy, what you talking about now?"

"Morgan Freeman was almost your daddy. I met him at a movie premier back in the day. I was a hot, young, tender and he was all over me. This was when he was first starting out. Then I looked over to my left and seen the most handsome man ever. Standing next to him was your father." They both laughed and continued to eat.

"I really enjoyed spending time with you, Ma. I'm about to head to bed now." After *Lean on Me,* the two watched *School Daze.* It's been a long time since they spent real quality time together and it was needed. Diamond took the plates to the kitchen and put the dishes in the dishwasher. She went over to give her mom a kiss before getting in the bed. Ms. Wallace followed suit and went to sleep herself. "I love you, Diamond."

"I love you too, Ma. Goodnight."

Chapter 7

"How nice of you to finally come home," said Ms. Wallace as Steven entered the house after five in the morning. "You know how it go, Ma. I have a business to run."

"You know, Steven, we never had a talk about your business. When I first met you, I was introduced to you as a young, successful architect. I feel like I may have gotten my daughter involved in something she can't get out of."

"Why would you say something like that? Do you not see your daughter happy?"

"Happiness is in the eye of the beholder, son. I haven't seen my daughter happy since the day she came to my house with a bloody face. What exactly is it that you do, Steven?"

"Ms. Wallace, no disrespect meant, but this is my house. You're a visitor in my home. To answer your question, I run a restaurant and lounge. I've had a long day at work and I'm tired. Have a good night," said Steven before walking upstairs. One thing he was not about to tolerate was someone questioning him in his home. It was his idea for Ms. Wallace to come and stay, to help Diamond out and hopefully teach her how to cook, but now he was second guessing that. He jumped in the shower washing off the remnants of his evening. Mostly the smell of Fiah. He couldn't dare let the night end without getting what he wanted.

He got in the bed and pulled Diamond to him. He whispered, "I love you," to her before falling asleep. Diamond snuggled up against her man enjoying his tight embrace he had her in. The two woke up the next day around noon. "You up, baby?" asked Steven. Diamond smiled as she felt her man's hard rod against her leg. So, she pushed her butt up against him and started moving her hips around. "I want your mouth, baby. Give Daddy his mouth." Diamond was never one to deny her man anything sexually. She always believed that what she wouldn't give him, someone else would. If she only knew. She turned around to face him and gave him a kiss before she disappeared under the covers. She always knew just what to do to get her man there. Right before he came, he pulled the sheet back so he could watch her get covered with his love. Then he pulled her up next to him and slid into her from behind. "You thought I was going to let you go without giving you this dick, baby? Oh, you feel so good. Look at your sexy ass with my cum dripping all down your face. Who pussy is this? I don't hear you, D, who pussy is this?"

"It's yours, Daddy."

"Say my name."

"Steven."

"Say my name, bitch."

"Oh, Steven."

"Give Daddy his cum. Yeah, let me feel you cum all over this big dick. Yeah, baby, just like that. You cumming again. I feel you getting wet. I feel your pussy grabbing this dick. Get fucked, Diamond. Take all of Daddy dick." Steven grabbed Diamond by the neck before he finally came inside of her. "You are so good to me, baby. I been waiting all night to get inside of you. Now go wash your face," he said while slapping her ass.

While she went in the bathroom, Steven began to have flashbacks of the night before. He knew he fucked Fiah, but he couldn't remember what happened. He did remember cumming all over her fat ass. The only thing he could think about is what happened to the rubber. Did he even wear one? Wait, he always wears one. *Why can't I remember nothing*, he thought to himself. After calling him a few times, Diamond walked in the room to see what he was doing. "Hey, babe, I been calling you. What you doing?"

"Come here, love. I'm sorry, I didn't hear you. What's up?"

"Your sister called yesterday. Your mom wants us to come over for Sunday dinner."

"Why do I feel like there is more to it than that?"

"Well, she said it would be nice if we came to church first."

"I knew there was more." Diamond kissed Steven on the lips. "We haven't been to church in months babe. I've been thinking that we should start going again, more regularly."

"Diamond, you know if my mom wants me there, I'm there."

"I love you, baby," she said before kissing him again. "There is something I want to talk to you about, though."

"What's up, baby?"

"So, I came in the house this morning and your moms came at me kind of crazy. Talking about it's about time I came home and how you not happy. You not happy, D?"

"I'm happy, baby. I'm just lonely. Since the doctor wants me to take it easy, I stopped working."

"Well, what are you telling your mother, because she thinks I'm the cause for all things wrong with Diamond. What do you need me to do to make you happy, baby?" Diamond looked at Steven with the saddest eyes, "I just want you to spend some time with me. The other night you said you were thinking about opening up a new restaurant. Maybe I can help with that. I just want to see you around more. I just feel so alone."

"So, you telling your moms I'm making you unhappy?"

"That's not what I said. Are you even listening to me?"

"I'm out here busting my ass to make sure you don't have to want for anything and you out here complaining trying to make me look bad?"

"Steven, that's not what happened." Out of nowhere Steven back-hands her. "Are you fucking kidding me, Steven?"

"I'm out of here. I got stuff to do. Make sure your mom is gone when I get back home. I will make it easier for her and tell her she can come back when the baby comes." Diamond sat on the bed holding her face as she watched Steven get dressed. Steven knew he messed up. He did tell Diamond he wouldn't hit her again, but he just had too much on his mind and he needed to go put together the pieces to this puzzle. When he got downstairs he saw Ms. Wallace in the kitchen. "Ms. Wallace, can I have a moment?"

"Before you do, baby, I just wanted to apologize for last night. You came in the house smelling like liquor and women and I just wouldn't be a good mother if I didn't say anything. This is your house, so I'm leaving today. I just ask that you do right by my daughter. If I find out anything different, I will have a talk with your daddy and he will have to straighten that right out."

"The same way he used to straighten you out, Ms. Wallace? Thanks for the apology. I will see you after the baby gets here." Steven kissed Ms. Wallace before leaving the house.

Ms. Wallace was in utter shock. Her and Mr. Thompson agreed that their private life would stay private. She knew that Steven didn't know the whole story, because if he did, he would know that Mr. Thompson is really Diamond's father. She made a mental note to have a talk with Mr. Thompson at a later time regarding this situation. Back upstairs Diamond was now in the mirror staring at her face. She hated that after everything she had been though with Steven, he still insisted on putting his hands on her. She thought with him knowing about the baby that things would've gotten better. For the most part they have. It just seems like every now and then something just snaps in him and he just doesn't care. She was actually happy that her mother was leaving. Her mom was becoming a hound, always on her back about something. Her mother caught her numerous times texting and smiling and of course she would just lie and say it was Steven, knowing that it was really Kashmere.

Diamond didn't know how she was going to handle her current situation. It was still early in the pregnancy and she wasn't showing yet, but what was she to do when she delivers? How does she tell her fiancée that she can possibly be having another man's child? She couldn't. Steven would kill her. Literally. Right now, that didn't matter. Right now, she just wanted to be in the arms of the man who said he loves her.

Kash: Hey beautiful. I miss you

Diamond: I miss you too baby. I wish you could be here right now.

Kash: Just say the word and I will be right there. It's been a while since I had you and I want to taste you

Diamond: My mom is leaving today. As soon as she's gone, I will let you know and we can link up

Kash: Can you do something for me first?

Diamond: Anything. What do you want?

Kash: I want you to spread your legs open and watch me kiss those pretty lips between your legs

Diamond: What else baby?

Kash: I want you to open her wide for me

Diamond: What you going to do now papi?

Kash: Spread her lips wide, so I can trace them gently with my tongue

Diamond: Mmmmm

Kash: Slide forward so I can wrap that delicious clit with my lips

Diamond: Papi

Kash: Feel me suck and lick on her slowly as I grab your thighs and spread your legs wider

Diamond: I wish you could hear her talking to you <biting bottom lip>

Kash: Let me respond to what she is saying by sliding my tongue deep inside her

Diamond: You are going to make me cum so hard just off the anticipation. I will definitely let you feel this

Kash: Mami, I'm on my knees right now sucking the juices dripping from you over and over again

Diamond: And I'm giving it all to you. Arching my back every time you bring me to a climax

Kash: I'm sliding my hands under your voluptuous ass and sliding you closer as I suck you harder and longer

Diamond: And I'm grabbing the back of your head as I say your name over and over again

Ms. Wallace begins banging on the door. "What you doing in there, girl? I've been calling you for the last ten minutes."

"I'm coming, Ma, I fell back asleep."

"I just wanted to tell you I'm going back home. This is you and Steven's place and how you two live just doesn't work for me. So, I'm going home."

"I understand, Ma. I will be sure to keep you posted and you are always welcome to come with me to my doctors' visits."

"So, you're not even going to fight with me to stay. Here I thought my presence was wanted."

"It was when you first got here, but Ma, you're a bit extra. I know you miss your home."

"Mmmm-hmmm. Just walk me to the door. I already called my cab. I'm just going to tell you this one thing, Diamond. If you ever need to come back home, your old room will always be waiting for you. You are nobody's doormat. You are a princess and you should be treated as such."

"Thanks, Ma," said Diamond as she walked her mom down to the door. "I almost forgot. Mrs. Thompson invited us all over for Sunday dinner. We are going straight to her house from church."

"Sounds good to me. Does that mean I will be seeing you in church finally?"

"Yes, Ma. That's what that means."

"Take care of yourself and my grandbaby. See you on Sunday." Diamond gave her mom a kiss. "I love you, Mama."

"I love you too, baby."

Diamond ran upstairs to get back on her phone.

Kash: Tell me you want it mami

Diamond: I want it papi

Kash: How you want daddy to give it to you

Diamond: I want it hard and deep baby

Kash: I want to fill you up right now. I want to feel you dripping all over my hard dick

Diamond: Come over

Kash: Open the door

Diamond ran downstairs and Kash was at the door. They started kissing immediately. Then he stood back to look at her face. "D, stop, why is the side of your face red?"

"Not now, Kash, please. Fill me up, baby. I need you right now." Kash remembering how Diamond used to be from when they were together years ago knew to just let it go right now. He sat on the couch and pulled her down on top of him. Diamond rode him up and down, hard and fast, as he kissed and licked her neck and her breast. "Oh, you feel so good, baby."

"I'm going to make you mine again, Diamond."

"Make me cum, Kash." Kash began fucking her harder, grabbing on her ass making sure she felt all of him inside of her. "I'm about to cum, Papi. Ooooohhhh. Fuck, Papi, I'm cumming, I'm cumming, Fu-uuuucccckkkk!!!"

"Now it's my turn," said Kash, as he turned over so they were on now laying on their sides. He lifted her leg in the air and gave her what she wanted. Since she was already pregnant, he didn't have to worry about pulling out. He came and stayed inside of her as he kissed her on the back of her neck. Then he said, "Start talking, D."

"Not now, Kash. Can we just enjoy the moment?"

"No, Diamond. I'm not going to keep standing by while this nigga thinks it's okay to put his hands on you."

"Kash, please, not right now."

"So, when, D? You need to leave that nigga and come be with me. You know I would never do anything to hurt you, baby."

"I know, but you have to go. Tomorrow we can meet up and spend the day together. I promise," said Diamond before giving Kash a kiss. She opened the door and he left out as quickly as he came. Diamond took the sheet off the couch and threw it in the hamper as she went upstairs to shower.

Diamond was in the bathroom jamming to her nineties music as she heard Steven slamming doors. "You better be lucky your pretty ass is in the shower. I been trying to call you for the last hour."

"Well, here I am. You know I'm in the house. Where the hell else am I going to be?"

"Don't get smart with me, D."

"Fuck you, Steven. You cop an attitude, hit me, kick my mom out and then you leave. Now you want to come back here with that same stank-ass attitude? Fuck you," said Diamond before closing back the shower door. Steven opened the shower door back up, and started unzipping his pants, "You know I like when you talk to me crazy."

"So what."

"So, you just going to turn me on more and not want to give it to me?"

"Ain't nobody thinking about you, Steven. You said you wouldn't hit me anymore."

"You know what. Fuck you, Diamond. Next time I'm calling you, answer your damn phone." Diamond just stood in the shower replaying the scene of events. If Steven would've came home just a little bit sooner this would've been a whole different situation. She was so happy she had Kash leave when she did. After about fifteen minutes she came out the shower and went into her bedroom.

She began drying off until she turned around and noticed Steven sitting in a chair in the corner. She jumped at the sight of him. "I thought you left. Why you sitting here in silence like a madman?"

"Because I am a madman, D. The other day before I came home from work, Dawne told me that Kashmere had asked her about you. Now, I wondered for a minute. Why is this nigga asking about my lady? How do you and that nigga even know each other?"

"Before Kash was a pimp, he was a regular guy. Well, as close to regular as any teenage boy could be. Me and him dated for a couple of years in high school until he decided that this was the life he wanted for himself. I dressed his first hoe and I went on my way. The night in the club was the first time I'd seen him in almost ten years. Maybe he was asking one of your hoes about me because he thought I was your hoe. I mean, what respectable woman would be in a place like that?"

"I don't want that nigga asking no one about you, ever. I will deliver that message to him personally. Is there anything else you want to add right now?"

"That's it, Steven." Diamond could tell from the look in Steven's eye that there was something that he wasn't sharing with her. "If I find out that you're lying to me, you're going to regret it. You and that nigga both."

"I heard you the first time, Steven. Now can I finish drying off?"

"As soon as you tell me why my house smelled like a man when I walked in."

"What are you talking about now? Go ahead with that dumb shit, man." Steven got up and headed in Diamond's direction. "You had some man in my house, Diamond?"

"Really, Steven? This is what you want to ask me? The woman who you claim to love, the woman that is carrying your child?" Diamond threw her hands up, which made her towel fall to the floor, and looked up to the sky, "This just isn't my day. The only man that has been in this house today was the cab driver who took my mom's bags to the car. Maybe if you didn't kick her out today we wouldn't be having this conversation." Steven pulled Diamond to him grabbing her by the neck, "Don't for one minute think I'm sleeping on this. Something doesn't feel right and I will find out what it is. Maybe I need to put a tracker on your phone. I think that would put me at ease." Diamond pulled away from him. "Here you go with that bullshit again. I'm going to tell you this for the last time. I am nobody's property. If you don't trust me, leave me. You are not putting a tracker on my phone. If I recall correctly, you were the one fucking your hoes and getting bitches pregnant. I just asked you this morning to spend more time with me and you come back with this shit? I don't even have time for this."

"You have time for whatever I say you have time for. I don't want to hear anything else about this nigga asking about you or we going to have a serious problem."

"You jealous, Steven? Does it make you mad to think that someone out there wants to love me? That someone wants to make me their only priority? That someone else might think about touching me right here?" she said pointing to her pleasure palace. "Get your shit together, Steven. Your late-night adventures are catching up to you.

One thing I've learned from my past relationships is this, the one who starts pointing fingers is usually the one who's doing the dirt. You better pray I don't catch nothing," said Diamond before walking out the room naked.

Was she right? thought Steven. *Nah, she dead wrong. I can feel it. I'm going to catch her. She not smarter than me. She's trying to turn me into my father. This bitch wants me to kill her. Nah, I'm bugging. Diamond loves me. She rides for me. She's having my baby. Maybe she is right. I gotta find Fiah and find out what happened last night. This shit got me bugging out.*

Diamond was scared as hell for a minute. Why did he ask about Kash? Why the hell was Kash at The Spot asking about her? What the hell is this nigga trying to do? What if Steven had gotten home just a few minutes sooner? How the hell did Kash get to the house so quick? Was Kash outside the whole time? Is he still outside now? Oh, shit, I left my phone in the room with this nigga! Fuck!

"So, what you doing, Steven? You coming, you going, you hungry? What's up? It's way too early for you to be home right now. Especially after the shit you pulled this morning."

"Diamond. You know that I love you, right?"

"Yes. I know you love me."

"And you know that I will do anything not to lose you, right?" he said now looking into her eyes. "Well, you need to act like it then."

"Baby, come here," he said while motioning for her to come sit on his lap. "I need you to understand something, D. We are forever. This right here," he said while rubbing her belly, "this is us. This is life. Our life. Forever, baby." Then he held her in his arms. "You know I never mean to hurt you, baby. I love you," he said while kissing her all over her face, now fully erect from her nakedness laying his arms. "I love you too, but I'm still mad at you and I'm not having sex with you."

"You sure you don't just want to kiss it?"

"Really, Steven?" said Diamond jumping up off his lap. Pulling her back down while laughing he says, "I was just playing, baby. I think it's time for me to buy you something nice. It's been a while. Tell Daddy what you want, babygirl." Diamond knew this side of Steven all too well. She knew this type of niceness, always ended up with a surprise. "I don't have anything in mind right now, but you know I will get back to you," she said before kissing him on the lips. "Go put some clothes on and then make me something to eat," he said, slapping her butt as she walked away. "All that ass and you don't want to share," he said as she threw on some boy shorts and a t-shirt. Diamond shot him that look that said, be happy I'm even cooking for you right now. He laughed and said, "Damn, babe. I'm just playing. Let's go downstairs. What you cooking for Daddy?" Walking down the stairs she said, "We just going to have to see what's in the fridge." Diamond opened the refrigerator and began to go through the shelves. "Looks like Mama was planning on making spaghetti. Hamburgers it is." Steven started laughing. "So, you can't just make spaghetti, babe? Why are you making burgers?"

"If you wanted spaghetti you shouldn't have kicked Mommy out. As for me and my hands, they about to make some burgers."

Steven walked over to the stove, where Diamond was seasoning the meat. "So, baby, I was thinking, we should have a threesome. Better yet, a foursome."

"Here you go now. Like, I just want to know, where do you come up with this stuff. You just go from one thing to the next."

"When you walked out of the room earlier on your superstar exit, you left your phone behind. It buzzed a couple of times, and I was about to look at it until I heard you coming back up the stairs, so I stayed in my chair. When we were coming downstairs I noticed that you never picked it up to look at, so I said you know what, I'm just tripping. Then I looked on the dresser and seen Kashmere pop up on your screen. Now, the first thing I thought was the vibrator didn't go off. You must've turned it off when you got dressed. Pretty quick there. Didn't I ask you if there was anything else that I needed to know?"

"Yes, you did, Steven, and I told you there wasn't."

"So why the fuck is this nigga's number stored in your phone? Take your password off this phone. I swear if there is anything here I shouldn't see we are going to have a problem."

"Give me the phone." Diamond unlocked the phone and handed it back to him. "What do you see? What's so important that you wanted to see?"

"So, you delete your messages, I see."

"Steven, don't be petty. Yes, I delete my messages daily. Do you see what it is that you are looking for?"

"Why is this nigga texting you asking if you're okay? That sounds real friendly, like y'all been talking lately."

"Now you're just being paranoid. How about I just respond to the message," she said taking the phone.

> Diamond: Hey Kash. How surprising it is to hear from you since I haven't seen you since The Spot
>
> Kash: Yes. That's right. You just crossed my mind, thought I would check on you.
>
> Diamond: That was nice of you. Maybe me, you and Steven can get together one evening
>
> Kash: That would be cool. I can introduce you both to my little sister Sophie
>
> Diamond: Great. I will put it together than. Talk to you soon
>
> Kash: Take care D

"Why that nigga gotta call you D, though? Why he acting all familiar?"

"Yo, you tripping, Steven. When you want to go out so this can be done with already?"

"Monday night. Dinner with the family Sunday then dinner with the ex on Monday. This should be an interesting weekend."

"It should. We haven't been to your parents' house in a while. Definitely not since I found out about the baby. And how you trying to have threesomes and foursomes with your pregnant fiancée?"

"I want to get it out the way before you become my wife. I can't dare say I allowed my wife to have sex with another man."

"Just to entertain this thought of yours for a minute. Who would be in the bed with us?"

"I have a new girl name Fiah. I want to fuck her, but I told you I wouldn't do anything else that you didn't know about. Now before you say no, she is not on my squad. She's an employee of the restaurant. She only deals with table service. You probably think I'm tripping, babe, but I'm trying to show you that I want to do better, baby. I just can't resist this woman. I have to have her." Diamond's eyes began to tear up as she heard her man share these desires he had for another woman. "Who's the other person?" she finally managed to get out. "Your boy. Kashmere. I want to see exactly how familiar he is with you."

"You're absolutely crazy. I don't know how I've dealt with you so long. You want to fuck that hoe, go ahead. Enjoy. Finish your own fucking burgers," said an angry Diamond walking upstairs. *Something is definitely wrong with this nigga,* thought Diamond as she went upstairs to grab her purse and her keys. Steven stood at the counter thinking, *Damn, how she just try to turn this shit around like I didn't just catch her out there? Wait, I didn't catch her out there. But I will.*

"Yo, where you think you going in those little-ass shorts? You better go put some clothes on." Diamond went upstairs grabbed some sweatpants and was back out the door. *This girl is a trip. The fuck she mad for? She better be happy I didn't just do with her what I wanted to do. That baby just saved her life, trying to play me like I don't know what's up. What the hell is wrong with her?* thought Steven. He picked up his phone to call Fiah. This was the second time he was calling her for the day and he didn't appreciate it. She answered on the second ring. "Hey, baby, what's up?"

"I told you don't call me that shit, call me Daddy. Why you didn't answer when I called you earlier?"

"Daddy, I was still sleep. You know I been working these late hours. Still getting used to it."

"What happened last night?"

"What do you mean? You talking about us going to the basement early this morning? You don't remember that?"

"No, I don't remember. Why the fuck don't I remember, Fiah?"

"You was drinking and getting high with Vanilla all night. You just asked me to meet you in the Champagne Room in the basement and I did."

"Okay. So, what happened?"

"We got in the room and you told me to stand in front of you, then you pushed me down to my knees. You told me to kiss your dick, to suck it, to lick it. Then you grabbed the back of my head while you fucked my mouth. You told me to stand up and you grabbed me from behind and pulled me into you. You began kissing me and grabbing my neck with one hand, while you used the other hand to put the condom on. Then you placed yourself inside of me. Hard and fast. You continued grabbing my neck while your other hand grabbed my hip pushing yourself all the way inside of me. You wanted to cum on my face, so you turned me around and sat me on the chair and came all over me while standing over me."

"Damn. I must've really been fucked up. I thought I came on your ass."

"So, you don't remember none of that, Daddy?"

"Nah. None of it. At least I know what happened now. I knew I wasn't crazy enough to fuck you without a rubber." Fiah was now in her feelings. She knew Steven had a girl at home, but he had her thinking that she could be his second choice. How could he not remember their first time together? Fiah was the first girl to work at The Spot and only host. She thought she was special because of that. "Was there anything else you wanted? I was about to run out to the store."

"There was, but I'd rather tell your sexy ass when I see you tonight."

"Okay, cool. Talk to you later, Daddy."

"Lata," said Steven before hanging up the phone. He felt so relieved about what he just heard. He laughed to himself as he thought about how fun life was. He went upstairs and took a nap.

It was dark outside when Steven woke up and realized that he was still in his bed alone. He picked up his phone to check the time. It was almost eleven o'clock, where the hell was Diamond at, he thought? He jumped out of the bed and turned the shower on. He let the hot water run, letting the bathroom became steamy. It was customary for Steven to come in the spot rocking a suit and some gators, but tonight, he felt like letting loose. He took out a pair of Gucci jeans and a fresh white Ralph Lauren Polo. Steven was feeling himself, as he usually is. As he washed his body he wondered if Diamond would let him have his threesome. It seemed like a win-win situation and this way he knew for sure the reason why he had to take her life. The thought of her having sex with another man while she was pregnant with his child made him snap a little. He had a plan, but it would have to wait until Monday. It was Friday night and he was trying to get into some more Fiah. This time he wanted to make sure he remembers what happening. *Mental note. Don't get too fucked up with Vanilla.* He must admit, he did miss having a white girl around. *Maybe tonight she could lick that coke off my dick before I smash Fiah. So many decisions,* thought Steven.

After a long, hot shower, Steven finally got out and got dressed. He threw on his white uptowns, white Gucci fitted, Gucci shades, a couple of chains and his Cartier watch. He was ready to go after that. He called Diamond's phone on the way downstairs and was surprised to hear it ringing from the living room. He didn't even get made when he seen her reach for the phone and push the button to stop it from ringing. He just kissed her on the forehead and watched her sleep for a second. He took her half smoked blunt out the ashtray and walked out of the house. As soon as he got in the car his phone was ringing. "Yo."

"Yo, bring your ass, man. Got a little situation with your new Firestarter."

"Damn, man. Already?"

"I told you don't be fucking these hoes. She acting just like Dream was."

"I'm leaving the house now. See you in a minute."

"One." Then off Steven went to The Spot.

As soon as his car pulled off Diamond's phone was ringing a familiar tune. 'Boyfriend number two' began playing. She smiled as she answered the phone. "Hey, beautiful."

"Hey, baby. What you up to?"

"Come open the door and find out."

"I'm sleeping. I'm not about to get up to see you not at the door."

"D, get your ass up. If I said I'm here, I'm here."

"I'm coming." Diamond went to the door and there stood Kashmere looking fine as ever. He came inside and asked, "You okay, baby? I been worried about you ever since that nigga came back home so soon after I left."

"How you know he came home as soon as you left? How you know to pop up when you do? You been watching me, Kash?"

"Yes, I have, D. When I'm not personally out here, I have a car that does twenty-four-hour surveillance. I'm not playing when I tell you that I love you. If anything was to happen to you after I found you again, I would never forgive myself, baby." Diamond just hugged Kash and told him that she loved him. "I don't want to be here. Let's go, D." Diamond grabbed her keys and her purse and they were off. "You want to come to my crib, baby? We could stop by the store. Get something to cook."

"We can do that if you the one cooking. You see what time it is?" It was after twelve. "I'm hungry, baby."

"I got something you can eat, Daddy."

"I bet you do, nasty," said Kash as Diamond got in his car and he closed the door. When he got in she says, "I'm thinking I should follow you. That way I don't have to get up so early in the morning. I can sleep in late with you," she said before kissing him on the lips. "Sounds like a plan, baby. Meet me at my crib on the east."

"Bet," she said before kissing him again and opening the car door. "Before she could close her door, he was already gone. She smiled at the thought of spending time with someone who loved her and wanted to please her. Steven used to be like that.

Diamond had no intentions on having sex tonight. She just wanted to be in the presence of someone who wanted and needed her the way a significant other should. Every time she told herself there was nothing left that Steven could do to make her feel like shit, he came back with something new. This right here was the last straw. Between him feeling like he some investigator and him confessing his lust for a woman he sees more than her, she was definitely in her bag and Kashmere was the only one who could get her back on track. She pulled up to Kash's condo in the east and was very happy to see him standing by his car waiting for her. He came over and opened her car door. He held his hand out for her to grab. "Baby, you still want to go to store before we go upstairs?"

"Nah, unlike you, I do go grocery shopping. I have a few things in the fridge." They both started laughing. "Oh, so you got jokes tonight, I see," said Diamond, hitting Kash playfully. He pushed her against her car and said, "Nah, D. Tonight I got you, baby." *Damn, I wasn't planning on having sex,* thought Diamond. This man just knew how to take her there. He always did the right thing, at the right time. "Let's go upstairs," said Kash as he threw Diamond across his shoulder. She laughed, as he caught her off guard and carried her upstairs.

Steven walked in The Spot, saying what's up to all his people. The only people he wanted to see right now was Calvin and Fiah. When he didn't see either of them on the floor, he went straight to his office. Calvin was sitting at the desk and Fiah was sitting on the couch with a drink in her hand. "What the fuck is going on with you, B? Like why is my brother calling me, telling me you being a bugout?"

"One of these ratchet-ass hoes you got in here tried to play me. So I told her to know her place."

"And who the fuck is you to tell her to know her place. It seems like you don't know your place."

"Yo, Calvin, I need the room for a minute."

"Aight, bro, I'm outta here," said Calvin before stepping out. Steven walked over to Fiah and slapped the fire out her ass. She lost hearing in her ear for a second as she grabbed her face. "You don't have the right to be checking nobody in this motherfucker, you hear me? The only reason I don't have you selling your ass like the rest of them hoes is because I want to fuck you. Don't you for a second think that because you get the dick you special. You are whatever the fuck I tell you you are. Do you hear me, bitch?" he said looking down over her while she still holding her face. "Yes, I hear you."

"Yes who?"

"Yes, Daddy."

"I see I'm a have to break you in like the rest of these bitches." He grabbed her by her hair and threw her over the back of the couch. He put two fingers inside his mouth, then placed them inside of her. "Look at your pussy wet for me," he whispered in her ear before placing himself inside of her. "Tell me you love this dick, bitch," he said grabbing her neck with one hand and grabbing her ass with the other one. "I love your dick, Daddy. Follarme, Papi."

"Talk that shit, bitch."

"Te quiero tanto. Quiero sentirte dentro de mi."

"I knew you had some good pussy. I knew I had to have you. You gotta stop tripping or you will never get this dick again. You hear me, bitch?"

"Yes, Daddy. I hear you."

"You about to cum, hoe?"

"Yes, Daddy. I'm about to cum."

"Good. So am I." Steven pulled out of her just before she came and put his dick in her mouth. Making her swallow every bit of his cum. He took his dick out her mouth and looked at her. "I don't care how good your pussy is. I will cancel your ass if you get out of pocket again. If you want to feel this big dick actually make you cum, your better play your position and keep your fucking mouth shut. Do you understand me?"

"Yes, Daddy."

"Now go get a rag so you can clean me up. When you finish I will call Dawne up here, so she can put some make up on that pretty face of yours."

As Steven sat on the couch waiting for Fiah to come back, he realized that Diamond had him tripping right now. Diamond was the only woman he ever had sex with unprotected since they been together. *What the fuck am I doing?* he thought. Fiah walked over to Steven with a hot, wet rag. "Get on your knees and clean me up." Fiah went to use the rag, but Steven stopped her. "Use your mouth. I want to see you lick yourself off of me." So Fiah did as she was told. At that moment there was a knock at the door. "Who the fuck is it?"

"It's Dawne."

"Open the door. Come here, Dawne, you couldn't have come at a better time. I need you to show this girl something about sucking a dick. Make me a drink first."

"Keep licking my dick till she gets over here. Make sure that you pay attention. I don't care how good your pussy is, I like getting my dick sucked. If you don't improve I will replace you." He never let a moment go by without letting Fiah know that she was replaceable.

Even though he knew he has no intentions of letting her go, he wouldn't dare let her know that. "Come have a seat right here," he said to Fiah, tapping on a space on the couch next to him. Dawne passed him his drink, took the pin out of her hair and dropped to her knees. "You see this shit? I don't even have to tell her to get down. This is how you supposed to greet me. Lay back on the pillow and play with your pussy. Maybe this time we can cum together," he said with a handful of Dawne's hair in his hand, guiding her head up and down his dick. "You see how she taking all of me. Fuck, that shit feel good, baby." He would never call Fiah baby. He knew she wouldn't know how to act if that happened. Hearing Steven call Dawn baby made Fiah want to learn the art of it all. She wanted him. All of him. She wanted to become his main lady, she just hadn't figured out how to do it yet. Fiah watched as Steven moaned, while stroking Dawne's mouth. She began rubbing on her clit while using her other hand to rub her nipple as she watched Dawne's tongue travel up and down Steven's shaft, then watched her lick his balls before placing them in her mouth one at time and then both at once. Looking at Steven being pleased turned Fiah on more than she anticipated. "I see you enjoying yourself over there. How many times have you came?" asked Steven putting two fingers inside of Fiah's wet box. "I came three times, Daddy."

"Well, let me make it four." Feeling Dawne sucking on his balls while stroking his manhood while playing with Fiah's wet, hot box, was about to make Steven cum in the worse way. He held it in because he wasn't ready for this party to be over. After making Fiah have an orgasm he instructed her to get on her knees behind Dawne and make her have orgasm. Watching Fiah eat Dawne out from behind was so sexy to him. Steven stood up and moved everyone with him. He made Fiah lay on the couch, while Dawne sat on her face and finished him off. The vibrations from Dawne's mouth as she came had his dick hard as ever. He grabbed her in his fist as he started giving her long, deep strokes, feeling the back of her throat. He fucked her throat until he came. He sat on a chair across from the couch as he watched

Dawne and Fiah finish up. He picked up the phone and called Calvin. "Yo, bro, I handled that situation."

"I bet you did, bro," replied Calvin before laughing. "Find Vanilla and tell her to come up here with that white girl."

"Damn, bro, you still going? I saw Dawn go up there about an hour ago."

"You can watch the tape whenever you like, bro. You know how I do."

"I hear that one. I will send Vanilla up in a minute."

"Lata, bro."

"One."

Kash threw Diamond on the couch once they got upstairs. "Why you play so much?" she asked him laughing. "Because it's you, baby. Do you know how long it's been since I've been with someone I love?" He bent down next to her, looked her in the eyes and said, "not since you left me." Then he kissed her on the lips. "Now I'm about to cook. I'm starving, baby," said Kash walking over to the kitchen from the living room. Diamond took her sneakers off and sat up on the couch looking at Kash. "What you about to cook, babe?" As soon as she seen him pull out ground beef from the fridge, she started laughing. "What you laughing at, crazy lady?"

"This evening before Steven proposed to me that you and one of his hoes have a foursome with us, I was seasoning some burgers. After he said what he did, I left him there to make his own damn burgers."

"Go back to this foursome. What's that about?"

"He thinks we fucking, Kash. He really freaked me out today. If he finds out about us, he's going to kill us both, you know."

"Don't worry about that, baby. I got it all under control. Did he mention the name of this hoe?"

"No, he didn't. He just kept saying how irresistible she is and how he just has to have her. He has never come out his face like that before. That's why I think he think he knows something about us."

"So, you mean to tell me, you was going to make that lame-ass nigga some burgers and you can't make me none?"

"You better go ahead with that there."

"I'm just playing with you, D. I know what you need. Check the drawer under the coffee table in front of you." Diamond smiled at the lovely aroma that hit her nose as soon as the drawer opened. She rolled up and watched TV while Kash made burgers.

He came over to the couch with two plates. He handed Diamond the plate with the one burger while he sat the plate with the two burgers in front of the empty spot on the couch. "Damn, D, you couldn't save a nigga none of that bud?"

"Come on, baby." She looked at him before pointing to a fresh rolled blunt on the table. "Oh, okay. I was about to say."

"You wasn't about to say shit," she said leaning in for him to kiss her. He kissed her on the lips and said, "I got something that you can kiss, baby."

"I bet you do," she said. "You better eat your burger while it's hot and juicy. I know you like it to squirt when you put your mouth on it."

"You making me hungry for something else right now."

"What you want, Daddy?" said Diamond after pulling her pants off. "I want you to squirt while I put my mouth on you. Lay back on the couch, baby." Diamond laid back and began to pull of her panties until Kash stopped her. "I got this, baby." Kash rubbed his fingers down Diamond's thigh. Right from the crease of her thigh till he got to her ankles. Then he went from her ankle back to the crease of her inner thigh, licking and sucking down the same path he just stroked with his fingers. Diamond moaned as his tongue and lips began to make her pleasure palace start calling. He then followed the path back to her ankle, this time nibbling on her inner thigh and kissing up her leg. This time he kissed his way to her toes before sucking each one. Her body began to shake under him as she felt the warmth and wetness of his mouth teasing her toes. He used his other hand to trace from her neck to her clit, where he stayed and played. While he began sucking her big toe, he placed one finger in her, then two, feeling her body move to his rhythm. He was at a full erection at this point, but all he wanted to do was to make her orgasm. After she came for the seventh time he felt her body tighten as her back arched. He knew this was what he was waiting for. He began to stroke her faster and deeper while running his tongue up and down her thigh. When he felt her began to orgasm, he stroked her faster while he began sucking on her clit, causing her to have multiple orgasms. Diamond couldn't remember the last time she had come like that. She was asleep within minutes.

Chapter 8

Diamond had got up in the middle of the night to use the bathroom. She felt good waking up next to Kash, who was holding her with his head laid in her breast. As soon as he felt her move, he woke up. "Where you going, baby?" he asked. "I'm going to the bathroom. I'll be right back." Diamond went to the bathroom and came back. When she came in the room, she looked at Kash sleeping in his king-size bed. She smiled before walking over to kiss him. As she was about to walk out of the room, he woke up again. "Baby, where are you going? You said you was coming right back."

"I know, Kash. Something don't feel right, so I'm gonna head back to my house."

"Come give Daddy a kiss." She walked over to give Kash another kiss. "I will wait to hear from you in the morning, beautiful."

"The morning? You don't want to know when I get inside?"

"Baby, I will know as soon as your car gets in the driveway." Diamond shot him a look before their earlier conversation came back to mind. "Get home safe, D." Diamond went in the living room to put on her sneakers and sweatpants, then she was on her way out the door.

It was almost four-thirty in the morning when Diamond got home. She was very happy to see that Steven hadn't made it in yet.

All of a sudden, she began to panic, she smelled Kashmere. She began smelling her clothes and realized that this man was all over her. As soon as she got in the house, she took off all her clothes and went upstairs. When she got in her room, she placed the clothes in a gym bag she kept in the closet before getting in the shower. As soon as she got out the bathroom, she heard Steven's car pull up in the driveway. She could hear him finishing up a conversation from the car phone. She dried off and quickly got in the bed. She heard Steven come through the door, but he never came up the stairs. She was actually happy about that. The more her and Kash spent time together, the less she wanted to be with Steven. She did want to try to make things work with Steven. When she found out she was pregnant, she had only been with Kash one time, so she really didn't think the baby could've been his. The most they really did was send some raunchy text messages. But last night, the way he made her body excited without using his penis, had her wanting more of him.

Steven came in the house twisted as usual. He was so done, he didn't even feel like going upstairs to get in the bed. He sat on the couch and took out his phone. There were three cameras inside the office at The Spot. The cameras have a direct feed to his phone. He began going through the videos from tonight. He went back all the way to before he got to the club. He was curious to see what Fiah and Calvin were doing before he got there. He fast-forwarded through since he seen that his brother was never close enough to her to touch her. When he got to the part where he entered the office, he let it play. He looked at himself as he backhanded Fiah and laughed as he seen her whole face turn. *Damn, I slapped the fire out that hoe,* he thought to himself. Then he put the video to slow motion as he watched himself take her roughly, enjoying the way she wanted it. After he came in her mouth, he fast-forwarded the video again and stopped when he moved everybody to couch, watching himself cum in Dawne's mouth, which turned him on. He felt his manhood grow, as he remembered how good her vibrating throat felt on his dick. Then he fast-forwarded the video again to when Vanilla came in the room with the white girl. His dick was rock hard now. He began stroking himself as he watched Vanilla lick the coke off his dick. Then he fast-forwarded the video to when he bust all over her face. That was enough to bring him to a climax. He fell asleep just like that. His dick in his hand, with cum dripping all over the place.

Diamond woke up about twelve, Saturday afternoon. She woke up feeling good until she looked up and seen Steven sitting in the chair staring at her in his wife beater and boxers. "Yo, what's up with you, Steven? This the second day you doing this stop and stare bullshit."

"Relax, baby. I was just admiring how beautiful you are. Even with the scars. You know I could've killed your ass that night, right? But what if I did? Then we wouldn't be here right now. You, having my baby." Diamond could tell this nigga was on some next shit. The whole time he was talking to her, it was like he was looking right through her. "I have every reason to believe that I should fuck you up right now. You think I'm fucking stupid, D, don't you?"

"What is wrong with you, Steven? You're really starting to scare me."

"No, I'm not. If I was, you wouldn't be trying to play me right now. I'm around bad bitches all day, but yet I stay faithful to you. Do you understand that you're my life, Diamond? I put a ring on your finger and you treating me like I'm some lame-ass, bitch nigga. I thought you would've learned from the first time not to fuck with me, but you didn't." Steven got up and walked over to the bed and pulled the blanket back.

When he seen her naked body, he began to rub his already hardened penis through his boxers. "Move over," he said to her. She slid over so he could get in the bed. "You have to be kidding me right now. You going to get in the bed with me smelling like some cheap female?"

"Shut your hoe ass up. This dick don't smell like perfume. Turn the fuck over," he said rolling her on her side so her ass was now facing him. Diamond knew now wasn't the time to be tough. She didn't know what he was about to do, but she knew she wouldn't be able to get out of this one. Steven scooted down in the bed and spread Diamond's ass cheeks apart, as he began to lick and suck her asshole. Diamond wasn't expecting this, but she was very turned on as he began fucking her ass with his tongue while placing two fingers inside of her wet pussy. Then he took the fingers out of her pussy and put them in her ass, while moving back up on the bed. "See me being a gentleman," he whispered in her ear, now moving his fingers in and out of her ass at a faster pace. He began biting on her neck as he added another finger. When he seen that she was gyrating her ass, he knew she was ready. He placed his dick in her ass slowly this time. He didn't want her to black out like before. He placed the two fingers back in her dripping, hot pussy, while inching all of himself inside of her tight asshole. "I told you that you would give me this ass and love it. I hear you moaning, bitch. Your pussy is so wet right now. Look at you taking all this big, hard cock up your ass. You like that shit, don't you? Tell Daddy you like it. Say that shit louder, bitch," said Steven as he began choking Diamond. "Now I'm going to fuck you the hoe you want to be." Diamond tried to loosen the grip he had around her neck. "I can't breathe," she managed to get out while gasping for air. Steven didn't hear her anymore. He was extremely turned on and only wanted to cum. He took his hand off her neck when he seen she didn't have the strength to fight him anymore. Then he punched her in the ribs twice before cumming all over her ass. "You want to act like a hoe, then that's how the fuck I'm going to treat you."

Diamond laid in the bed with tears in her eyes. She knew better than to let him hear her cry. When she heard him get in the shower, she pulled the blanket over head and began to cry more. This was it. She knew she had to go, but how was she going to do it. She knew wherever she went, he would be right there to find her. What Diamond didn't know, was that Steven had sent Calvin to the house around two that morning, to pick up something. Steven became furious when Calvin came back to The Spot and told him that Diamond wasn't home. While Steven was in the shower he closed his eyes and said, "God, I know I'm not perfect, but I try to do the right thing. Why this girl trying to play me like some sucker? I just wanted to love her and give her everything and she goes and steps out on me. God, please don't let me kill her today." Steven placed his head on the shower wall letting the water run down his body as the tears came out his eyes. He stayed in there for about twenty minutes before getting out.

"Why the fuck you still in the bed," is the first thing he said when he comes back in the room. Diamond didn't reply, she just got out of the bed with the comforter wrapped around her and slowly walked to the bathroom. Steven felt sick to his stomach once the comforter was off the bed and he saw the all the blood on the sheets. This was all too much for him. He got dressed and left. He needed to be anywhere but here right now. When Diamond heard the door close behind him, she began to cry, loud and hard. *Why is this happening to me? What did I do to deserve this? I should've left after the first time. I always leave. Why didn't I just leave?* She went back in her room to get her phone. She picked it up and texted Kash.

> Diamond: Being with you again has been one of the best things that has happened to me in a long time. Now I'm sitting here thinking about what could've happened if you never decided to choose the lifestyle you did. We would've probably been somewhere married right now. With children. Happy. Know that I loved you. I wish things would've ended differently.

Diamond pushed send and turned her phone off. She went back into the bathroom and grabbed a blade out of the medicine cabinet. *Looks like this is the only way I can leave.* Diamond started crying as she began slitting her wrist. She laid in the comforter as she began to bleed out.

Steven felt bad for leaving like he did, so he decided to give Diamond a call to check on her. When the phone went straight to voicemail, he knew something was wrong and headed back to the house.

Kash was at his home in the west, chilling when he got Diamond's message. As soon as he read it, he felt a sharp pain in his chest. He just felt like something bad had happened. He called her immediately. He instantly became enraged as the phone went to voicemail. He called the guy he had watching the house and told him to go ring the bell. The guy was just about to get out the car when Steven pulled up driving erratically. He got back on the phone to let Kash know that Steven had just gotten home. Since Steven wasn't home, Kash thought maybe it wasn't that bad. Then the driver heard Steven screaming from inside the house. He called Kash back to let him know that something was wrong. For the first time since he was a child, Kash began to cry. Kash was about an hour away from Diamond. He stayed on the phone with the driver, as he kept him informed of what was going on. "Boss, the ambulance just pulled up."

"No, Troy, don't tell me that."

"Go see what's going on."

"Kash, just be easy, man. I can't blast this fool in front of the cops. Okay, I see they bringing her out on the stretcher."

"How is she, man? How bad does it look?"

"I can't really tell. Looks like she's wrapped up in a blanket."

"Follow the ambulance. I'm heading to the hospital now."

When Steven pulled up to the house, he jumped out the car immediately and went inside. It had been about ten minutes since he first tried calling Diamond. He called her name as he ran up the stairs and headed to the bathroom. He screamed when he first saw her wrapped in the blanket with blood everywhere. He seen her eyes flicker before he ran to call the ambulance. He picked her up in the blanket and carried her downstairs to the couch, with tears running down his face. "Diamond, you better not die on me. You hear me, D?" He laid her on the couch and ran to the kitchen to grab some towels. He wrapped the towels around her wrist, in efforts to stop the bleeding. Her skin was pale, but she still had a pulse. Steven just sat with her, trying his best to apply pressure on the now covered wounds. He was relieved when he heard the ambulance pull up. He ran to the door to let them inside and they took over. Before he knew it, they had her on the stretcher putting her in the ambulette. "Are you riding with us, sir?"

"No. I will meet you at the hospital. I need to call her mom."

Ms. Wallace was in the house getting ready for church when her phone began to ring. She seen it was Steven and picked up immediately. Steven never calls her, so she knew it had to be an emergency. "Ms. Wallace, there's been an accident." Ms. Wallace could hear in his voice that he had been crying. "Steven, talk to me. What's going on?"

"Ms. Wallace, I don't know. I came home and...."

"What, Steven? You came home and what?" Steven was trying to talk through his tears. "I came home, and she was on the floor. Bleeding."

"Oh, no, don't tell me she had another miscarriage."

"No, Ms. Wallace, she didn't. Meet me at the hospital."

"Steven. What happened to my baby?"

"Just meet me at the hospital," said Steven before hanging up the phone. Ms. Wallace dropped down to her knees and began to pray. "God, please don't take my baby. She is all I have left." Ms. Wallace began to cry as she prayed to God, begging him to save her child. She stayed on the floor and prayed for about an hour. She knew there was nothing she could do at the hospital to save her daughter. What she did know was that the God she served would never put more on her than she could bear. Her prayers right now, would do more than any doctor could ever do. Two hours later Ms. Wallace was out the door, on her way to the hospital.

"Troy, you at the hospital?"

"Yeah, I'm here, boss. All I can tell you is that she's alive."

"That's all I need to know. Hit me when that bitch-ass nigga leaves. I know he had something to do with this shit. That nigga is about to be somebody." Troy quickly heard Biggie smalls song in his head, "You're nobody, till somebody, kills you." He knew immediately what that last statement meant. "He not even here. I haven't seen him since I been here. What you need me to do?"

"For now, just stay at the hospital. I gotta put some things in motion real quick." As soon as Troy hung up, he seen Ms. Wallace come through the door. He could overhear her asking where her daughter was. Once the receptionist responded, she was on her way to see her baby. Ms. Wallace made sure she held it together for her baby girl.

When she got to the room and saw her daughter with breathing tubes and her wrist wrapped up she lost it. Troy heard her crying loudly from the room. "Noooooo. Not my baby. God, noooo." The nurses ran to the room to assist her. They tried their best to calm her down before she caused any harm to herself. "What happened to my baby?" she asked the nurse, with tears pouring out her eyes. "Tell me now. What happened to my baby? Oh, God, nooo," she said still crying. "Ma'am, your daughter tried to commit suicide." Ms. Wallace froze. All she could think about was the conversation she had with Steven the day before. All she felt right now was guilt. She blamed herself for everything that was happening with her daughter. "Ma'am. Are you okay?" The nurse waved her hand in front of Ms. Wallace's face. "Ma'am, do you hear me."

"I'm sorry. Where's the man that came in with my daughter?"

"Ma'am, there was no man that came in with her. The ambulance brought her in here alone. There is one person who has been in the waiting room since your daughter has been here."

"Can you show them to me?"

"Sure. Come this way." As they walked back to the waiting room, Ms. Wallace felt a feeling she has never felt before. She didn't even feel like she was in her body anymore. She felt like she was watching herself move. Before she knew it, they were standing in front of Troy.

"Excuse me, sir, the nurse told me you've been here since my daughter was admitted. Do you know Diamond?"

"Hi, ma'am. I don't know your daughter, but my employer does."

"Who is your employer?"

"His name is Kashmere. I'm not sure if you know him. Him and your daughter went to high school together. Him and Diamond have reconnected recently. When he heard that something happened to Diamond he told me to come and check on her since he couldn't make it." Ms. Wallace was pissed that Steven wasn't there, but she was grateful that someone was looking out for her child. Ms. Wallace couldn't take anymore. Troy caught her before she passed out.

Kash jumped up abruptly, awakened by Diamond's screams. "Diamond. Wake up. I'm here, babe," he said while he rocked her in his arms. Diamond grabbed him tight, as she cried. Happy that this was all just a bad dream. Kash stroked Diamond's hair, as he told her everything would be alright. "I have to leave him, Kash."

"So, leave, baby. You know I got you. Whatever you need."

"Just hold me," said Diamond as she continued to cry. She looked up at Kash and said, "You really love me, don't you?"

"More than you know, D. More than you know." Then he kissed her on the lips before he began stroking her hair again. "I'm about to leave in a few and head to my mom's house."

"Nah, baby. Not right now you not. Just chill for a minute. Get your head right." Diamond looked over at the clock. It was now three in the morning. "You know I'm not going to let anyone hurt you, right, babe?"

"Yes, Kash, I know."

"Go back to sleep then." And she did.

Diamond rolled over and squinted her eyes as the sun was shining through the half-pulled-back curtains. "Kash?" she called out after seeing she was in the bed alone. She got out the bed and followed her nose straight to the kitchen. She smiled as she seen Kash at the stove making breakfast. "Babe, you sure you know what you doing over there?"

"Hey, baby. I got this right here. Go in the bathroom and get straight. I got everything laid out for you." Diamond was surprised to go in the bathroom and not just see a towel, washcloth and toothbrush, but there was also an outfit, socks and a matching panty and bra set. She smiled, feeling loved. She had washed her face and brushed her teeth before calling Kash in the bathroom to turn on this fancy shower. The thing had jets on the side, coming from the top and bottom. Diamond knew she could definitely get used to this feeling. The feeling of freedom and love.

Before Diamond got in the shower she checked her phone. She couldn't believe it was eight o'clock in the morning. Diamond was never up that early. *Damn, how long was he up?* she thought. She turned on her radio app and jumped in the shower. *Ohhh, this shower feels so good,* she thought. When she looked on the rack in the shower and seen her Vanilla Lace shower gel, she smiled instantly. *He remembered.* She stayed in there for about thirty minutes before finally getting out. She dried off and looked in the cabinet for some lotion and there it was, the matching lotion and body spray. She lotioned up and got dressed. She brushed her wet hair back and put it in a ponytail, before heading back to the kitchen.

As soon as she walked out the bathroom, she heard Kash immediately. "Damn, baby. You smell so good. I can smell you all the way in here." He had the table set when she came to the dining room. "This is all so nice, babe, and it smells good." He walked to the table and pulled the chair out for her. "Anything for you, beautiful," he said before kissing her on the lips. He loved her lips and he made it his business to kiss them every time he had the chance. He sat in the seat across from her so he could admire her beauty, even with the scars. Kash had made some grits with cheese, sausage, bacon, eggs and toast. Diamond was loving the fact that he cooked and did it well. "Baby, these grits are perfect. I see you remember I like sugar in my grits."

"I remember everything about you, Diamond. I should've married you then."

"Mmm-hmm. You say that now," she said with a sausage link in her mouth. "I like how you got that link in your mouth."

"I bet you do. What time is it, babe?"

"It's almost nine-thirty. You got somewhere to be?"

"Yeah. I gotta head to my mom's house. Steven is probably going to be over there soon looking for me."

"Can I ask you a question, Diamond?"

"Of course, baby, what's up?"

"What was you dreaming about this morning?"

"I don't even want to think about it right now. Can we talk about it another time?"

"Anything for you, baby. I won't press it." When Diamond was done, Kash offered her something to drink while he took her plate. "I will take some apple juice, please. Got me sitting here like a kid. Gotta finish my meal before I get something to drink," she said before laughing.

"Yep. That's right," he said while handing her the cup and smiling. "Breakfast was really good, baby." Diamond stood up and wrapped her arms around Kash's neck, and said, "I remember when we were teenagers. We would sit up and talk about our wedding and all of our kids. You always said you wanted to be rich, so you could spoil me, give me everything I want. I always told you," Kash interjected, "You always told me, all you want is me." He looked in Diamond's eyes, lifted her chin up and kissed her passionately. After a few minutes he stopped. "You just said you have to go to your mom's crib. Don't start nothing you can't finish."

"You right, baby."

"Get your things together. I'm about to put these dishes in the dishwasher." He walked over to the dishwasher and began putting the dishes in. "You so damn lazy. You can't wash your own dishes?"

"I could, but I choose not to. That's what money did. Allowed me to make choices, as well as give you that wedding that we always talked about. Just give me a few days, baby. I'm taking you from that clown." Diamond put her sneakers on and got all her things. She rolled up a blunt and was ready to head out. Kash walked her downstairs to her car. He gave her a kiss before she pulled off.

It was almost eleven-thirty when Diamond pulled up to her mother's house. She was so happy she had that blunt to hold her down in all that traffic she got caught in. She was a little relieved to see her mom's car was gone when she got there. She was full, high and just wanted to take a nap. She used her key, went straight upstairs to her room, turned the TV on and laid down. She looked at her phone and seen she had missed a call from Steven about ten minutes ago. She figured she would wait a few minutes before calling him back. Before she knew it, she was sleep. She woke to hear Steven and her mom downstairs talking. *Oh, shit! What time is it? I forgot to call him back!* thought Diamond. Diamond looked at her phone and seen that it was now after four. And that she had five missed calls from Steven and a message from Kash.

Kash: My spot still smells like Vanilla. I can't wait to taste you again.

She smiled before deleting her messages and made her way downstairs. As soon as Steven seen her, he got up to greet her. "Look who finally woke up. That's a nice outfit too, I don't remember that," said Steven before giving Diamond a hug and a kiss. "Thanks, baby. It was something I picked up when I was working."

"Come have a seat and talk with us. I was just telling your mom how you had me worried about you," said Steven while sitting on the loveseat across the couch from Ms. Wallace. He patted his hand next to him gesturing for Diamond to sit beside him. "I'm sorry, Steven," said Diamond as she sat down. "Last night I just got so sick and I didn't want to be home alone, so I came over here."

"What's wrong with you, babe? When I left you was asleep on the couch, you looked okay."

"Yeah, it was probably something I ate."

Ms. Wallace interjected, "When I got in from church my phone rung, to my surprise it was Steven. Any other time, I would've thought something was wrong. Then he told me he was looking for you, so I told him you were here, sleeping and he came on over."

"Thanks, Ma. For easing his mind," said Diamond as she looked from her mother to Steven. "What time did you get here, baby?" she asked Steven. "I been here for about an hour now. I didn't want to wake you up. Then your mom told me she was cooking, so I just sat back and looked at some pictures of my beautiful lady," he said as he pointed to the photo albums on the coffee table. "Ma, I know you didn't bring out the albums!!" Ms. Wallace started laughing. "You know I did. I wanted him to get an idea of how beautiful my little grandbaby is going to be." Steven smiled as he looked at Diamond and rubbed her belly. "I can't wait until you start showing, baby." Diamond just smiled as she thought about how crazy this nigga really is.

"Let me go check on the food," said Ms. Wallace as she got up and walked to the kitchen. "It sure smells good," said Steven. As soon as she was out of eyesight, he turned to Diamond. "You better be glad your mother picked up her phone, D. First, Calvin goes to the house for something and you not there, then I get home and you not there, I wake up and you still not there," Steven stopped and took a breath. "I'm just happy you're okay and where you are supposed to be." He softened his tone as he stroked her cheek. "Are you coming home tonight? I was thinking of taking the night off since we have to go to church in the morning. Maybe we can read the bible or something." Diamond looked at Steven like he was crazy. She has never even heard him say the word bible for as long as she knew him. "I wanted to spend some time with my mom today. I should be back home before it gets too late." Ms. Wallace walked in the dining room with a big pot. "I hope you guys are ready to eat."

"I sure am," said Steven getting up from his seat. "That smells good, Ma," said Diamond walking behind him. "Diamond, come help your mama out in the kitchen."

"I'm right behind you," said Diamond following her. Once they were in the kitchen Ms. Wallace said softly, "You got some explaining to do." Then in her regular tone she said, "Get the bowls out the cabinet, while I get this cornbread."

Diamond set the bowls on the table before filling each one with chicken and dumplings. Diamond could never resist her mom's cooking. Once all the bowls were filled she took her seat. Ms. Wallace says, "Steven, will you do the honor of blessing the food?"

"Of course, Ms. Wallace." Diamond looked at Steven as if to say, "You know how to pray?" He looked back at her as if to say, "I got this."

"Can we all bow our heads. God, we want to say thank you for this meal. Bless the hands that prepared the food as well as the mouths that will partake of it. Amen." Ms. Wallace looked at Diamond and said, "Girl, pick your face up. All he did was pray." Then she began laughing as she cut the cornbread. Diamond just couldn't get over the fact of how crazy this man was. There were just too many sides to him.

As Ms. Wallace cut the cornbread, the doorbell began to ring. "You expecting somebody, Ma?"

"No, I'm not. If it's those Jehovah's Witness people, tell them we aren't interested." Diamond went to the door. "Who is it?"

"It's Charles. Is Diamond home?" Diamond almost peed on herself. She didn't know how to react. *What was he doing here and why was he here now? Of all times to come, he shows up while this crazy man is here. What do I do?*

"Who's at the door, baby?"

"It's for me, Ma. I'm going to step outside for a minute." Steven looked at Ms. Wallace before getting up to go to the door. By the time he got to the door, Diamond was already outside. He opened the door in time to see Diamond giving Charles a hug. Steven stepped outside and closed the door behind him. "Who the fuck is this nigga?" he says. "My bad, brother. I'm Charles, just an old friend," he said while extending his hand to Steven. When Steven didn't reciprocate, he pulled his hand back. "I was in town and I wanted to see how Diamond was doing. I don't want any problems."

"Well, if you just an old friend why don't you come in and eat with us?"

"Nah, that's cool. Ms. Wallace doesn't care for me too much."

"What kind of friend are you exactly?"

"Me and Diamond dated for a while. Things didn't end too well. I actually came over to see if we could try over again," said Charles while looking at Diamond. Diamond just stood there nervous as hell, not knowing which Steven was standing before her. Steven took Diamond's hand and held it up, showing Charles her engagement ring. "I'm sorry, my man. I didn't know. Congratulations to you both."

"Thanks, bruh," said Steven as he opened the door and led Diamond inside. "Be safe, my man," said Steven before closing the door behind him.

Ms. Wallace was at the table praying the whole time. She had no idea who could've been at the door, but they were outside a little too long for her. She was happy when she heard the door open and no arguing going on. "Is everything okay?" she asked as they made their way back to the table. She could tell by the look on Diamond's face that something had just happened. Diamond put on a fake smile and said, "Yes, Ma, everything is fine. That was Charles at the door." Ms. Wallace turned her face up, as she remembered how many days Diamond was stuck in her room over that man. "What did his sorry ass want?" Steven laughed to himself as he thought, *Damn, that nigga wasn't joking. She really don't like his ass.* "He said he was in town and he just wanted to see how I was doing." Steven interjected. "Actually, Ms. Wallace, he said he wanted to see if him and Diamond could get back together."

"I know he didn't," said Ms. Wallace becoming more upset. "He sure did," said Steven. This was the first time Steven had seen Ms. Wallace upset and he was loving it. "So, you know I had to make sure he seen this big rock I put on her finger," he said smiling, looking at Diamond. Diamond just smiled back. *Could this day get any worse?* she thought.

Diamond knew it took a lot for her mom to get upset. Even though she didn't know the details of what happened with Charles, her mom saw the effects that it left on her daughter. So, she tried to lighten the mood by changing the conversation. "I'm looking forward to going to church tomorrow, Ma. I was just telling Steven that we need to start going back regularly."

"Well, I've been telling you that for the longest, young lady. You grew up in church, but you sure wouldn't think so."

"Ma, I talk to God. I don't always have to physically be in the building. Besides, half of those people in there do worse things than me. Does it make them better people because they go to church?" said Diamond before eating a piece of cornbread. "Diamond, you know I raised you to always worry about yourself. You can't live your life according to what other people do. God is going to judge you for you, not for anybody else." Diamond began looking down at her food wondering why she chose to talk about church. "Look, baby. Diamond, pick up your eyes and look at me. I'm not trying to come down on you. I just want so much more for you. I want you to really experience love. Nobody can love you like Jesus can, baby. Nobody."

Just then Steven's phone began to ring. "Excuse me, ladies, it's my brother." Steven went into the living room to talk. "Hey, man, what's up?"

"I just wanted to check on you and make sure everything was good."

"What's up, Calvin? Quit the small talk."

"Mommy went to the doctor yesterday, she not doing too good, man."

"What you talking about? I just spoke to her the other day."

"Just stop by the house when you get a chance."

"I'm at D's mother's house, I will be there in a few." Steven hung up the phone and went back into the dining room. "I hate to leave so soon, I have to go by mother's house. Ms. Wallace, the food was great," said Steven as he gave her a kiss on the cheek. "Can you send me a plate home with Diamond?"

"Of course I can. Give your parents my love," replied Ms. Wallace. "Come walk me to the door, babe," he said looking at Diamond. She got up from the table and walked him to the door. "You sure everything is good, babe?" she said to Steven. "I don't know, D. Give me a call when you on your way home. I love you," he said before giving her a kiss and heading out the door.

Diamond walked back to the table. Her mom was clearing the table, taking the dishes to the kitchen. "Grab the pot for me, Diamond." Diamond grabbed the pot and headed to the kitchen. "You have some explaining to do, young lady," said Ms. Wallace as she began washing the dishes. "I know, Ma."

"So where were you last night?" Diamond walked over and sat on a stool right next to the sink. "I was with Kashmere." Ms. Wallace looked up from the dishes and said, "Who?"

"Kashmere, Ma. The guy from high school who I just knew I was going to marry."

"The pretty boy? How did this happen?" Diamond smiled and said, "I actually ran into him at Steven's restaurant." Ms. Wallace dropped the plate in the sink, "Girl, are you crazy? You playing with fire, Diamond." Ms. Wallace shook her head as she resumed washing the dishes. "I didn't mean for it to happen, Ma."

"From that smile on your face, it looks like you have gotten yourself caught up in a situation." Ms. Wallace turned the water off and faced her daughter. "Baby, you're grown, so I can't tell you what to do. I will just tell you to be careful. You are engaged with a baby on the way, what are you really doing right now?" Diamond's eyes began to tear up. She wanted to tell her mother what had been going on, she just didn't think now was the right time. "I don't know, Ma."

Ms. Wallace went over to her daughter and hugged her. "Diamond, I know something is going on that you are not telling me. I won't push you. When you ready to talk, I'm here, baby."

"Thanks, Ma," she said never letting her mom go. "Now wipe them tears off your beautiful face," she said, holding Diamond's face in her hands. "All I want is for you to be happy, baby. You have some choices to make. You cannot go into marriage uncertain. Just because you are having this man's baby, doesn't mean you have to be with him. You hear me?"

"Yes, Ma, I hear you." Ms. Wallace walked to the cabinet and pulled out a bottle of wine. "My daughter, is just wanted by all. You remind me of myself when I was younger." She got a wine glass out of another cabinet. "Should I take one out for you?"

"Only if you got something stronger than that."

"Now you got jokes. You know I don't. I know you about to go roll up them herbs anyway." Diamond began laughing. "Really, Ma? Herbs?"

"Call it what you want. I call it herb. I know your nerves was shot when that fool came over and Steven went outside." Diamond got up from the stool and stretched. "Ma, you have no idea. I thought I was about to pee on myself." They both laughed before exiting the kitchen. Ms. Wallace grabbed her glass and went and sat on the couch. Diamond went outside to her car to roll up.

Steven pulled up to his mother's house about twenty minutes after talking to Calvin. He used his key and went inside. His dad was on the couch watching TV with Calvin and his mom was in the kitchen getting dinner ready for tomorrow. He went into the living room to greet the men before going to see his mom. She was at the sink washing some collard greens when he walked in. "Is that my second fa-vorite son?" she said before turning around. "Hey, beautiful," he said before giving her a hug and kissing her on the cheek. "And why am I not your first favorite son?" he said laughing. "Boy. stop it. What brings you by, a whole day early?"

"Calvin gave me a call and told me you not doing good. What's up, Ma?"

"I told that boy not to say nothing. I don't need everyone worried over me." Ms. Thompson said as she walked back over to the sink. "I'm fine, Steven." At that moment Calvin appeared in the doorway. "That's as far as you got, Mommy? I thought I would've smelled something cooking by now."

"Well, if you would help instead of getting on the phone, running your mouth, maybe you would." She turned around to look at Calvin and said, "Didn't I tell you I wanted to wait to get a second opinion before you start worrying everybody?"

"Mommy, ain't nobody trying to hear that. Talking about a sec-ond opinion when they tell you have stage three breast cancer." Steven looked at Calvin and said, "What did you just say?"

"Mommy has breast cancer and she been keeping it a secret. The only reason I found out was because I'm smashing the receptionist at her doctor's office." Mrs. Thompson looked at him in shock, "That's how you know? I thought your father told you."

"No, he didn't. You know Daddy keep secrets just like you do." Mrs. Thompson went back to the sink to take her greens out and place them in the pot. "I don't want to talk about this right now. And you better not mention this to your sister, you hear me?"

"Why not? When are you going to feel like talking about it?" said Calvin. "After I get my second opinion. Now the two of you just get on out of my kitchen."

Mr. Thompson called the boys back in the living room. "Look, boys, you know how your mother is. She has an appointment next week with a different doctor. We will have to wait to see what happens." Steven sat on the recliner and Calvin sat on the couch next to his dad. "You okay, son?" Mr. Thompson asked Steven. "No, Dad. I'm not okay. This is too much right now. I gotta go." Steven got up and headed to the door. Mr. Thompson looked at Calvin and nodded his head in Steven's direction. "Hold up, Steven. Let me walk with you." The two walked out to Steven's car. Calvin knew exactly what Steven was about to do. They got in the car and Steven pulled out a blunt from the ashtray and lit it. "Calvin, I can't lose her. I can't lose another mother." He laid his head on the steering wheel as he began to weep. "Give me that blunt and get your shit together, nigga. Mommy ain't going nowhere." Calvin took a couple of pulls before passing the blunt back to Steven. "Remember what Mommy used to say whenever things would get bad?" They looked at each other and together they said, "God will never put more on us, than we can bear." Calvin says, "That's right, bro. He gave us a great mother. He not going to just take her away like that. So, get your mind right so we can keep getting this money." Steven passed the blunt back to Calvin before reaching for a folded bill in his arm rest.

"Steve, come on, man. Don't tell me you fucking with this shit again. Yo, what the fuck is going on with you? I understand you doing it with the hoes in The Spot, but you getting high by yourself now?" Calvin slapped the bill out of Steven's hand and coke flew all over the car. Steven looked at him and said, "You lucky you my brother, nigga. Get the fuck out my car." Calvin opened the door, before getting out the car he said, "You lucky you my brother, nigga. Now get your shit together. I'm not going to be doing business with no fucking coke-head." He slammed the door and finished smoking Steven's blunt before going inside the house.

Chapter 9

Steven sat in his car for a minute before pulling off. He knew his brother was right, but fuck what he was talking about, he wanted to get high. He wanted to forget that his mother was sick. He wanted to forget that his fiancé was cheating on him. He just wanted to forget it all. He reached in his armrest and pulled out an eighth of coke he had, put some back in the same hundred-dollar bill he had, crushed it up and took a couple of bumps. It was almost nine o'clock and he didn't feel like going home. He definitely didn't feel like being around Diamond right now. He picked up his phone and called Fiah. He figured some pussy would make him feel better. After calling her twice and she didn't answer, he became furious. So, he decided to go to her house. It took him almost an hour to get there. Five minutes before he reached her spot, she called him back. "Hi, Daddy, sorry I missed you. I was in the bathroom." The way Steven felt right now, he could've stomped this girl into a coma. He had a take a couple of breaths before he responded. "Hello, are you there?" said Fiah. "Yeah, I'm here. You taking the night off. I'm about to be at your house in two minutes. Open the door for me." Fiah smiled and said, "Okay, Daddy, see you in a few."

Fiah quickly looked for something sexy to put on. She had just gotten out the shower, so she had on her sheer floral robe. She was about to start getting ready for work when she looked at her phone and seen the missed calls from Steven. She ran through her closet going through outfit after outfit when she heard the door open. Steven was high as a kite by the time he got upstairs to her apartment. "Fiah, where you at?" said Steven after entering her spot. "I'm back here, Daddy." This was the first time he had been inside of her place. He dropped her off before, but never came upstairs. He walked to her room, stood in her doorway, and leaned on the door frame as he watched her going through her closet. "What you doing over there? Come here and greet me, baby." Fiah turned around with the biggest smile. How she longed to hear this man call her baby. She walked over to him and dropped to her knees as she unbuckled his pants. "I see you learning," said Steven. He stepped out of his pants and walked over to her bed. "Go make me a drink." Fiah got off her knees and walked to the kitchen. She came back with two bottles and said, "Light or dark?"

"Dark is good. Pass me my pants when you come back this way." Fiah placed both bottles on her dresser before going back to the kitchen to get two drinking glasses. She went back to her room and passed Steven his pants before making the drinks. "You want me to put the TV on, Daddy?"

"Not really. You can put some music on." Fiah had her ShaRae CD in right now. As soon as Steven heard it, he immediately told her to put something else on. He didn't want to hear or see anything that reminded him of Diamond.

Fiah put the radio on before placing Steven's drink next to him on the nightstand. Even though Steven was twisted, he did take notice of how clean her place was and how everything was put together. After she sat the drink down she went back to try and find something to put on for Steven. Steven rolled a blunt and took out his folded bill. "What you doing over there?" Steven asked her as he took a couple of bumps. "I'm trying to find something to put on for you, Daddy."

"Don't worry about that. Put on some heels and bring your sexy ass over here next to me." Fiah put on her clear, four-inch stilettos and laid on the bed next to Steven. He took the card he was using and placed some coke on it and put it in front of Fiah. "You know I don't mess with that." Steven looked at her and said, "Are you telling me no?" She looked down and said, "No, Daddy." Steven placed the card to her nose again, this time she snorted all the coke that was on it. She didn't know how she expected to feel. This wasn't the same high that she got from weed. When it hit her she knew it. All of sudden, she felt euphoric, she wanted more. "I do have another nostril over here, Daddy," she said tapping on her nose. Steven smiled as he gave her another bump.

Fiah never thought she would do any drug other than weed, but tonight changed her mind, quickly. Fiah loved this new feeling. She felt sexy, horny, happy and seductive all at the same time. She took the blunt from Steven as she stood up from the bed and started danc-ing in a sexy way. She walked over to get her drink and downed the cup, before pouring herself another one. Steven was laying on his stomach across the bed, with his head at the foot of the bed, watching Fiah run her hands down her neck, to her breast, before grabbing both breast in her hands. He felt himself harden as she bent her head down and flickered her tongue on her nipples. Steven seen the effect the coke was having on her. He hated to interrupt her flow, so he got up from the bed to look for something hard and flat. "What you look-ing for, baby?" asked Fiah. "I need something to spread this coke on. Looks like you ready to do some lines."

"Stay right there, Daddy, I got you." Steven went back and laid across the bed. Fiah, still dancing, walked over to her dresser and got her make-up case. On the other side of the foundation was a mirror. She swayed her way over to Steven, twirling the case on her fingertips. Before she got to him, she dropped the case on the floor. She bent down to get it, so that he could get a full view of her ass, as her robe rose up and her head went down. *Damn, her pussy look good,* thought Steven as he bit her butt.

"Ohhhh, Daddy!" said Fiah in response to what Steven had done. *It had to be the coke,* she thought to herself. That bite almost made her cum on herself. She couldn't wait to see what else he would do with his mouth tonight. Steven took the mirror from her and poured all the coke that was in the bill on the glass. He took his card and separated it into lines. Then he went in his wallet and pulled out a piece of a thin straw. While he was doing this, Fiah was still dancing seductively, taking the belt off of her robe, opening up the robe in a teasing way. Steven found her so irresistible right now. He passed her the straw and watched her do a line like a pro. "You are so sexy, baby," he whispered in her ear. *It has to be the coke,* she thought to herself. His whisper went straight to her vagina, and she became wet immediately. He passed her the blunt as he got up from the bed and pulled the comforter back. He kept looking at her in her own world, smoking her blunt and touching on herself while dancing sexily. "Come here Di, Fiah," He shook his head, thankful that she was high and didn't notice that he almost called her Diamond. "I'm coming, Daddy," said Fiah, as she crawled from the foot of the bed to the head of the bed.

"Lay down," said Steven. Fiah didn't know what was about to happen, but her sex levels were definitely on a thousand right now. Steven took the blunt from her and took a couple of pulls before putting the rest in the ashtray. He downed his drink and did a couple of lines, while he ran his fingers across Fiah's neck, straight down to her clit. While he played with her clit, he began kissing on her neck before biting it. Fiah moaned and arched her back, so turned on by his every touch. Steven was becoming more aroused at the way her body was responding to him. He placed two fingers inside of her as he began sucking and nibbling on her nipples. He felt her body shake, as she began to scream and orgasm. He just had to have to her. He put some coke on the card and poured it on her pussy before he began to take his time licking it all off. "Oh, baby, your mouth feels so good on me," said Fiah before she came. She grabbed Steven's head as she moved her hips, enjoying every orgasm that he gave her. And the slurping sound he made as he sucked her cum up, made her grab her nipples as she came for him harder each time. Steven did this until he couldn't take it anymore. He had to have her now. He got up, flipped her over and put her ass up before putting all of himself inside of her. Her pussy was so wet, tight and hot. "Damn, you feel good, baby," he said while stroking her, with one hand around her neck. The harder he fucked her, the tighter he began grabbing her neck, and the louder she moaned for him to fuck her harder. Before he knew it, he was cumming inside of her, hard. Not taking his dick out of her, he rolled to the side and whispered in her ear, "I love you, baby." She smiled from ear to ear, still gyrating on his semi-hardened penis. "I love you too, baby."

"I think I need a drink," said Steven before taking himself out of Fiah and slapping her hard, on the butt. In a whiny voice she replied, "Why did you take him out, Daddy? You felt so good inside of me." Steven looked at her pouty face and kissed her on the lips.

He looked her in the eyes and said, "Can you promise to always be honest no matter what?" She smiled back at him and said, "Yes, Daddy." He sat up, so his back was now resting against the back of the bed. "Go get my drink, babe." Fiah got up for the first time in a while. She felt a little lightheaded and she went back down. Steven smiled, remembering that this was her first time getting high. He looked at her trying to pull herself together. He moved the hair from in front of her face and said, "What's your real name?" Fiah looked up at him, smiled and said, "Sofia." "Sofia," he repeated before getting up to make his drink.

Ms. Wallace knocked on Diamond's old bedroom door. "Hold on, babe," she said to Kashmere on the phone. "Come in, Ma." Ms. Wallace opened the door and walked into Diamond's room. "It's almost eleven o'clock, baby. Are you going home tonight?" Diamond was laying across her bed. "No. I think I'm going to stay here, if that's okay with you." Ms. Wallace looked back at her with a smile. "Of course, it's okay with me. Who are you on the phone with?"

"I'm talking to Kashmere, Ma." On the other side of the phone Kash says, "You told your mom about me?" Diamond answered, "Yes, I told her about you."

"Does she remember me?" Diamond laughed and said, "No, she doesn't." Ms. Wallace enjoyed the look of happiness she seen on her daughter's face. "Tell Kashmere I said goodnight." She walked over to Diamond to give her a kiss, then left the room.

"Babe, you really told your mom about me?" Diamond was now grinning from ear to ear. "Yes, Kash, I really told her about you. I've decided that tomorrow is the day. I'm finally leaving Steven." This was the best news Kash had heard all day. "Marry me, Diamond."

"Kash, stop playing."

"I'm not playing, D. Send me your mom's address." As soon as Diamond gave him the address he hung up the phone. Kash jumped in the shower and got dressed. He stopped at his spot in the east to pick up the ring and he was on his way to Ms. Wallace's house. From the first day Kash seen Diamond again, he knew that she would be his. The very next day he went out and brought her a ring. Diamond became very excited as she rolled around her bed and kicked her feet. She got up, took Steven's ring off, placed it on her dresser and got in the shower. When she got out of the shower it was almost twelve. She dried off, put on her Victoria's Secret Vanilla lace lotion and her black and white, penguin onesie. She loved that the onesie had an easy access, back entrance flap. She did have plans once she seen Kash. Ten minutes after she had finished getting dressed, she heard her phone vibrate from a text.

Kash: Bring your sexy ass outside.

Diamond: Coming out.

Diamond smiled as she walked up to Kash's black Range Rover. When she got inside she said to herself, *Damn, he smells so good.* "You do too, baby," Kash replied. Diamond looked confused, "Did I just say that out loud?" He leaned in and kissed her. "No, baby, I'm just reading your mind." Kash got out of his vehicle and walked over to Diamond's side. He opened the door and helped her get out. "This onesie is kind of cute," he said, as he spun her around to get the full view. Then he pulled her into him and wrapped his arms around her tight. "I told you I wasn't going to lose you this time, babe." That's when he dropped to one knee and pulled the ring from inside his jacket pocket. He took her hand and said, "Diamond Nicole Wallace, will you marry me?" With the biggest smile, Diamond said, "Yes," as she looked down at her three-carat Princess Halo diamond ring. Kashmere got off of his knees, feeling the happiest he has ever felt in life. He picked her up and swung her around as they both kissed each other. "We have to be quiet before my mom comes out here," said Diamond. Kash helped her back inside and closed her door. Then he walked back around to his side and got in.

"I'm sorry I didn't get dressed to go out. I told my mom I would go to church with her tomorrow."

"It's cool, D. I have the rest of my life to take you out." He grabbed her face and began kissing her from her forehead, to her nose, to her lips. "I'm going to make you the happiest woman in the world, baby. You will never regret this decision."

"I know I won't," said Diamond as she reached for Kash's belt buckle. He knew what was up, so he pushed his seat back as he lit the blunt that was in his ashtray. After she had unzipped his pants, he passed her the blunt, so he could take them off. He noticed the flap in the back of the onesie when he spun her around, so he knew he was about to get more than just head. When he was done, Diamond got on her knees in her seat, pulled his hardened cock out and began kissing it. "Damn, D, your kisses feel so good."

"You sure you ready to have this mouth only, for the rest of your life?" she said, now licking up and down his shaft. "Yes, baby, Daddy is ready for you, and only you." Something about his words made Diamond hornier than ever. She moved his right hand to her flap as he used his left hand to push her head up and down on his dick. Once the flap was open, his fingers found their way to her moist, hot spot. His dick became rock hard as his fingers made their way to her pleasure palace. After he made her cum, he took his fingers out of her and placed them in his mouth. He loved the taste of her love.

"Daddy wants to be inside of you, baby," he said while Diamond made her mouth pop off the head of his manhood. Diamond kissed the head, before climbing over the seat. She sat on Kash, so her back was facing him. She sat on him slow, while he filled her up. He turned her face to him and began kissing her, while she rode him up and down. He kissed and sucked the right side of her neck, which turned her on. The more turned on she became, the faster her ass bounced up and down on his rod. "You about to make me cum, D," moaned Kash. Diamond made sure all of him was inside of her as she clenched her hot box and began whining her body up on him. Within minutes they were both cumming together. Kash pulled Diamond to him and buried his face in her neck before kissing it. "I'm not letting you go this time, baby." He turned her face to him and said, "Did you hear what I said?" She smiled and said, "Yes, baby, I heard you. I'm not letting you go either." She kissed him on the lips and laid her head back on him.

Still inside of her, he began to stroke her hair. "When are you getting your stuff out his house?" She closed her eyes, dreading this conversation. "Soon, baby."

"How about now? He's not at the house. We can get your things and just be done with this once and for all." For the first time tonight, Diamond realized that she hadn't heard from Steven since he left the house earlier that day. She looked at the clock, it was now almost two in the morning. For a second, she wondered if he was okay, then she realized this was Steven she was thinking about. "Okay. Let me put some clothes on. I will be right back." She kissed Kash before reaching in his glove compartment for a wet wipe. She took out one for her and one for him. Kash was almost mad he said something once he was out of his warm, comfortable place. Diamond snapped back her flap and got out of the car. She got inside and ran up the stairs. She put on some sweats, a t-shirt and her sneakers. She was on her way downstairs when he remembered the ring. She went back to her old bedroom and got Steven's engagement ring. She wanted to be sure that would be the first thing he seen when he got home.

When she got back in the Range, Kash looked at her and said, "You ready?" She replied, "As ready as I will ever be, baby." He kissed her on the lips and they headed out. He turned on the radio and pulled out a blunt from the ashtray. "Here, baby," he said, as he passed it to Diamond. She put the back of her seat back and put her feet up on the dash before lighting the blunt. Once the blunt was lit, Kash pulled off. He always made it his business to take care of business, so his time with Diamond wouldn't be interfered with. Tonight, his phone just wouldn't stop blowing up. "I'm sorry, D, I have to take this."

"Go ahead, baby," she said. Diamond's thoughts were consumed right now. Even though she wasn't looking forward to being alone with Steven, he said he wasn't working tonight and he wanted to spend time with her. *His ass ain't even home. I bet he with that raggedy-ass hoe right now. I hate that nigga,* she thought. "What the fuck are you talking about right now?" she heard Kash say into the phone. "Fuck that shit. I will be right there." Diamond looked at Kash and said, "Is everything okay?"

"Nah, D. I can't wait to give all this shit up for you. I have to go take care of something real quick, you coming with me?" Diamond passed him the blunt and said, "Let's go, baby."

Kash took a couple of pulls before he spoke again. "I give these hoes one simple thing to do. One simple thing. Fuck, suck and get my money. Shit is fucking simple as hell." He passes the blunt back to Diamond. "As soon as we set a date, I'm leaving all this shit behind. Dumb-ass hoes, man."

"Baby, what happened?"

"Remember the hoe you met in The Spot that night? Cookie? Well, this bitch decided she wants to take my new hoe. Now I have to teach both these hoes a lesson." Kash reached out for Diamond to pass him the blunt. "This game is all about respect, D. Now I gotta go and lay down my pimp hand. I hate fucking these hoes up." Kash looked at his phone which was ringing off the hook now. He picked it up very angry, "What the fuck you want? I don't even wanna hear that shit, bitch, you fucking know better." Then he hung up the phone. "D, I'm going to take you by your spot first. What do you even need to get from there?"

"I just wanted my jewelry and some of my outfits and shoes."

"Dead that. You can take whatever clothes and shoes you want. Everything else, I will buy back for you. You're my Diamond now, fuck that corny-ass nigga. I don't want shit he got for you in my crib." Diamond just sat back as she wondered if she was doing the right thing.

Twenty minutes later, they pulled up in front of her and Steven's home. "You got some time. I will be back in an hour. If I'm not back in an hour, Troy will come bring you home." Kash notice a look in Diamond's eyes that he hadn't seen before, sadness. "Babe, this will soon be over. All I want is you, D." He stroked her cheek and said, "Come give me a kiss." Diamond gave him a kiss before getting out of the car. As she walked in the house, she had a cold chill come across her. She just figured it had to do with the dream she had. This was her first time being in the house since then. She went upstairs and began packing. She didn't want to be in this house any longer than she had to.

❈

When Steven came back in the room, he walked in to see Fiah doing lines. "Look who's a big girl now. You don't need Daddy no more." She smiled with coke on her nose, "I'm always going to need you, Daddy." Steven smiled as he walked over to get some bud and a dutch out of his pants. He split the dutch and dumped the insides in the garbage. Then he put his boxers back on before sitting in a chair next to the bed. Fiah got up and poured herself a drink. "You want one, Daddy?"

"Sure," he replied. She walked over and gave him his drink. "Sit right here," said Steven, tapping the bed, the spot directly in front of him. He rolled up, then downed his drink before lighting the blunt. He sat up in the chair, so that he was now arms distance from Fiah. He took two pulls and blew the smoke in Fiah's face, before he passed the blunt to her. "Who sent you?" Fiah took two pulls before she started coughing. She looked confused as she passed the blunt back to Steven. "I'm only going to ask you one more time. Who sent you?"

"Baby, I don't know what you talking about." Steven took another pull before slapping Fiah sober. "I'm not your baby, hoe." Then he slapped her again. "I'm really trying to be nice right now." Steven stood up and began pacing in the space in front of his chair. "How can you afford this place, Fiah?" Fiah was now crying with her head in her hands. Steven slapped her again. This time he had a little more force with it, which caused Fiah's nose to start bleeding. "Go get some tissue and clean that shit up," he said pointing to the nightstand which held the coke and liquor. Fiah still crying, walked over to the table and got some tissue for her nose. "So, I'm walking around your place and notice how nicely it's furnished and I think, damn, this bitch must have some real paper. Then I pass the china cabinet, and there it is. A picture of you and an old friend of mine." Steven stood directly in front of Fiah, "I really don't want to hurt you, but I will. Who sent you?"

Not wanting to be hit anymore, Fiah finally told Steven what he wanted to hear. "Kashmere sent me to your spot to get a job."

"Now we getting somewhere. Keep talking," said Steven before making another drink and having a seat back in the chair. "I just moved here from Maryland three months ago. My brother, Kashmere...."

"Wait, did you say your brother?" Looking at the floor, Fiah said, "Yes. Kash is my brother. He told me if I came to New York, he would put me down with the family business. He said he would give me a place to stay and I could make a lot of money. When I found out that the family business meant I would have to stand on a corner and sell my body, I told him to buy me a ticket back to Maryland." Steven sat back in the chair and crossed his legs, while he continued smoking his blunt. Fiah looked at Steven and continued talking. "My brother said he had a friend who could put me in a better working environment, since I thought I was too good for the street. He gave me the address to The Spot and told me to ask for a job." He sat up in the chair and said, "That's all it was? He only sent you to work?"

"Yes, Daddy. He said I could make a lot of money working for you, and that I would need it if I wanted to keep staying here. After seeing how people live out here, I knew I didn't want to lose this crib." He stood up again and walked over to where Fiah was sitting on the bed. He sat beside her and lifted her head up. "Sofia, I really want to believe you right now." Fiah looked at Steven with tears in her eyes and got on her knees. "Daddy, I told you I wouldn't lie to you. My brother would kick my ass if he knew I was sleeping with you right now. He told me that he is the only person who could ever fuck me for free." Fiah really began crying now. This was the first time she had ever shared that with anyone. Steven really wanted to believe her, but he felt like there was more to the story. "Fiah, if I find out that you're lying to me, you're going to regret it." Still on her knees crying, Fiah says, "I'm not lying. I just don't want to be anybody's property anymore. I just want to be a normal person. This life isn't for me." Steven reached his hand out to help Fiah get off the floor. He laid on the bed and Fiah laid next to him. "If I find out that you're lying, I'm going to kill you. You and the baby." Confused, Fiah asked, "What baby?"

"The one I put inside of you." Steven turned Fiah over to her side before reaching over to turn the light off.

Neither one of them fell asleep for a while. Steven laid with this girl in his arms, wondering if all women lied. He looked over at the clock to see that it was almost four in the morning. He knew he wasn't making it to church. Then he told Fiah to reach over and get his phone off the nightstand. When he seen that he only had missed calls from Calvin, he became furious. Diamond hadn't called him or texted him. *That fucking whore. She's probably with this nigga Kash right now or better yet Charlie. I got something for her ass,* he thought.

What did Kash get me into this time? He told me this was a quick mark. He told me to get in good and take over. He never said this could cost me my life. Baby? Pregnant? Me pregnant? This is going too far. I just wanted diamonds and money. I'm going to be stuck with this crazy nigga for the rest of my life? Kash fucking owes me big time. All over a fucking girl. He had me do all of this over a fucking girl. Diamond, your ass better be worth it. Fiah let silent cries leave her, as she wondered what was in store for her. Just then she felt Steven's fingers make their way inside of her. Despite how she felt emotionally, she still had coke in her system and his fingers had her wanting the real thing. So, she took her hand and began stroking him before placing him back inside of her. Steven lifted her leg up as he put himself all the way inside of her. He tried to stop thinking about Diamond, but he couldn't. He kept seeing someone else inside of her, stroking her, touching her, tasting her, taking her. He began choking Fiah as he fucked her. The more he envisioned Diamond, the harder he choked her and fucked her. When he no longer felt her fighting back, he loosened his grip and held her as he filled her with more of his cum. "I love you, baby," he whispered in her ear before closing his eyes to escape Diamond.

"Hey, baby, I'm about fifteen minutes away. You almost finished?" Diamond was now in the living room with four suitcases full of clothes and shoes. And although Kash told her to leave all the jewelry behind, there were a few pieces that she just couldn't let go of. She decided she would leave them at her mom's house, so Kash wouldn't know. She went over to the coffee table and took the weed out that was in the drawer underneath. She was very surprised when she seen the bag of cocaine that was sitting next to it. At this moment, she knew she was making the right choice by leaving. She never even knew that Steven ever used coke. She felt so stupid right now. *Who is this man that I loved all this time? Who is this man that I almost married?* At this moment, for the first time, she actually hoped that Steven wasn't this child's father. Just then a horn blew outside. She took the coke out of the drawer and placed Steven's engagement ring on top of it on the coffee table. She went to open the door and instead of Kash getting out of the car, she seen that it was Charlie.

She walked out the door and closed it behind her. "Charles? What are you doing here? Did you follow me?" Diamond began walking away from her door, towards him, as she didn't want Kash to drive up and think the wrong thing. Charles was just staring at her with red, teary eyes. So, Diamond repeated, "Charles, what the fuck are you doing here?" He began walking closer to Diamond. "Do you know how long I thought about this moment, baby?" Diamond began backing away from him. "Are you drunk, Charles?"

"Diamond," said Charles slurred, "how you going to play me for these street niggas? You know you not even about that life. You should take me back, baby. I'm still in love with you." Diamond took out her phone and called Kash. "Come on, D. What you doing? Who you calling, baby?" Diamond hung up when the phone went to voicemail. "Charles, you really need to leave before my man gets here."

He looks from the ground back up at Diamond and says, "Your man? Which one would that be?"

"You have been following me." Just then Diamond sees a man getting out of a car. *That must be Troy,* she thought. "I'm telling you right now, Charlie, you should just go." Charles went to reach for her and fell on the ground. He looked up to her from his knees and said, "Baby, I know I messed up, but I love you. None of them niggas will ever love you like I did." Diamond looked at him with pity, as she seen this person in the shadows getting closer to them. Out of nowhere, he took a gun out from his jacket and put it to his head. "Come on, Charlie. Are you kidding me right now? Charles, I don't have time for this. I bet it's not even loaded, is it."

"D, there's only one way to find out." By this time Troy had made his way quietly behind Charles and disarmed him.

"Please don't hurt him," Diamond said to the man she assumed to be Troy. Troy never responded. He simply helped Charles off the ground and walked him to his car. He kept the gun and walked back to his vehicle. Diamond went inside and rolled up. *What the hell is going on right now? This has been a crazy-ass day.* As soon as she lit the blunt, she heard her phone vibrate.

Kash: Who car is in front of your crib?

Diamond: Baby, just pull up in the driveway

Kash: D, do you need to tell me something?

Diamond: Just pull up and help me with these bags

Being that Kash just left a crazy situation, he was already in a different state of mind from when he first seen her that night. It was almost five in the morning and he was tired. He just wanted to get his lady home and get in the bed with her. So, he decided to listen to her. Troy had already put him on about what had happened just minutes before, so he knew there was no real reason to react right now. Diamond opened the door and started rolling out her suitcases. Kash got out to help her. He opened the trunk and started loading the suitcases inside. When he seen her going back inside, he said, "Damn, babe.

You have more stuff?" She came back out smiling with her last two suitcases in hand. "It looks like I'm going to have to get you a house soon," he said seriously joking. Diamond gave him a kiss as he made room for the luggage and she went back inside for a last goodbye. *Damn, I almost forgot my Double Stuf Golden Oreos,* she thought as she walked to the kitchen and took the package off the top of the fridge. When she got back to the living room, she went in her purse to take out Steven's ring and placed it on the coffee table. Right on top of the bag of coke she found. Before she got out the door, she heard her phone vibrate.

Steven: I'm not making it to church in the morning. See you at my mom's house.

Diamond didn't even respond. It was after five in the morning and he was just now texting her. She refused to get upset. She decided it would be best for her to break up with him at his mom's house. At least this way he wouldn't try to put his hands on her, she thought. She grabbed her blunt and placed the Ziplock bag with the weed in her purse. She smiled as she walked out of that house, leaving Steven and all the bad memories that came with him behind.

She walked to the Range and got inside. Kash looked at her and said, "You're all mine now," before giving her a kiss. She smiled back at him and said, "Yes, I am, baby. I just have this one more thing to do tomorrow and it's over." She held her hand up and admired her new engagement ring. Kash smiled as he backed out of the driveway. Charles car was gone by the time they left and Kash made sure to make mention of it. "You know, Troy hit me and told me some nigga was over here bothering you. That's why I didn't answer when you called, I was on the phone with him." Diamond passed him the blunt and said, "It's nothing, baby. Just an ex trying to get me back." Kash smiled and said, "My beautiful Diamond. I guess I have to get used to having a girl that everybody wants." She laughed and said, "I don't know about that, baby. Besides, I only have eyes for you." Kash smiled at that one. Being with Diamond made him think a lot about his teenage years and all the choices he made at that time. He couldn't be more happier than he was at this moment. He had his secrets, but doesn't everybody? He knew he had to call his sister and thank her for being a beautiful distraction. He knew if he had someone take Steven's attention away, getting Diamond back would be that much easier. And it was. "Hey, baby," he said. "Yes, baby?" she asked. "You feel like rubbing my back when we get home?" She looked at him with seductive eyes and said, "Is that all you want me to rub, Daddy?" He smiled and said, "Yes, baby. It's been a long day. I will give you some more of this D when you wake up. Just roll over and put it in ya," he said in a joking way. They both laughed.

When they pulled up to the condo, it was after six in the morning and they were both tired. They took off their shoes and got in the bed fully clothed. Diamond snuggled up in Kash's arms and they both fell asleep.

Chapter 10

"Good morning, beautiful. Or should I say good afternoon." Diamond smiled as she heard Kash in her ear followed by a kiss to her neck. She smiled and said, "Hey, baby."

"Don't move," he whispered in her ear. "I promised you I was going to give you this D when you got up." He unzipped his pants and pulled them down, enough to get his stiff rod through the opening of his boxers. Diamond, following his lead, began pulling down her sweats and her panties. While still holding her close, he placed his hard cock rub in between her thighs, letting it rub against her pleasure palace. When he felt her become moist, he put himself inside of her, nice and slow. Diamond moaned in ecstasy as he took her from behind. Inch by inch. Deep and slow. She loved how Kash took his time with her, making her cum over and over and over again, until they finally came together. They laid like this for a while, Kash still inside of her, holding her close to him. He brushed the hair from her face and kissed her cheek before saying, "You know I love you, baby." She turned her head, so she could look at him and said, "Yes, I know, baby," followed by a kiss to his lips. "So, why you have to go and have dinner with this dude family? Why you can't just stay here with me?" Diamond didn't really feel like having to explain herself. Totally turned off, she said, "I just do, babe," before pulling up her panties and sweats and getting out of the bed. As she headed to get her phone off the dresser, Kash pulled his clothes up and sat up in the bed. He took out a dutch and began breaking up some weed. "I don't get it, D. You say you want to be with me, right?" She picked up her phone and sat on the bed. "Kash, you know I want to be with you. I showed you that last night," said Diamond as she held up her ring finger. She looked through her phone and seen there were several missed calls from her mom. She was surprised that none of them were from Steven, but that just let her know that he never went home last night. He would certainly have called her if he came home and seen the ring on the table.

Diamond gave Kash a kiss before trying to call her mom back. The phone went immediately to voicemail, so she knew she was still in church. Then she sent a text to Aleese to find out what time she should get to the house. Aleese text her back telling her to be there by five. So she had to be out of the house by three thirty since she still had to go to her mom's house to pick up her car. She looked over at Kash who was now smoking his blunt and watching TV. "Are you big mad or little mad?" she asked. He smiled at her and said, "Big mad." They both smiled as she straddled him and began kissing him all over his face. He looked at her and said, "You know I can't stay mad at you, baby. I just have a bad feeling about this." She looked him in the eyes and said, "I got this, Kash. I'm can't just walk away without saying anything. There is a great chance that I'm having this man's baby, I can't just disappear." Kash knew there was a big chance that the baby wasn't his, but he didn't want to think about that. Kash picked Diamond up from on top of him and moved her to the space in the bed beside him. He passed her the blunt and went to get in the shower. Diamond took a couple of pulls and sat there in deep thought. For the first time since everything has happened, she stopped and thought about if she was doing the right thing jumping into a relationship with Kash. She must have been zoned out for a while. The next thing she knew she heard Kash calling her name. He threw a hundred dollars on the bed and told her to take a cab to her car because he had something to take care of. She looked at his back as he walked out of the bedroom. Before she could make it out the bed, she heard the front door slam.

What the hell is wrong with these men in my life? For a quick minute she thought about Charlie last night. On his knees in front of her with a gun to his head. Telling her that she isn't about this life. She shook her head and thought, *Do I just make everybody crazy?* She relit the blunt and walked into the living room. There sat every bag she had packed before leaving. *At least he brought my things inside. Damn, how long was sitting there?* She sat the blunt in the ashtray before going through her bags to find something to wear today. She chose one of her black cashmere tops with a pair of dark blue jeans and some black heels before getting in the shower. She turned on her radio app and began getting ready. It was almost three o'clock when she got out of the shower. She dried off and put some lotion on. Today she decided to put on her Cashmere mist. When she was done she put her towel back on and walked to the living room to get her clothes. Then she went to the bedroom to get dressed. While in the shower, Diamond decided that she wasn't ready for this. She didn't like how Kash just dipped out on her. So, she decided when she left today, she wasn't coming back. After she got dressed, she called her cab. While waiting for the cab, she wrote a letter to Kash.

Hey Kash,

I think we rushed into this too fast. I do love you, but I'm not ready to jump into another crazy situation. Hold this ring until we are really ready.

Diamond
xoxoxo

She placed the letter on his dresser and placed the beautiful ring he just gave her on top of it. As soon as the cab came, she gathered all her belongings and closed the door behind her. As she got all her things on the elevator, she wondered if she was doing the right thing. She looked down at her empty ring finger and felt freedom instead of sadness. She smiled as she began getting her bags off the elevator. She was grateful to the driver for meeting her at the door and helping her get her things in the van. She looked back as she pulled away thinking how everything was all good just a day ago. Then she sat back in the seat and took a nap as the cab took the hour drive to her mom's house.

Fiah woke up the next afternoon very sore. Her neck and her love box felt like it been battered. She woke up to Steven's hot breath breathing down her neck. The first thing her eyes saw was the nightstand which held the coke, weed and liquor. She really didn't remember much of what happened after they had sex the first time. The way she felt, she didn't know if she wanted to remember. Then she jumped out the bed and ran to the bathroom to pee. She had to catch herself from falling when her foot hit the floor. She felt a little dizzy, but she didn't want to pee on her white carpeted floors. She sat on the toilet for a little while wondering why her vagina felt the way that it did. She had to wipe herself softly, that's when she felt how swollen she was down there. *What did this guy do to me last night?* she thought to herself. She got off the toilet and went back to her bedroom. She went to get her phone off the nightstand, then headed to her living room. She lit a clip she had in the ashtray and checked her phone. She had two messages from Kash.

Kash: Hey Sophie, I haven't heard from you since earlier yesterday. You good?

Kash: I heard you didn't go to work last night. Why I still haven't heard from you?

Fiah was about to text him back, then she changed her mind. He's the reason she was in this predicament in the first place. *Maybe she should text him back. He's probably worried about me.* Then she heard Steven calling her and she forget about Kash altogether. "Fiah, where you at, baby?" She yelled back in the other room, "I'm in here on the couch." He yelled back at her, "I'm lonely in here without you. Come back to bed." She slowly got off the couch and walked back to the bedroom. She called herself going into the living room to get away from this man. He was stroking his hard rod when she came in the room. "Look what Daddy got here waiting for you, baby." She looked at him and said, "Where do you plan on putting that?" He replied, "In your mouth. Now bring your sexy ass over here." He seen how slow she was moving and said, "Why you walking like that?" When she got to the bed she sat down and said, "Why don't you tell me, Steven? You see these marks on my neck?" He put some coke on his dick and said, "All I want to see right now is my dick going in and out of your mouth. Now give it to me, baby." He knew she wasn't in the mood, but he didn't care. He knew once she got that coke back in her system, he could fuck her throat like she was Dawne. Fiah was not in the mood to do anything sexual, but she knew she shouldn't tell this nigga no. She began licking the coke off his dick before she put it all in her mouth. Within minutes her mouth was numb and Steven was taking advantage of it. He began stroking it slow at first, then he began to pick up the speed. He was fucking her mouth the same way he fucked her pussy just hours before. He slapped her face hard every time she gagged on it, which turned him on more. So, he got on his knees in the bed and had her lay on her stomach as he held her face and stroked her mouth, hard and fast. He was kneeling straight up at first before bending over in doggy style position. Since she said her pussy was sore, he put his finger in her butt instead. He grabbed her ass with his free hand as he continued fucking her mouth. When he saw how she responded to his finger in her ass he figured she wanted him to put his manhood inside. He slid a second finger in and then a third as he prepared her for what was coming. He had no intentions on seeing her again after today, so he wanted to make sure he gave her everything she deserved. While Fiah was asleep, Steven went through her phone and seen all the messages between her and Kash. Messages that proved his suspicions were correct. Kash sent her to be a distraction while he went after Diamond.

As he remembered reading the messages, he began to become angry. He no longer cared that she was sore, now he just wanted to hurt her. He took his fingers out of her ass and took his dick out of her mouth and told her to lay down as he walked over to the candy table. He did a couple of lines before making her do some. Then he poured her a drink and made her down it. Then he poured her another drink. This cup containing more than the last, but he made her down it. He took a shot himself while jiggling her ass cheek in his hand. "You know I'm about to get up in that ass, right, baby?" She looked at him with glassy eyes and said, "Yes, Daddy." He took another shot before he laid back on the bed. He stroked his dick, till it got back hard and then called her over to him. He sat her swollen hot box right on his hard cock and made sure he put it all the way inside with the first stroke. She let out a slight scream as he filled her up. She felt as if he was ripping her open. He could see that she was in pain and it turned him on more and more. He continued giving her deep strokes while he began choking her and sucking on her breast. Fiah didn't know how to feel right now. Even though she didn't want to be sexed right now, Steven felt so good inside of her. The pain turned into pleasure as the drugs and alcohol took over her body. Just when she thought he was almost done, he put his fingers back in her ass. One, then two, then three, then four. By now she was screaming again as he rammed his four fingers in and out of her ass while fucking her pussy hard and fast. With his free hand, he began to punch her in the rib. The first time he hit her, it took her breath away. Then he followed that with two more blows before he came inside of her. Then he took his four fingers out of her ass and put them in her mouth forcefully as he flipped himself around, so that he was now on top of her.

"Didn't I tell you I would kill you if I found out you was lying to me about your brother?" Immediately Fiah began to panic, so she bit down on his four fingers he still had in her mouth. Steven screamed in pain, "You dumb bitch." He followed that with multiple blows to the face. Steven hit her like she was a hoe who tried to steal his money. He couldn't believe he allowed himself to be played by this hoe. When he realized what he was doing, he stopped hitting her. He looked at her lifeless body and seen that Fiah wasn't breathing. Both her eyes were swollen shut, she now had a bloody nose and a split, swollen lip. He quickly went to check her pulse. When felt it, he knew she was still alive. He looked at her lying there, no longer looking like the beautiful lady he was infatuated with. *Why none of these chicks can't keep it real these days. I told her, don't lie to me.* "Why your dumb ass just couldn't tell me the truth? I could've had something with you, Fiah," said Steven before taking another shot. Then it hit him, he needed to get out of here. He did a couple of more lines before going in the bathroom to wash his hands and face. While washing his hands he looked in the mirror and was very sad at the man he saw looking back at him. He punched the mirror before going back into the bedroom. He quickly got dressed. He took the make-up case with the coke, the rest of the weed and the open bottle and he headed out the door. He checked his watch as he walked down the stairs, it was now three thirty. He figured he had enough time to run to the house and change clothes then head to his mom's house for dinner. As soon as he got in the car, he realized that he still hadn't heard from Diamond since he left her at her mother's house. This only made him mad all over again. He lit his blunt and headed to the highway.

Kashmere got to Fiah's place less than five minutes after Steven left. If he hadn't stopped to get gas, he would've caught him before he left. The last time he spoke to Sophia, she was getting ready for work. He knew something was wrong when he spoke to Dawne this afternoon and she told him that Fiah never made it in. He parked his car and went upstairs to her place. He didn't even think to knock, he used his key and went right inside. As soon as he opened the door he started calling her, "Sophia, yo Sophia, where the hell you at?" in an angry tone. He seen her phone sitting on the couch, which let him know that she was home. He then headed to her bedroom still calling her name. When he got to the bedroom door and seen his sister's naked, battered body lying there, tears immediately began to fill his eyes. He ran over to her thinking that she was dead. He laid her head in his lap as he stroked her hair, "Who the fuck—" He was so angry he couldn't finish his thought. He grabbed his phone and called nine-one-one. "I need an ambulance right away. It's my sister, I don't know if she's dead or what," he managed to get out through tears. "The address is four-sixty-one Willows Road. I'm on the third floor. Please hurry.... You asking mad questions right now, I don't know what happened. Just hurry the fuck up," he yelled before hanging up the phone.

Just then he saw her arm move. He began rocking her and said, "Sophia. Come on, baby girl. I got you, you going to be okay." He ran in the bathroom to get a wet rag to clean her face. When he seen the shattered mirror, he really began to wonder what happened. He told his sister countless times to never let anyone into her home. No one was supposed to even know where she lived. He rushed back in the room and seen the blood come from Sophia's mouth as she tried to talk. "Shhhh. Don't talk. The ambulance will be here soon. I got you, baby girl." Kashmere's heart broke as he seen the tears fall down his beautiful sister's swollen eyes. As he heard the sirens get closer, he wrapped his sister in the comforter and carried her down the stairs.

He got downstairs just in time to see the guys at the entrance door putting up the gurney. He placed her on the gurney and they wheeled her back to the ambulance. "Sir, are you riding with us?"

"No, I'm going to follow you," Kash replied. Two police cars rolled up as they were putting Fiah in the ambulette. When the police seen the blood on Kash's clothes they began to question him as they stepped out of their vehicle. "Sir, is everything okay?" He looked at the officer with tears in his eyes and said, "No, Officer. Everything is not okay. I came over to check on my sister. When I got here...." Kash grabbed his chest as he began to feel a pain shoot through his heart. The officer ran over to Kash to make sure he was okay. "Are you okay, sir?" Kash looked at him still holding his chest and said, "I'm okay, I'm okay. I just need a second." The partner of the officer who came to his aid said, "How about we go upstairs and you can run us through what happened."

"I don't know what happened. I got here and found her like this." He put his head down in his hands and said, "That's the only family I have left," while the tears fell from his eyes. "Do you want us to give you a ride?"

"No. I got it," said Kash wiping the tears off his face. "We will follow you to the hospital then."

"Do whatever you want. I have to go," said Kash walking over to his Rover. One of the police cars followed Kash to the hospital as the others looked around. Since he brought her downstairs, they had no idea what apartment to search. After knocking on a few doors and not getting much help from the neighbors, they eventually left.

Kash sat in his ride for a minute as he got his mind right. He didn't care that the police were around, he needed to smoke some bud before he caught a case. He sat there and wondered who would do something like this to his sister. Then Steven came to mind. *Nah, that nigga not that crazy*, he thought. He gave Troy a call anyway and told him to go back and watch Steven's house. After Diamond left this morning, Kash let him know he didn't need him there anymore. But just in case this nigga was crazy enough to have hurt his sister, he wanted to know where he was. While he was driving to the hospital he thought of all types of things he had planned for whoever had done this. He became dark quick, his sadness now turning into rage. He knew he had to pull it together before he got in front of all these people at the hospital. He looked down at his clothes and seen all the blood on his clothes. He thought about going home to change until he looked in his rearview mirror and seen the cops were still following him.

About ten minutes later he pulled up to the Emergency Room parking area. He rushed inside and said to the receptionist, "I'm looking for Sophia Thompson." She was on the phone in her own conversation. He slammed his hand on the desk space in front of her. "Maybe you didn't hear me the first time. I'm looking for Sophia Thompson." The receptionist was startled from the loud noise his hand made from hitting the desk. She said, "Hold on," before moving the phone away from her mouth. "You can have a seat over there, the doctor will be out to talk to you in a few minutes, sir." He turned around and walked away from her. The way he was feeling right now, he knew that was the best thing to do. As soon as he walked away, she rolled her eyes and proceeded with her conversation after she paged the doctor that was on call.

The doctor came down a few minutes later and asked the receptionist, "Where was the patient's relative?" She pointed to Kash and said, "He's right over there, sir." He walked over to Kash and said, "Hi, I'm Doctor Robinson. I'm sorry to tell you this, but the young lady we just brought in didn't make it."

"I think you got me confused with somebody else, Doc. My sister was fine when I put her in the ambulance." Dr. Robinson looked at Kashmere with sadness in his eyes. "Why don't you have a seat, son."

"I don't want to sit down, Doc. I just want to see my sister." Being that she had just died moments ago, they hadn't removed her from the room yet. "Okay. Let's go," said Dr. Robinson. When they got to the close door to the room where Fiah's body lied, the doctor said, "Prepare yourself for what you are about to see." The tears were already coming down Kash's eyes before the doctor opened the door. When he walked in the room and seen his sister's face and body covered with a sheet he lost it. "Why the fuck you got this sheet on her like that? How's she supposed to breathe?" He walked over and moved the sheet. He looked at her and said, "Come on, sis. I'm taking you home. These people don't know what they are doing here," he said looking at Dr. Robinson. Dr. Robinson didn't know what to say, but he knew he couldn't allow Kash to move this body. At this time Kash was now pushing a wheelchair from the corner to the side of Fiah's bed. When he went to pick her up out of the bed, that's when the doctor yelled for security. He ran over to Kash and tried to stop him. Kash pushed the doctor to the side and continued to get his sister out of the bed. "I'm going to take you home, sis. I'm going to cook your favorite food and…." When Fiah's lifeless arms fell on his, he knew it was time to let go. He grabbed her in his arms and cried. By this time the security guards were at the door helping the doctor get up. Dr. Robinson said, "I'm okay, guys. I thought we had a situation, but everything is okay." The guards looked at him as if to say are you sure. He looked at Kash holding his sister crying and said, "Yes, I'm sure." Dr. Robinson walked over to Kash and said, "Son, are you okay?" Kash started feeling that pain in his heart again. "I'm okay, Doc."

"I'm going to need you to let go, son. I know it's hard but you have to let go. If you don't mind me asking, who is she to you?" He looked at the doctor and said, "She was my sister." He looked back down at her somberly and said, "The only family I had left." He gave her a final kiss and whispered in her ear, "I'm going to find out who did this to you. Word to everything I love, Sophie. They ass is dead." He let her go and walked out the room.

As soon as he hit the doorway, he felt his whole world had just crumbled. He had to get out of this hospital. Everything started feeling small to him. Small and dark. He began to feel that anger again and all he could think about was Steven. The officers that followed him, approached him as he headed out the door. "Hey there, we really need to get into your sister's apartment so we can investigate." When Kash turned around the officer seen his blood shot eyes. "Look, man, you got a card or something? I need to get ready to plan a funeral." The officer put his head down as he reached in his pocket to get a card. He handed Kash the card and said, "I'm sorry for your loss, man," and gave him a hug before walking away. Kash took the card and walked to his car. All he saw was red, somebody had to die. He got in his car and made two phone calls. One was to Dawne and the other was to Troy. He called Dawne to see if Steven went to work last night. He called Troy to see where Steven was. Troy let him know that he hadn't seen Steven since he had gotten there. Dawne let him know that Steven wasn't in last night. He sat back in his seat and tried to figure everything out. During his phone call with Dawne, she had also shared with him that Fiah and Steven were having sex. This was something he didn't know. *Even if the nigga found out that I was using her to distract him why would he do that to her?* He decided to call Steven. Steven picked up on the first ring and said, "You got some big balls calling me. I know you been fucking my wife."

"This ain't even about that. You been fucking my sister?"

"Yeah, I fucked that hoe. Then I cancelled her ass. You mad that somebody been fucking her besides you?"

After that all Kash heard was Steven laughing on the other side of the phone before hearing a dial tone. *What the fuck that nigga just say? I'm going to seriously hurt this nigga.* Kash sped to his house on the south side to get ready for war. He was going to make sure Steven died a slow and painful death.

Diamond got to her mom's house around four-thirty. The cab driver helped her take all of her things to the front door. "Thank you so much for all of your help," said Diamond as she gave the driver a ten-dollar tip. He smiled and said, "Thank you." The house was so quiet when she had gotten inside. She took all her bags upstairs before calling her mom again. This time she answered.

"Well, look who finally decided to pick up a phone and call me."

"I tried to call you earlier but it went to voicemail."

"I'm over at Diane's house. What time will you be here?"

"I just got to your house to get my car. I should be there in a few."

"Okay. Love you, baby. See you when you get here."

Diamond really hoped everything went well today at this dinner. She didn't have anything planned to say. She just knew that she liked her life and knew that if she stayed with him her dream would come true. Either he would kill her or force her to kill herself. She felt his parents' home would be a safe zone and she could be able to enjoy one last meal with the whole family. Diamond thought about calling Kash to check on him. But he hadn't checked on her since he left her in his bed, so she changed her mind. She rolled a blunt and went out to get in her car. As she smoked, she had the strangest vision. She just seen Steven with a bat smashing her windows out. She had come to love her car and she couldn't let that happen. After she finished smoking, she went next door and asked her neighbors if she could leave her car in their garage. Even though they hadn't spoken in years, they knew Diamond since she was a little girl. The middle-aged couple were more than happy to help her out. She parked the car then walked across the grass back to her house before calling her cab. While waiting for the cab to come Diamond said a short prayer. "Lord, I really can't take another crazy day. Please let this dinner go well." A few minutes later Diamond was on her way to the Thompsons' house.

Steven was still a little twisted when he walked through his door. The whole drive back home, he just kept seeing Fiah's disformed face. *I should've killed her ass,* he thought to himself. He pulled into his driveway and went inside the house. He came in the house and went straight upstairs to get in the shower. He knew a nice cold shower was all he needed to get him going. That and some more coke. He couldn't wait to see Diamond's trifling ass, so he could expose her to his family. Her and her hoe-ass mother. He finally found the woman of his dreams and she betrayed him. So what, he put his hands on her. If she got out of pocket she deserved to get checked. *I gave this girl my heart and she played me for some lame-ass, incestuous-ass nigga. She gonna wish she stayed with me after I'm done with her ass.* He got out the shower, wrapped his towel around his waist and headed to his bedroom. When he got there he noticed that his bed still looked the same way he left it. He just thought Diamond stayed at her mom's house until he looked in the closet and seen that there was stuff thrown everywhere and half of Diamond's things were gone. All her stuff was still on the dresser. He checked her jewelry box, looked like everything was still there. *Smart girl,* he thought. *If she left at least she didn't leave with anything I brought her.* He didn't care about the clothes, just the jewelry that he spent so much money on.

This simple-ass bitch think she can just leave that easily? Steven took the weed and the make-up case out of the pants he had on. He looked in a sock in his top drawer and pulled out a gram of cocaine. He went back over to the bed, put some coke on the mirror and did some lines while he rolled up. *How dare her fuck around on me and try to leave me. I own that bitch. The only way she leaving me is in a body bag.* He continued to get high as his thoughts got crazier. Halfway through the blunt he got a phone call from Aleese.

"Hey, big brother. You still coming today, right?"

"Hey, A. Yes, I will be there. Have you heard from Diamond today?"

"I sure did. She hit me up earlier asking what time she should be here."

"What did you hear in her background? Did you hear anybody talking?"

Aleese laughed and said, "Let me find out you don't have your lady in check."

Steven laughed too and said, "You know better than that, baby girl. I didn't come home last night, I think she's mad at me."

"Oh, God!! Y'all better not spoil this day for Mama. Y'all already both done missed church."

"Shut your face, little girl. Ain't nobody spoiling nothing. See you in a few, big head."

"Whatever. See you when you get here," said Aleese before hanging up the phone.

Steven got dressed. He was feeling like a boss today, so he put on his off-white linen suit and his tan Gucci loafers. He didn't know how to explain his knuckles, but they didn't look as bad as they did a few hours ago. He looked at himself in the mirror and smiled. "There you go, baby," he said to himself before throwing on his Gucci glasses. He liked the touch of professionalism the non-prescription glasses gave him. He took another bump, wiped his nose, grabbed the clip and headed down the stairs. He went straight out the door never looking on the coffee table in the living room. He got in his ride, lit his blunt and headed to the highway. About twenty minutes into the drive, the phone rings and its Kashmere. He said his peace before banging it on him. *Fucking dweeb. How you take my bitch?* he thought to himself as he began laughing. "I have a feeling today is going to be an interesting day," he said to himself.

Chapter 11

This was the first time Ms. Wallace had been to the Thompsons' house in years. She and Mrs. Thompson were thick as thieves until the night she first slept with Joe. It was supposed to be a one-time thing, but the affair went on for almost year. Because of their cautiousness, neither Mrs. Thompson or Mr. Wallace ever knew what was going on, so she thought. The only reminder of their secret love affair was her beautiful daughter Diamond. Joe tried to get Julie to get rid of the baby, but he changed his mind after finding out his wife couldn't conceive children. Even though he had to love Diamond from a distance, he felt good seeing the woman she had become. He couldn't be there for birthdays, holidays or special events, but financially he was always there. Mr. Thompson was the one who put Ms. Wallace in the house she was still living in that was now paid off. So, you can only imagine how happy he was when he found out that Diamond was dating his adopted son. He was even happier when he found out he was going to be a grandfather. He was looking forward to experiencing the happiness that a newborn baby would bring. And he was even more excited that he could now show Diamond the kind of love that he has always wanted to give her.

Ms. Wallace was in the kitchen helping Mrs. Thompson get things together for dinner. Ms. Wallace said, "Diane, your house is beautiful.

When did you get it remodeled?" Taking the cornbread out of the oven she said, "The boys did it for me. They wanted to buy us a new house, but I couldn't leave here." She began cutting the cornbread into squares before placing the pieces in a big bowl. "Don't forget to let me show you the third floor before you leave, girl."

"I thought the house looked a little higher when I pulled up. I haven't been here in so long I couldn't remember."

"It has been a while, J. We family now, so that's about to change," she said smiling. "Can you put the yams and the collard greens in these bowls while I start setting the table?"

"Sure, Diane," said Ms. Wallace walking over to the stove.

Aleese came downstairs in a pair of tight sweatpants, a midriff shirt and a scarf on her head. "Hey, Ma, what do you need me to do?" Mrs. Thompson looked at her daughter and said, "You can start by getting dressed." Aleese put her hand on her hip and said, "What's wrong with what I have on, Ma?"

"Let's start with that pouch you got hanging out. Don't nobody want to see that." Aleese started laughing. "So, you gonna clown me like that, Ma?" Diane called her husband who was in the living room watching TV. "Joe, come in here and tell your daughter what's wrong with what she has on." Joe knew that Aleese had on something she shouldn't have if he was being summoned. He walked into the dining room and looked at Aleese and said, "Baby girl, go put on something that fits," and he went back and sat on the couch. Aleese made a face and went upstairs to change her shirt. She knew not to argue with dad.

Diane walked back in the kitchen still laughing, "I don't know what's wrong with that girl. She knows daggone well she don't need to be wearing no belly shirt looking like she in her first trimester." Ms. Wallace laughed and said, "Diane, stop. It couldn't have been that bad." Diane picked up the bowls with the yams and collards greens in them and said, "If Joe had something to say, it was definitely a problem." She started laughing again as she went to place the bowls on the table. It was now almost four-thirty. Mrs. Thompson wanted to make sure everything was in place when the children arrived. Ms. Wallace was in the kitchen placing the string beans in a bowl when Diane came back in. "Are you excited, girl? We are finally going to be grandparents. I don't know about you, but I'm ready to start shopping for some cute baby clothes."

Ms. Wallace responded, "So am I. It's been so long since I've had to change a diaper and make a bottle." She looked over at Diane, whose smile had disappeared. "I'm sorry, Diane. I didn't—"

Mrs. Thompson interjected, "It's okay, Julie. I used to be sad that I wasn't able to have any children of my own. More like I felt like a failure to Joe. I know that he always wanted to be a father." Then she smiled and said, "But that wasn't God's plan for me. God blessed me with three wonderful children. Even though I can't get this last one out the house," she said laughing. While Julie was in the kitchen she had been eyeing the bottle of wine at the end of the counter. "How about we pop that bottle open and toast to God giving us some good children," said Ms. Wallace. "I am all for that one," said Diane walking over to get the bottle. "Can you look in the cabinet to your left and get two wineglasses?" Ms. Wallace took the glasses out of the cabinet and placed them on the island. "I have been waiting to pop this bottle. Who better than to be sharing this moment with," said Diane looking at Julie. She filled the glasses up before taking one for herself and passing the other to Julia. "To our beautiful blessings," said Diane. They raised their glasses, then clinked them together before sipping on their wine.

Mr. Thompson came into the kitchen to see what the two ladies were giggling so much about. He leaned against the wall in the doorway and said, "Well, well, well. Looks like the dynamic duo is back together again." Joe often thought about his time with Julie. If it was up to him he still would've had her on the side, but she ended their affair when she found out about the baby. "It's good having you back, Jules. Diane always seems so happy when you're around." Julie had to stop looking at Joe. His voice always did something to her. She looked at Diane and said, "It's good to be back." Twenty years ago, this would've been a moment Joe would've taken advantage of. This moment did remind him of the time he asked Diane if she would be interested in a threesome with Julie. Diane of course said no, and Joe just assumed she wasn't about that life. Diane declined because she was afraid that Joe would favor Julia over her. Diane was more focused on her career before the children came. Julia brought the fun into both of their lives. Even though all these years have passed, Joe still remembered how Julia felt and how she tasted. "Diane, can you get me a beer out of the fridge?" He had to break his thoughts of Ms. Wallace. His thoughts had him feeling his manhood about to rise. Diane put her drink down before going in the fridge and taking out a beer for her husband. Joe and Julie's eyes locked briefly before Julie went to finish putting the food in the bowls.

"Here you go, baby," said Diane handing Joe his beer. "I love you, baby," said Joe, giving Diane a kiss before walking back into the living room. Julie smiled and said, "All these years later and he still looks at you the same way."

"Girl, stop it. You know if Frank was alive it would be the same with you two." As Julie put rice in the bowl she said, "That seems like forever ago." Sipping on her wine Diane asked, "How long has he been gone now?" Placing the bowl on the counter Diane replied, "It's been over fifteen years."

"And you haven't been with anybody else in all that time?" Julie smiled and said, "No. I've been letting Diamond keep my focus." Diane put her glass down and went to get the bottle for a refill. "I tell you what, if anything ever happens to me, I want you to be with Joe." Julie looked at Diane in a confused way. Diane took another sip and said, "I know why you stopped coming around, J. Diamond is Joe's daughter, isn't she?" Julie couldn't even respond. Her throat got dry as tears filled her eyes. "Maybe I should leave," said Julie. Diane put her glass down, walked over to Julie and hugged her. "I forgive you, Julie. I forgave you a long time ago. Only a fool wouldn't know that she is his." With tears now flowing down her face Julie said, "I'm sorry, Diane. It was a mistake, but I couldn't get rid of her." Diane looked her in the eyes and said, "I'm happy you didn't. You were able to give Joe something I never could. Now wipe these tears off your face." Diane went to get some tissue for Julie. "You knew all this time and you never said anything. Why now, D?" Diane walked close to Julie and said, "I'm dying, I have cancer." Julie started crying all over again. "Stop it, Julie. I don't want you crying for me. You're the first person I've told."

"You didn't tell Joe?"

"No, I didn't. I just said you're the first person I've told."

"D, you have to tell him."

"Look, Julie, I have kept your secret for over twenty years, surely you can keep mine for a few more weeks."

"Weeks? That soon?"

"Yes. Now get your face wiped off and take another drink with me. Not another word of this. Okay?" Diane looked at Julie's face and said, "The same energy you had while you was sleeping with my husband, is the same energy I need you to have right now." Julie wasn't expecting that at all.

The doorbell rang. "Joe, get the door. That must be Diamond because the boys both have keys." Diane looked at Julie and said, "There's a bathroom down the hall. Get yourself together, girl, we have a dinner to get ready for." Diane smiled and continued drinking her wine. Mr. Thompson went to get the door. He opened it and seen Diamond standing there with a big smile on her face. He gave her a hug as she came through the door. "Where did you park at? I don't see that pretty car of yours." She wasn't expecting him to be paying so much attention. "I decided not to drive. I left the car at Mom's house." Mr. Thompson found this very strange since Diamond has been driving that car all around town since she got it. He decided to not make a big deal about it. "Let me look at you," he said smiling. "You are beautiful just like your mother."

"Yes, she certainly is," said Mrs. Thompson. "Come give me a hug, baby." Diane rubbed her belly and said, "When are you going to start showing? Aleese look more pregnant than you do." Diane laughed as Diamond covered her mouth embarrassed for Aleese. "Mrs. Thompson, that's not nice," said Diamond smiling. "Oh, chile, please, she does. I had to make her go upstairs and change her clothes. Coming down here in a belly shirt looking four months pregnant." Mr. Thompson went to take the wineglass out of Diane's hand. "I think you had enough, baby." Diane grabbed her glass back and said, "I'm just getting started, baby." She gave Joe a kiss and walked back into the kitchen. Diamond looked at Mr. Thompson as he stood there shaking his head. "That's your wife," she said laughing. "Yes, it is," he replied.

Mrs. Thompson yelled from the kitchen, "Diamond, can I get you some wine?" Diamond walked to the island and said, "I don't think I'm supposed to be drinking wine, ma'am."

"Girl, please, I don't think you're supposed to be smoking weed either but I still smell it on you." Diamond could tell that Mrs. Thompson was on a roll today. Mrs. Thompson went and pulled out some red wine and poured Diamond a glass. "Fix your face, we family now." She handed her the glass and said, "It's red wine. You can drink red wine while you're pregnant. Don't worry, we will be eating soon. I know you probably have the munchies." Diamond almost choked as she took a sip of her wine. Aleese came down the stairs in a whole new outfit and her hair was now done. Diamond ran over to her and gave her a hug. "Am I happy to see you." Aleese seen her mom with the wineglass in her hand and said, "Mommy must've said something to you." Diamond laughed and said, "Your mother is a fireball." Aleese looked at her and said, "You have no idea, girl." She walked into the kitchen and said, "Mommy, how many glasses have you had already?" Diane looked at her and said, "Little girl, I'm the parent here. Now come take these bowls to the table. Diamond, put your glass down and you come help too." Diamond was walking into the kitchen as Aleese was coming out. "Welcome to the family, girl," said Aleese passing by her with the bowls in her hand.

When Diamond got in the kitchen Mrs. Thompson said, "You have any of that herb with you?" Diamond looked at her confused and said, "Excuse me, ma'am?"

"I'm going to need you to stop ma'aming me. Call me Ma or Mom. Either is better than ma'am."

"Okay, Ma. No, I do not have any herb with me. I'm sure Steven will have some when he gets here." Mrs. Thompson handed Diamond the bowl with the string beans in it before saying, "Why didn't you and Steven come together?"

"To be honest with you, I haven't seen Steven since he left me at my mom's house yesterday. He said he had to come and check on you and that was it." Mrs. Thompson shook her head and said, "I notice you don't have your ring on." Diamond quickly tried to hide her hand under the bowl. "I know my son is a lot to deal with. If for whatever reason things don't work out with you two, you will always have us. As long as you are carrying my grandbaby, you will always be a part of this family." Mrs. Thompson seen the tears in Diamond's eyes. She took the bowl from her and gave her a big hug. "These Thompson men are a trip, girl. It takes a strong woman to handle them." She wiped the tears from her eyes and said, "You are a strong woman, you hear me?"

"Yes, Ma," said Diamond.

Ms. Wallace walked into the kitchen nervous when she seen Diamond crying, talking to Diane. "Is everything okay in here?" asked Julie. "Everything is fine," said Diane as Diamond went to give her mom a hug. "We were just having a talk about these Thompson men." Julie smiled as Diamond grabbed the bowl and walked into the dining room. Aleese was setting the table when Diamond came back in the dining room. "Don't pay Mommy no mind. She has no filter in general, so when she gets that wine in her system, girl!" Diamond put the bowl down and smiled. "Your mom is cool. You need some help with that?"

"I got this, girl. Watch this. Hey, Ma, I invited somebody over for dinner." Diane looked at Julie and said, "Is it a man or a woman?" before she broke out in laughter. Diane looked at Julie and whispered, "I think Aleese is a lesbian, she just don't want to tell us." Julie dropped her head and said, "I can't with you, girl." Diamond looked at Aleese with a confused face. Aleese whispered, "My mom thinks I'm a lesbian because I've never brought a man home." Diamond laughed and said, "Ohhhhh."

"It's a man, Ma. Although I think he used to be a woman." They all started laughing except for Joe. He didn't like when Diane teased Aleese about her sexual preference. He just wanted his daughter to be happy. He was also nervous about what might come out of Diane's mouth during dinner. He wasn't sure how many glasses of wine she had, but he was sure she was past one.

Mr. Thompson heard the door open and in came Calvin. "Hey, Pop," said Calvin walking over to give his dad a hug. "Finally, some testosterone in this house. I'm going to warn you now; your mom has been sipping." Calvin laughed, "That means we going to have some fun today." Calvin walked into the kitchen. "Hey, Ma," he said giving his mother a big hug and a kiss. "Hey, son, nice of you to finally make it," said Mrs. Thompson looking at her watch. It was now five-twenty. "Where is that brother of yours?"

"Fu—" Mrs. Thompson backed up and looked at him. "I'm sorry, Ma. I don't know where that nigga is. Your son been tripping, Ma. Word." Calvin walked over to Ms. Wallace and said, "You know you aging like fine wine, beautiful." Ms. Wallace started blushing. "Boy, cut it out. She old enough to be your mother," said Mrs. Thompson. Calvin spun Julie around and said, "She is definitely somebody's mother, but she damn sure ain't mine." Ms. Wallace was turning red now. Mr. Thompson yelled from the living room, "Boy, if you don't get your ass in here. And bring me a beer on your way." "God give me strength today," said Joe. "You better get your father his beer," said Mrs. Thompson laughing.

"Aleese, you got that table set?" asked Mrs. Thompson from the kitchen. "I'm almost done, Ma."

"Let's go in the dining room, Julie. And grab the bottle," said Mrs. Thompson. Ms. Wallace was still smiling from what Calvin just said. "My boys are something else," she said as they walked to the table. "Has anybody heard from Steven? I'm ready to eat now," said Mrs. Thompson. Nobody said anything. "Oh, so now y'all going to act like y'all can't hear me." In a much louder voice Diane yelled, "Has anybody heard from my child Steven Marquis Thompson?" Joe got up and said, "Diane, nobody has heard from him. You're making that your last glass for the evening."

"Joe, call my son and see where he is," said Diane before swallowing the rest of her wine and pouring another glass. "Okay, Diane." Joe hadn't seen his wife drink this much in a long time. He knew if he went and took the wine away from her, dinner would be over before it began, so he let her have her way. He went ahead and gave Steven a call. The phone rang and went to voicemail. "Let's just get started. I'm sure he's on his way," said Joe walking to the dining room.

"Come here, Joe. You can sit here at the head of the table. Julie, you can sit over there to the left of him. Diamond, you sit next to your mom and Steven can sit beside you. Calvin, you sit there, so your across from your dad. Aleese, is your friend slim or on the hefty side? Don't want to sit them in the middle and they are uncomfortable," Diane said while around the table. Before Aleese could respond Diane continued talking. "Never mind. Just keep the seat open next to your brother. You can sit in the middle right next to me." Mrs. Thompson looked at her watch and it was now five-thirty. "Well, I guess we can start now. Nobody wants to eat cold food. Joe, can you bless the food?"

"Can we all bow our—" Steven came through the door just in time. He walked in with the biggest grin on his face. He walked over to the table and said, "So y'all were going to eat without me?" Anybody who looked at Steven could tell he was high off of something right now. Diane cut her eyes at him and said, "Sit your black ass down. Coming in here late and flying. Them herbs don't do that, son," said Diane cutting her eyes at him.

"That's all that cocaine he been snorting," said Calvin. "Yo, mind your business, chump. Ain't nobody say nothing to you."

"Y'all both quit it. Daddy about to bless the food," said Aleese. Steven went to take his seat next to Diamond. Mr. Thompson was about to continue his prayer, until Diane got up from the table. "Come on, Diane, not now," said Joe. Diane walked over to Steven and slapped him so hard his glasses flew across the table. Steven immediately stood up, shocked and embarrassed. "You better sit your five-dollar ass down before I make change," said Joe from his seat. Steven sat back down. Diane looked at Steven with tears in her eyes and said, "You're breaking my heart, boy. I didn't raise you like this. You got this beautiful young lady here, who is about to have your baby, and this is what you want to do? Cocaine, son?" Mrs. Thompson walked away from the table and went into the bathroom. "Now look what you did," said Calvin. Steven just sat there with his head down. "Jules, go check on Diane. Steven, come take a walk with me," said Mr. Thompson walking to the front door.

Julie went to check on Diane as Joe had asked. As soon as Mr. Thompson closed the front door behind him and Steven the questions began. "Calvin, how you know that Steven is doing cocaine?" asked Aleese. "Because I've seen him do it. I didn't pay it no mind when I saw him fuck with it at the club. But yesterday when I told him about mom and he tried to do it in front of me, I knocked that shit out of his hand." Aleese looked at Diamond and said, "Diamond, did you know about this?"

"I found out this morning."

"How did you find out?" asked Aleese. "I wanted to tell every-body at the same time." Diamond put her head down and started fidgeting a bit. "I'm leaving Steven." The tears began coming out of her eyes. "For the last year and a half, Steven has been very abusive and it's just been getting worse." Aleese got up from her seat and walked over to Diamond, "I'm so sorry, Diamond. You know we had no idea."

"I know y'all didn't. A few months ago, when my face got messed up, that was all him. He made up that story about me getting into a fight at the club. The next day, I lost our first child." Calvin held his head in hands not believing what he was hearing right now. "Dia-mond, that's my brother and all, but I will kill that nigga if he puts his hands on you again. Do you hear me?"

"Calvin, it's not going to get to that. That's why I'm leaving."

Mr. Thompson took a pack of cigarettes out of his shirt pocket and lit one, then he passed one to Steven and lit it for him. Even though he didn't smoke cigarettes, he took it anyway. Up until right now, he never knew his dad smoked cigarettes. "I don't know what's gotten into you lately, son, but you gotta stop this destructive path you're on. I know we are not your biological parents, but we have loved you as our own and given you the same opportunities we gave Calvin and Aleese. We didn't stress you about not going to college. We didn't stress you when you moved out and started pimping the white girl. We just supported you and let you know that we were al-ways here for you. We were so proud of you when you and our brother went into business with each other and opened the club. We thought you had finally got back on track. But today, showing up high and late and standing up to your mother, son, I can't have that. You will not disrespect that woman, do you hear me?" Looking at the ground Steven said, "Yes, Dad." He knew he was bugging out and he knew he needed to apologize to his mother. "Look at me, boy." Steven picked his up and looked at his dad. "You are about to lose Diamond. You didn't even notice she wasn't wearing her ring, did you?" Steven hadn't noticed and he really didn't care. "Dad, she's not who you think she is."

"Apparently neither are you, son. What you going to tell me, she stepped out on you? I don't blame her. You don't come home at night and I know you and your brother be having sex with them nasty girls at the club. I really don't care what she's done, son. I knew that girl all her life and she's always been a good girl. So, anything that has happened to change that, I'm sure was brought on by you and your actions." Steven couldn't say anything because his dad was right. Mr. Thompson flicked his cigarette and gave Steven a hug. "You know we love you. Whatever you need us to do to help you get off these drugs let us know." Looking at Steven in the face he says, "You better make a decision before it's too late, son. When you get in this house you better apologize to your mama."

"I know, Dad. I love you too." Steven flicked his cigarette and they both went in the house.

Steven couldn't help but see the hate-filled eyes looking at him when he came back in the house. Aleese had got up from sitting next to Diamond and went back to her seat. Nobody said a word. Steven and his dad went back to their seats. Then Diane and Julie came out the bathroom laughing and went back to their seats. Diane says, "Why everybody looking so serious? I'm ready to eat now. Joe, say the prayer." Steven stood up and walked over to his mother and gave her a hug and asked her to forgive him. She looked at him smiling and said, "Baby, you are already forgiven. Now go have a seat so we can eat." Mrs. Thompson was high as kite right now. She had smoked a joint while they were in the bathroom and now she was hungry as ever. "Joe, take it away." Joe blessed the food and the bowls started being passed. "Calvin, you better fix your face," said Diane from across the table. "Maybe if you share some of that weed you had, I could." Aleese started laughing, "What are you talking about? Mommy don't smoke weed."

"Little sister, you don't know anything."

"Boy, go in the bathroom. Look in the Band-Aid case in the medicine cabinet." Calvin headed straight to the bathroom. "I don't need any of y'all messing up my dinner today." Aleese looked at her mom and said, "When you start smoking weed, Ma?"

"Don't worry about that, baby. It was prescribed from my doctor for my anxiety."

"Since when you been anxious, Ma? I've never seen you have a problem with anxiety." Then Steven says, "Why you lying, Ma? Aleese, Mommy has cancer. She's sick." Aleese looked at her mother with tears in her eyes, "Mama, tell me this ain't true." Diane cut her eyes at Steven and said, "Didn't I just say I didn't want anybody messing up my dinner today?" Steven replied, "I'm just tired of everybody keeping secrets." Then Aleese says, "Oh, like how you been putting your hands on Diamond?" Everybody stopped what they were doing and looked at Steven. Diamond sitting next to him with her head down. "Yo, mind your business, Aleese."

"Son, what is your sister talking about?" Aleese says, "Go ahead, Diamond. Tell them how Steven was the one who did that to your face." Immediately tears just started flowing from Diamond's face as she began feeling scared and embarrassed. She was going to bring it up at the right time. Now just didn't feel like the right time. Mr. Thompson was so angry he got up and punched Steven in his face.

Diane jumped up and started yelling, "Don't hurt him, Joe." Julia went over to her daughter and hugged her with tears in her eyes. "Why you didn't tell me, Diamond? I sent you back home with him. Why you didn't tell me?" Hearing all the commotion, Calvin comes out the bathroom and sees his dad on top of Steven throwing blows. "Calvin, get your father," said Mrs. Thompson. Calvin pulls his dad off of Steven and Steven gets off the floor. "This family is built on secrets. You know why Daddy is all mad right now? Because unlike us, Diamond is his real daughter." Calvin immediately said, "What you talking about now?"

"Go ahead and ask him yourself," he said while wiping the blood from his nose. Joe looked at Diane with tears in his eyes and said, "I'm sorry, baby." Diane walked over to her husband and put her finger on his lips and said, "Don't, babe. I already knew. I've always known." Joe fell to her feet on his knees crying, hugging Diane's waist. Now Diamond, Aleese and Calvin are all looking confused. Diamond looks at her mom and says, "Mommy, what's going on right now?"

"Baby, I'm sorry you had to find out like this. It wasn't supposed to happen this way."

"So, you're telling me that the man I thought was my father for all these years isn't my father?"

"Yes, Diamond, that's what I'm telling you," said Ms. Wallace crying.

"Tell them how you been cheating on me, Diamond. Tell them about your little boyfriend. Is that even my baby?" Diamond looked at Steven with hate in her eyes and said, "I fucking hate you." As the tears began to fall from her eyes she began to bring up everything she had been holding inside. "Yes, I have been cheating on you. With a man who loves me more than you ever could. You think you can just do whatever you want to me and I'm just supposed to take it? Tell your family about that hoe you got pregnant. Tell your family about the hoes you been sleeping with all this time. Tell your family how you have raped me and all the times you put your hands on me. I should've been left you. I was so stupid to think that you could change." Just then Diamond's phone started ringing. Steven went to her bag unphased by anything she just said and pulled her phone out. "Look who it is. Kashmere, your boyfriend." Calvin's eyes got wide not believing that Kash is who she had been sleeping with. Steven answered Diamond's phone and put it on speaker for everyone to hear.

Kash: Yo D, you still with that nigga at his mom's house?

Steven: What up fam. Why you still calling my girl?

Kash: Diamond, get away from that nigga. I just left my sisters dead body at the hospital. That crazy nigga killed my sister yo.

Diamond: Steven what is he talking about?

Kash hung the phone up. "Steven, give me my phone."

"Nah, B, you ain't getting this back."

"So Calvin, remember Fiah from the club? Why did Kash send her there to distract me while he got his paws on Diamond?" Calvin looked at Steven and said, "Bruh, did you really kill her?" Steven put his head down for a minute, then said, "It was an accident, bro. I told her ass not to lie to me. She was alive when I left her. A little unrecognizable, but alive."

"Yo, bro, what the hell happened to you, man? You killed this man's sister? You know he coming for you, right?"

"All this shit is Diamond's fault. He sent Fiah to the club because of Diamond."

"Nah, B, he didn't make you have sex with her or fall for her. You can't blame this on Diamond.."

Mrs. Thompson started yelling, "You murderer. Get out of my house right now. I don't want you here anymore. I don't want you to ever step foot in this house again. I'm calling the police."

"Ma, I'm leaving, you don't have to do that." Mrs. Thompson picked up the phone. Before she could even dial the number she started grabbing her chest and fell to the ground. Aleese grabbed the phone and called the ambulance. Mr. Thompson picked up his wife and carried her to the couch. "Baby, are you okay?" Her eyes were open and she gave him a smile. "I don't want you to remember me like this. I want you to remember me spicy, baby. I told Julia when I die I want her to be there for you in every way."

"You're not going anywhere, Diane. Don't talk like that."

"Just remember what I told you, honey. You were always a great husband and father. You have to be strong for the kids. You have to get Steven some help. Promise me that." Diane's eyes started closing. "Diane, stay with me. The ambulance is on the way. Hold on, baby."

Aleese was on her knees sitting next to her mother, holding her hand. "If something happens to Mommy, I will never forgive you, Steven." Just then the doorbell rang. Calvin rushed to the door thinking it was the ambulance. He was very shocked to see Pastor Johnson standing on the end of the door. "Hey, son, Aleese invited me to dinner. Sorry I'm just getting here." Calvin opened the door all the way, so Pastor Johnson could come inside. He immediately saw Diane on couch with Joe and Aleese by her side. "Joe, what happened?"

"She was holding her chest and she just fell out. We are waiting for the ambulance right now. Aleese, move over, honey, so I can say a prayer for your mother." Pastor Johnson took his oil out of his inner jacket pocket and laid his hands on Mrs. Thompson's head and began praying.

With all that was going on Aleese had forgotten that she invited the pastor to dinner. It was just like God to send someone when you need them the most. After he prayed for Diane he asked Joe to step to the side so they could have a conversation. "Julia, can you and Diamond go over there with Aleese, please, while me and the Pastor talk?"

"Sure, Joe," said Julia. Him and the pastor stepped into the dining room where Calvin and Steven were having a conversation. Calvin knew his brother was tripping on the drugs, but putting his hands on women and even now finding out that he killed someone made him more empathetic toward him. They got up from the table when they seen their dad and the pastor coming that way. Pastor Johnson looked at Steven and said, "Son, I see a darkness over your life right now. The devil has been taking you for a ride and you have just been allowing it to happen. You are going to be the cause of a lot of sadness to come. You need to give your life to God before it's too late. This is not the plan that God had for you, but it's not too late to get back on track. Do you want me to pray with you?"

"I'm good, Pastor. I will come see you when I'm ready."

"Son, tomorrow isn't promised to you. You can walk out of this door right now and not make it to tonight. I made the offer to you. And just because you don't want me to pray with you, doesn't stop me from praying for you." Pastor Johnson gave Steven a hug. He held him for a minute. Steven didn't know he was praying at that time, but he did begin to feel something stirring up inside of him and he immediately began to cry. "Hold your head up, son. It's still not too late." The pastor walked over to the table to where Joe was sitting and had a seat. Calvin put his arm around his brother and they walked into the kitchen.

"You know God works in mysterious ways, Joe."

"Tell me about it, Pastor. Today was just supposed to be us having a nice family dinner and it seems like all hell just broke loose."

"It's times like this when God shows up and shows out Joe. Over the last few months Diane has been coming to see me for counseling. Her cancer has gotten worse and she only has a few weeks to live."

"Pastor Johnson, what are you talking about? Diane said she was getting better."

"You know how your wife is, Joe. She didn't want anyone to worry about her. You see how long she waited to tell the kids. I know this isn't what you want to hear right now, but Diane has already planned her funeral and paid for it. She knew you all would be heart broken and she wanted that to be one less thing that you would have to do." Joe couldn't believe what he was hearing right now. He thought to himself, *This day just can't get any worse.*

Joe heard everyone at the couch laughing, then Aleese called him over. He came over in time to see Diane trying to sit up. He ran over to her smiling. He bent down on the floor next to her. She stroked his face, smiled and said, "You can't get rid of me that easy, baby." He began kissing and hugging her, telling her how much he loved her. Seeing Diane up and smiling made everyone forget about all the craziness that just happened. "Where's my baby? Steven, come here." Steven came and sat next to his mom on the couch. He laid his head on her shoulder and began to cry. She put her arm around him and held him in her arms. "You know we haven't sat like this in a long time. When you first came home, I would hold you for hours while you cried. I told you then that I would always be here for you and I would never leave you. I can tell from your behavior today that you finding out about me being sick has had you feeling some type of way."

"It has, Ma, you said you would never leave me. I can't lose another mother." Steven hugged his mom back and they both began crying. While hugging him she said, "I will always be here with you. As long as you live, you keep me alive through you. Don't you ever forget it." Joe put his back to the couch, put his head back and wept silently. "Come here, kids," said Mrs. Thompson. Aleese and Calvin came over by their mother. "Diamond, you come here too. You're a part of this crazy family of mine." Diamond smiled as she walked over and sat next to Aleese.

"Since Steven has put it out there, I might as well tell you guys what's going on. I went to the doctor a couple of weeks ago and they told me my cancer has gotten worse. They are only giving me a few more weeks to live." Everybody immediately got sad and began crying. "This right here is what I don't want. I've lived my life and want you all to live yours. Diamond, don't get rid of my grandchild. She is going to be as beautiful as her mother is. And you better name her after me," said Diane playfully. Up until that moment, Diamond already had in her mind to have an abortion as soon as she could. Diamond smiled and gave Mrs. Thompson her word that she wouldn't get rid of the child. She didn't know what she was going to do as far as Steven was concerned, but she would cross that bridge when it came. "Calvin and Aleese, I want you guys to get your brother some help. He needs your love more than ever right now. And promise me, that you guys will be there for each other. Especially Daddy. When I'm gone, he's going to need all of you. Julia, come here, girl." Ms. Wallace made her way to the couch right next to Joe. "You already know what I've asked of you. You just keep him happy and you better be there for all of my children. I know today a lot was said, and even though we all want to kick Steven's ass right now, we have to show him compassion at this time." Julia looked at Diane and said, "Whatever you want, D." She walked over to her and gave her a kiss on her cheek.

Right after that they heard the ambulance pulling up, so Aleese went to open the door. The paramedics pulled up and got the gurney out the back before heading to the door. Once they got inside the house Diane quickly told them she was okay and didn't need to go to the hospital. They took her vitals and checked her out. Once they seen how high her blood pressure was, they talked her into coming with them. She told them to take the gurney back to the ambulance and she would meet them at the hospital. They told her they would take the gurney back, but she had to leave with them. One EMT worker took the gurney back while the other one waited for Mrs. Thompson to get her coat and say her goodbyes. Everybody walked outside with Mrs. Thompson except for Aleese. She went upstairs to get her coat, so she could go with her mom to the hospital.

Mrs. Thompson had a lot of pride. She didn't want her neighbors talking about her or knowing she was sick. Mr. Thompson gave her a kiss once she was inside the ambulette. He asked the drivers to wait for his daughter who was going to accompany her mom for the ride. While he was still inside with her, Diamond and Ms. Wallace decided that they were going back home. They were saying their goodbyes to Pastor Johnson when Diamond seen Kashmere's Range Rover driving up. She immediately yelled at Steven, "Go in the house, Steven. Now." Even though she no longer wanted to be with him, she didn't want any harm to come to him either. Steven didn't understand what was happening until Calvin shouted, "Everybody get down." Calvin seen the guns coming from the passenger side of the front and back windows of the Rover. While bullets went flying in the direction of the Thompson house everyone ducked for cover and the ambulance pulled off. A few seconds later, so did the Rover. Calvin was the first one to get up. Then everyone else started getting up. Calvin went to help up Diamond and Ms. Wallace as Steven focused his attention to the front door. He screamed as he seen Aleese lying in the doorway bleeding.

Once he screamed, everyone turned around to see what had happened. They ran to the door to try and help her. Diamond took out her phone to call nine-one-one. *This cannot be happening*, she thought to herself as she gave them the address to the house. By this time Calvin had Aleese in his arms crying, while he held her limp body. Steven was pacing the living room, hitting himself in the head, saying how it was all his fault. Then his phone rang and he saw it was Kashmere. He quickly picked up the phone. Before he could speak, Kash said, "Now you see how I feel, nigga. You got one minute to tell me that this shit is over before my boys spray up this ambulance in front of me." Steven's heart stopped beating at the thought of his sister and his parents dying because of his actions. Calvin saw Steven's face and asked who was on the phone. Steven replied, "It's Kash. He said if I don't say it's over right now, he going to kill our parents."

"What the fuck is you stuck for, nigga? Tell that man this shit is over."

"But he killed Aleese."

"You know the code of the streets, Steven. What the fuck you thought was gonna happen? You took out that nigga sister. Nobody else is dying because of your dumb ass. Tell that man this is over right now." Steven paused before saying, "You got it, Kash. It's over."

"That's the smartest decision you made today, my man," said Kash before hanging up the phone.

Once Steven said that, he stopped following the ambulette and went to drop his people off before heading home. He knew after this, him and Diamond was over, but that was okay. He didn't love Diamond more than he loved his sister. Now that he had vengeance for her, he could be able to properly grieve. He held his tears in until he got to his crib.

The ambulance got to the house and rushed inside. They made Calvin let go of Aleese as they checked her vitals. They immediately pronounced Aleese dead and covered her with a white sheet before calling for the coroner to come. Ms. Wallace went to console Calvin while Pastor Johnson went to console Steven who was on the floor crying, yelling how this is all his fault. Diamond feeling like she had more than she could handle for the day went to the bathroom to find the band aid case in the medicine cabinet. She could not believe how this day turned out. As soon as she lit the joint her phone began to ring. She didn't recognize the number, but she answered anyway.

Diamond: Hello

Mr. Thompson: Diamond, it's Joe. Is everybody okay.

Diamond: (pauses before crying)

Mr. Thompson: Diamond, what happened honey? Talk to me.

Diamond: (in between the tears) She's gone. They shot her.

Mr. Thompson: Who Diamond? Who got shot?

She could hear Mrs. Thompson in the background asking who got shot.

Diamond: Aleese. They shot Aleese (said Diamond now crying hysterically)

Mr. Thompson: No, no, no. Not my baby Diamond. Tell me they didn't shoot my baby.

Diamond hung up the phone as she heard Mr. Thompson start crying. She sat on the bathroom floor as she began feeling wetness come from between her legs followed by sharp pains from her belly. "Mama, help!!" She couldn't even make it off the floor she was in so much pain. There was so much going on that Ms. Wallace didn't hear her. When Diamond seen no one was coming she started kicking the door. Everyone heard that, then they heard Diamond screaming from the bathroom. Calvin rushed to the bathroom and opened the door to see Diamond on the floor bleeding. "D, you okay?" he asked as he went to pick her up. "Ms. Wallace, tell the paramedic we need them." She got nervous when she seen all the blood coming from Diamond. Calvin was already covered with blood from his sister and now he was covered with blood from his niece as well. He also couldn't believe how this day turned out. He walked past his sister's dead body as he carried Diamond to the ambulance. He knew they wouldn't be able to get the gurney past her body and they couldn't move her until the coroner came. Ms. Wallace followed behind him as he walked on the back of the ambulette and placed her on the gurney. He told her he loved her as he left them and went back to his sister.

Another ambulance had arrived as they pulled off. Calvin walked back to the house feeling empty. His sister was all he had left. He couldn't believe all of this could happen in one day. He looked up to the sky and said, "God, I can't lose nobody else. You can't take my momma too."

Chapter 12

Mrs. Thompson looked at her husband with tears in her eyes. As he stood in the hospital room door crying, his phone fell out of his hand. "Joe, what happened?" Joe just looked at her with his eyes full of sadness as he wept. Diane began crying, knowing that something terrible had just happened. Joe walked over to sit next to her on the hospital bed. He pulled her close to him and began crying like a baby. "I'm sorry, Diane. I'm so sorry, baby." Diane tightened her embrace. This was the first time she had ever seen Joe like this. "Baby, just tell me what happened."

"They shot her, D. They killed our baby." Diane felt her soul leave her body. "Nooooooo. Joe, not my baby girl. Not my baby, Joe." Mr. Thompson hugged Diane tighter as she tried to pull away from him. A nurse walking by the room stopped in to see what was going on. From the screams she heard, she knew it had to be serious. "Is everything okay?" When no one responded, she walked closer to the two and asked again, "Is everything okay?" Joe answered, "No. Can you let me know when my wife will be able to go home?"

"No problem, sir. We just need to run a few more tests and we will release her if everything comes back okay." The nurse left the room and went to find the doctor.

Still crying in Joe's arms Diane said, "I can't do this, Joe. I can't bury my baby. Why couldn't it have been me? Why would God do this to me?" Joe just held her tighter as the same thoughts ran through his head. As he sat there rocking his wife in his arms, all he could say was, "I don't know, baby." He looked Diane in the eyes and said, "All I know, is that you have to fight. I can't lose you right now, Diane." Diane looked back in his eyes and said, "This is too much right now. No parent should have to bury their child, Joe. It should've been me. It should've been me." Joe just wrapped her back in his arms as he began to rock her again. *This is unbelievable. I can't believe how this day is ending. God, you know I don't ask you for much, but I need you to give my wife more time. Me losing her and Aleese is more than I can bear. You told me you would never put more on me than I can bear.* "Everything is going to be okay, baby. I don't know how, but I believe God is going to work it out all. We just have to believe HE will," said Joe still rocking Diane.

Diamond screamed in pain as the ambulance zipped through the traffic to the hospital. Ms. Wallace sat next to Diamond, holding her hand as she told her everything would be okay. "It hurts, Mommy." Julie looked at the EMT who was sitting in the back with her. "Do you have anything you can give her?"

"We are almost at the hospital, ma'am. They will give her something when we get there." She cut her eyes at the guy then turned back to Diamond, "We are almost at the hospital, baby. Just hold on a little bit longer." Within minutes they were pulling into the emergency room entrance. The nurses immediately took charge rushing Diamond to the nearest available room. There was an aspiration technique used to remove any remaining tissue left behind to prevent infection. They hooked her up to an IV and within moments Diamond was knocked out from the medication.

Ms. Wallace sat in the chair in the corner of the room with so many mixed emotions. Although she was sad that Diamond had to experience her second miscarriage, she was happy that she was no longer going to be bound to Steven for the rest of her life. Yes, Julie was a Christian, but when she found out that Steven was the one who beat her daughter up like that she was ready to make some phone calls to get someone to teach this young man a lesson. Tears came out of her eyes as she looked at her daughter and felt like she was the cause of this all. If she didn't introduce Diamond to this man none of this would've ever happened. *What a day this has been. Here I thought I was just going over to the Thompsons' house for a nice Sunday dinner and all of this happens. First Diane tells me she's dying, and she wants me to be with Joe fine ass. Then she tells me she knows that all this time he was Diamond's father. Then Diamond loses another baby to Steven. God, the day can't get any worse. I do ask you to bring peace to the family for them losing a child and a sister. I don't know what I would do if you took my baby girl away from me.* Julie pulled her bible out of her pocketbook and began reading her favorite psalm, which was Psalm 121. *I will lift up mine eyes unto the hills, from whence cometh my help. My help cometh from the Lord, which made heaven and earth. He will not suffer thy foot to be moved: he that keepeth thee will not slumber. Behold, he that keepeth Israel shall neither slumber nor sleep. The Lord is thy keeper: The Lord is thy shade upon thy right hand. The sun shall not smite me by day nor the moon by night. The Lord shall preserve thee from all evil, he shall preserve thy soul. The Lord shall preserve thy going out and thy coming in from this forth, and even for evermore.* She laid her head back and closed her eyes.

A little while after Diamond pulled off in the ambulance the coroner had finally come. After they were done, Pastor Johnson took it upon himself to call the local funeral home to come pick up the body. Steven was still on his knees crying while Calvin was in the bathroom finishing that joint. Calvin was so gone that the blood on the floor didn't even phase him. He felt an emptiness that he had never felt in his life. As he sat on the toilet, he laid his head back and looked at the ceiling. *I know it's been a minute since you heard from me, but I need you right now,* thought Calvin, as the tears ran down the side of his face. *I know haven't been by to see you in a few years, but you said you only look after children and fools and I've definitely been foolish. You took my sister. You took my sister from me.* He wiped the tears from his eyes and took another pull from the joint. He felt so much rage at that moment. He stood up and looked in the mirror. All he saw behind his red eyes was emptiness.

Calvin was so angry over the fact that he couldn't do anything about this situation to make it right for his sister. A life for a life. Steven's dumb ass wiled out and it cost Aleese her life. Because Calvin knew that Steven also lost a sister, he couldn't even be mad at him. When Diane adopted Steven, it was one of the best day of Calvin's life. He always wanted a brother and now he had one. He saw the way that Steven looked out for Aleese when they were younger. He appreciated Steven for always being there for her and keeping her in line when he was away at college. They were a family. Blood didn't make them a family, but love did. What he knew right now more than anything, was that he had to get Steven off them drugs and get him back on track. He took another pull off the joint before putting it out. *God, you gotta help me with this here. I don't know what to do.* He sat back down on the toilet and put his head down in his hands as the tears came down his face. *You can't take my mom too. I can't lose nobody else.*

When Calvin came out of the bathroom, he saw Pastor Johnson had finally gotten Steven off of the floor. They were sitting at the dining room table which still contained the food and the plates that were made hours earlier. Pastor Johnson stood up when he saw Calvin heading their way. "How you holding up, son?" he asked with his arms extended to him. Calvin just walked into the hug and for the first time in his life, cried in front of people. "It's okay, son. Let it out," he said as he continued hugging Calvin. After a few minutes they sat down at the table with Steven. Pastor Johnson began talking to them both.

"I know there are things in life that happen, and we find ourselves asking why. Why did this happen this way? Why didn't I do this differently? Why did I let my emotions cause me to do what I did? The truth of the matter is, is that some things are just meant to be. It didn't matter if you made the right move or not because what happened, would've still happened. The one thing that I've learned about God in all my forty years of pastoring, is that our God doesn't make mistakes. You see I said our God, right? I've known you boys ever since Diane brought you both home. Diane had you three in church every Sunday. As you got older, you both went your separate ways. But God never did. God has been there with you both every step of the way. He said, he will never leave you nor forsake you and he hasn't. These are going to be some hard times coming up right now and your parents are going to need both of you to be their strength. You can't be strength to someone else before being it for yourselves. So, I need you both to work out whatever issues you may be facing within yourselves. Today was a tragedy. You both lost a sister, but Steven you also lost a child and your fiancé. You two are going to need each other like never before." He looked at both of them during this speech and said, "Am I my brother's keeper?" The boys looked at each other. "Maybe y'all didn't hear me. I said am I my brother's keeper?" Calvin and Steven both replied, "Yes, I am."

"Good, good. Now Steven, go give your brother a hug." Steven got out of his seat and walked over to Calvin who was already up and ready. The two brothers hugged, and both immediately cried.

"Calvin, man, I'm so sorry. You know Aleese was my heart. I don't know what I'm going to do without her, bro."

"You going to live, man, that's what you're going to do. We are going to live. She going to live through us." After a few minutes Pastor Johnson got ready to leave.

"You know, this is the first time I've been to the house for a Sunday dinner, in I don't know how long. When Aleese first asked me, I told her I couldn't make it because I had a prior engagement, but she insisted on how much she wanted me to be here. All I can say is God knows things we don't know and may never understand. What we do know is your precious, darling sister was an angel. God let me get here right on time. I will give your parents a call and let them know where your sisters remains are being held." He gave them both a hug as they thanked him for his love and support, and then he headed home. Pastor Johnson held it together for the sake of the boys, but as soon as he got in his car he began to cry. He knew Aleese almost her whole life. He had seen her grow from a little girl, into a beautiful young lady. She never got into any trouble, was never disrespectful, attended Sunday school, was part of the choir and a member of the hospitality committee. He would definitely miss her radiant smile that would always brighten up the room. He looked up to the sky and said, "Well, God, looks like you called another angel home." He wiped his face and drove away.

"What we going to do about this house, C? We can't let our parents come home to this." Steven grabbed his phone and got into work mode. They kind of both did. It was something about Pastor Johnson's presence that got them focused for the moment. "I'm about to call the cleaners. They will have all of this together in less than two hours. You send a text to everybody letting them know that The Spot will be closed for the next seven days in memory of Aleese. They should figure out what that means. Yo, Steven, I need you right now, man. Keep your nose clean."

"I got you, bro. Mommy got more weed rolled up in the bathroom?"

"Yeah, but let me get that for you. You don't want to go in there right now."

"Thanks for looking out for me, Calvin. I love you, man." Calvin was now walking to the bathroom. "Yeah, yeah, yeah. That emotional shit is over right now. Save it for the funeral." Just the thought of having to bury his sister made Steven punch the wall next to him. Calvin walked up to him and passed him a joint. "Light this up, man, and get your mind right. You just gave the cleaners something else to do. Your ass is paying for that one. Now send out that message, nigga."

Steven sat at the table and lit the joint. He sent the message out to Dawne telling her to inform everyone that The Spot would be closed due to the death of Aleese. Dawne just shook her head when she got the news. First, she got a call earlier about Fiah from one of the customers who worked at the hospital and now she hears about Aleese. She began to wonder if the two murders were connected. She just sent her condolences to Steven, then Calvin, before contacting all the girls. Dawne was management. She was who the girls called if they would be out or late, so it's only right that she let everyone know that they would be out of work for the next seven days. All of the girls responded asking Dawne to give Steven and Calvin their regrets and heartfelt condolences. And she of course responded to all of them saying that she would. She text Steven back when she was done and told him she would be around for another day before catching a vacation. Steven knew she deserved it. This would be the first one she had since she been down with him. He responded back to her, telling her to come by his crib tomorrow to pick up something for her trip. Her face lit up when she seen the message. She knew he would want something in return, but she also knew that whenever he told her to come through, he always left her pockets heavy.

Next, he sent a text to the cleaners. They were actually the same cleaners who cleaned The Spot twice a week. He had regular maintenance people who cleaned daily. But every now and then a situation may get out of hand and someone may need to be handled. The cleaners handled the problem and then cleaned up behind themselves. Of course they were very sad to hear the news. They had never met Aleese, but the respect they had for the Thompson brothers left them very remorseful for the family. They dropped what they were doing and headed to the address that Steven had given them.

Steven finished the joint and started heading up the stairs to check on Calvin. When he got to the top of the steps, he just saw Calvin standing in Aleese's doorway. "Yo, you good, C?" Calvin looked back at Steven and said, "You know, I still remember the day we first got here. I was eight and Aleese was only three. I came home one day and found my mom dead after watching my dad beat her ass day after day. And now, my brother whom I love with all my heart, is the cause of somebody's daughter being dead. Yo, Steven. What did you do to Fiah? I need to understand why I'm about to bury my, our baby sister." The tears flowed down Calvin's face as he stared at Steven waiting for an answer. Steven walked over to his brother and sat on the floor next to him. "To be honest, C, I was falling for Fiah. You know I haven't messed with none of these hoes like that after Kat. Especially after what happened with Dream. Then you call me and introduce me to one of the baddest chicks I seen in a long time. I had to have her, bro. All I did was tell her to be honest with me. I told her, C, just be honest with me and she said she was." Steven began wiping the tears off his face as he continued the story. "I put her to sleep, but that coke had me going. So, I get up to get a drink from the fridge. I just needed something cold in my stomach. I'm walking back to the room and I look over to the china cabinet and I see a picture of her and this nigga Kashmere. So now I starts going through her phone. I'm scrolling through days of messages with these two back and forth plotting on me. He sent her to the club to distract me while he took Diamond from me. To be honest, bro, I don't even know if that was my kid she lost."

"What you talking about, Steven? Diamond wouldn't do you like that."

"Man, I thought the same thing until I read them messages. He even proposed to her. The last message he sent to Fiah, was him saying, she said yes. C, I lost it, man. I watched my mom run around on my dad for years and treat him like a sucka. I wasn't going out like that."

Just then there was a knock at the door. "That must be the cleaners," said Calvin. Calvin extended his hand to his brother, helping him up off the floor. "We gonna get you some help, Steve. Don't tell nobody else what you just told me. If anybody ask what happen to Aleese, just say it's too painful to talk about. You hear me, man?"

"I got you, Calvin."

"Go wipe your face off and get it together."

"Aight, man, I will be down in a minute." Calvin went downstairs to greet the cleaners. They paid their respects and went straight to work. Steven went into the bathroom in his parents' room to wash his face. He hadn't been in here since they had it remodeled. He stood in the mirror and stared at the person he saw before him. Unlike before at Fiah's crib, he was no longer filled with anger and rage. This time he saw a scared little boy, who felt like his world was crumbling all around him. He grabbed a rag and wet it with cold water. He wiped his face a couple of times before pulling a folded bill out of his pocket. He just kept hearing his brother's voice in his head telling him to keep his nose clean. He opened the bill up, his hand was shaking so much, he ended up spilling all the coke out of the bill. He dropped the bill on the floor, then went and climbed in his parents' bed. He laid on his mom's side of the bed. Her scent made him feel comforted. How he wished to be in her arms right now. Since he couldn't, this would have to do. Calvin went to take a ride while the cleaners cleaned. He had already paid them but, let them know that Steven was upstairs if they needed anything. He also made a mental note to remind Steven to give him the money back for fixing that whole in the wall.

Calvin got in his car and started driving. He really didn't have a destination. Tonight, was the first time that he regretted not having a lady in his life. Someone who could hold him and console him and tell him that everything would be okay. He drove to a lake a couple of miles from his mom's house. When he pulled up, he got out of the car and walked over to look at the water. The water looked really dark and scary as the moon glistened on top of it. At that moment Calvin realized he wanted more out of life. He wanted to make a family of his own. A couple of hours had passed since he left. He called Steven to see if the cleaners had left. When Steven didn't answer his phone, he became worried and headed back to the house. He kept calling Steven the whole time he was driving. The more the phone kept ringing the more nervous he became. He pulled up and saw the cleaning van was gone. When he stepped inside the house, it looked cleaner than he ever remembered it being. It looked a little brighter too.

"Steven!!" yelled Calvin as he headed up the stairs. He followed the heavy snoring to his parents' room and saw Steven in the bed knocked out. He figured this was probably the first time Steven had been to sleep since everything happened. Especially since he been so coked up lately. Calvin headed back downstairs and called his dad to check on his mom. He let them know that the hospital decided to keep mom overnight for observation, but she was okay. Calvin let his dad know about the conversation that he and Steven had with Pastor Johnson. He also let him know that Pastor Johnson was taking care of all the funeral arrangements and that he would give them a call tomorrow to fill them in on everything. He told his dad he loved him and hung up the phone.

Mr. Thompson was very proud of his boys. He was happy for their accomplishments, even though he wasn't fully in the loop on what happened at The Spot. He knew they were successful business owners for years now. He was very impressed on how they were taking care of business. All Joe worried about now was going home the next day and his baby girl not being there to greet him with her warm, beautiful smile. He dropped his head as he sat in the chair across from his sleeping wife. He looked up to the ceiling and said, "I never left

you. The time you looked in the sand and only saw one set of footprints, those weren't yours. That was my footprints I made, while carrying you." For the first time since everything happened Joe felt a
peace come across him. He knew right then, that everything was going
to be okay. He closed his eyes and fell asleep.

Diamond had been released from the hospital once she was up
and walking. Her and Julie headed back to their home by cab. She
still had on the hospital gown since her clothes were filled with blood.
That was the first of many nights that Diamond spent in the bed with
her mom. She had so many things on her mind. How did her life get
so crazy? How did the man she loved kill someone? How could the
other man she was about to marry kill her friend? *Why do I keep
picking these crazy niggas,* she thought as she silently cried under the
covers. She felt bad about what came next, but she thanked God for
letting her lose this child. She would've hated to have been stuck with
any of these men for the rest of her life. All she wanted was love but
she ended up with black eyes and a hurt heart. Let's not forget the
shocking news that the man she thought was her father wasn't. The
man who was supposed to be her father-in-law was actually her real
dad. Once she found out she felt stupid for never putting it together
sooner. She looked just like Joe. She hoped in some way that she
would be able to begin a relationship with him. She didn't know how
that would work since she didn't want to be around Steven anymore.
But she knew time would heal all wounds. She also knew that she and
Joe would be spending a lot of time together if Diane had anything
to do with it. *What a day this has been. God, didn't I ask you for a
peaceful day?* Diamond laid there until she finally fell back asleep.
She was happy that she followed her mind earlier and took all her
stuff from Kashmere's crib. She was also happy that she didn't listen
to him and leave all her jewelry at Steven's place. *What's next?* was
her final thought.

Ms. Wallace was very surprised that Diamond wanted to get in
the bed with her. They hadn't been in the same bed since her husband

was alive. Julie didn't know how they were going to get through this situation. She didn't even know if her daughter was safe. These were dangerous men she was involved with. She said a prayer to God and fell off to sleep.

Calvin wanted to go home but for what? To be home alone? Even though his brother was upstairs knocked out, he was happy to know that someone else was around. He laid his head back on the couch and fell asleep within minutes.

"Talk to me."

"They just pulled up to the house, boss. Diamond had on a hospital gown."

"Did she look hurt? I told everyone to focus on that nigga and the sister."

"I don't think she hurt, boss. She was walking on her own. She was hunched over a little bit." Kashmere hung his head down, knowing that Diamond lost the baby. There was never a doubt in his mind that the baby was his. He knew he had lost her forever. "What should I do now, boss?"

"Go home, Troy. It's all over."

"Roger that," was the last thing Troy said before hanging up the phone. Kash hung up his phone as he held the engagement ring that he had just given to Diamond the night before. He threw it across the room before he ripped up the letter that she had left with it. Kash was enraged all over again. He did all of this and he still didn't end up with the girl. He knew he said no more bodies, but that may now be subject to change.

The next few days seemed to go by so fast. Diane met with the pastor and the funeral director to pick out a dress and casket for Aleese. She picked a beautiful pink casket with gold rose petals engraved around the sides. She found a beautiful white dress to adorn Aleese with, to honor her daughter's virtuousness. Diane wasn't really sure why an autopsy was done, but that was how they discovered that Aleese was still a virgin. As she took the last look at her daughter looking like an angel in her casket, she felt herself getting weak. Joe was right by her side and wasn't about to let her fall.

The day of the funeral was here, and everyone was in place except for Steven. The day after Aleese's death, was the first time Steven had been home in days, for more than just a couple of minutes. The first thing he did when he got in the house was sit on his couch. He sat back until he looked on the coffee table and seen Diamond's ring on top of an empty coke bag. Steven became furious as he blamed Diamond for all of this happening. When in actuality, all of this was his fault. If he never would've brought Diamond to The Spot, she wouldn't have run into Kash and Kash wouldn't have tried to send his sister in the mix to run game while he tried to get Diamond back. Steven didn't want to accept the blame for this. He didn't want to accept that he lost his fiancée because of his own arrogance and he definitely didn't want to accept the fact that he lost his sister because of his rage.

Without even realizing it, he picked up the glass table and threw it against the wall. He just stood there as glass shattered everywhere, before going upstairs and laying in his empty bed. He laid there and wondered what was left for him. This was the first time he really appreciated street justice. Yes, he lost his sister, but at least he wasn't in jail for murder. Steven really felt like the scum under the bottom of the barrel right now and all he wanted was something to take the edge off. He knew he could call Vanilla, but he didn't want none of them hoes knowing where he lived. Then he remembered that he told Dawne to come by that day. He sent her a text and told her to get an eight ball for him from Vanilla and to come as soon as possible. Dawne saw the desperation in his message. She hit Vanilla up, picked up the package and headed to Steven's crib.

She pulled up in the driveway and got out of her car. She was very surprised to see that the door was open. "Steven," she called as she came inside. "I'm up here, D." Dawne had been to the house a couple of times before, but she had never been inside. When she saw the glass all over the floor, she thought that Steven might be hurt, so she moved a little quicker. When she got upstairs and saw Steven sprawled across the bed, sweaty and bug eyed, she knew something was wrong. "Daddy, what's wrong with you?"

"I'm good, D. You got that for me?" She pulled the package out of her purse and handed it to Steven. She watched him as he took a bill out of his pocket and poured coke into it before crushing it up. Once he took a hit, he seemed to be back to himself immediately. He wiped his nose with the back of his hand before thanking Dawne for coming over so quickly. "Daddy, you don't look too good. How about I set my trip back a day and I take care of you."

"You can start by running me a hot bath. Then you can cook me some food." Then she stood up in front of him and unbuckled her trench coat and held it open for him to see the contents beneath. "You sure that's all you want, Daddy?" Steven smirked as he thought about how good his dick would feel in Dawne's throat right now. "You know you have always been my number-one girl. You know I'm going to give majestic to you before you leave me, bet that." She smiled as she took the coat off and walked in the bathroom to prepare his bath.

He did a couple of more lines while the tub filled up. She called him in once it was ready. He walked in the bathroom and took off all his clothes as he got in the tub one foot at a time. He sat back in his jacuzzi tub as Dawne took off her clothes to join him. First, she sat in front of him as she bathed him. Then she sat behind him as he laid back on her and she washed his hair. He closed his eyes while he enjoyed her hands massaging his head. As long as he liked it, she kept going. After another fifteen minutes, she got out and dried off before getting another towel for him. He tied the towel around his waist then walked back to his bed. He took the towel off and laid down as she dried him off and lotioned him up. When she was done, he told her what drawer to find his underwear and t-shirt in. He told her to take out a second shirt so she could put something on while she went downstairs to cook. "I'm sure you've seen the glass on the floor. If you walk in front of the couch you should be okay." She put her t-shirt on as she walked back over to the bed. She got on her knees as Steven stood up. She put his underwear on before putting his t-shirt on then she was headed downstairs. Steven made sure to slap her butt before she left his presence.

He felt good for the first time in days. This was all he needed, a little rest and pampering. Before he knew it, he was back asleep. Dawne had made her way downstairs and walked in front of the couch like he said. She saw a pair of slippers at the bottom of the steps which she put on her feet, then proceeded to the kitchen. She thought about what she could make that was quick and easy. She looked in the fridge and saw some chicken that had been seasoned. Since she didn't smell any bad odors, she figured it must not have been in there that long. She saw cheese and spaghetti sauce, so she decided to make some chicken ziti. Once the ziti was almost done, she made some garlic bread and also prepared a salad. Dawne had been employed by Steven for a long time. She was one of his originals that was trained by Kat, so she knew how to take care of Steven like he was accustomed to. She found a serving tray under the cabinet. She placed his food on the tray and headed upstairs. She placed the tray on the dresser as she woke Steven up. He smiled as the smell of the food hit his stomach, then his nose. He had just realized that he hadn't had a meal in two days. Dawne was happy to see him eating. When he was done, she made him a second plate. He was very content with all she had done. After he finished eating, he went to his safe and pulled out a thousand dollars. He handed it to Dawne and said, "I want to thank you for always being there when I need you. I'm not in the mood for any other services right now. So, take this and enjoy your vacation." She smiled as she ran to give him a hug. "Thanks, Daddy." "I'm about to go back to sleep. Clean up the kitchen for me and make sure the door is closed when you leave." Dawne had no problem doing what Steven asked. By the time she got back upstairs, Steven was snoring again. She got dressed, kissed him on the forehead and headed out the door.

When Steven woke back up, he couldn't believe what the clock said. It was ten o'clock the next night. How did he sleep a whole day away? He went to check his phone, but it was dead. He sat up and felt eyes staring at him. He looked over at the chair in the corner and saw that it was occupied by somebody. For the first time in life Steven felt fear. Then he heard a voice say, "I sat here and watched you sleep, wondering if I should just blow your brains out or wait for you to wake up so I could beat you to death like you did my sister." Steven went to get out of the bed, but Kash quickly suggested he didn't do that as he cocked his gun. "I used to respect you, Steven, you used to be an honest business man. You and your brother built a whole business off of selling pussy. Who in the game can't love that? But you had to get greedy and cocky. I wanted to let you live, I really did. Then I came home and found a letter with the ring I gave to Diamond. So, all of this is now for nothing. My sister is dead, and Diamond doesn't want anything to do with me. Sorry it had to end this way." Kash pulled the trigger twice. "That's for Sophia. Only I was supposed to know how good her pussy was," he said as he walked over to Steven's bleeding body. He picked up Steven's phone and said, "You should've never started fucking your hoes. We probably wouldn't be here right now if you just stuck to your rules. I'm going to let you lay here and bleed out. No one's coming to save you. You're going to die by yourself, just like my sister did." He closed the bedroom door, headed down the stairs, then left.

He jumped in the car parked across the street and Troy pulled off. He immediately charged Steven's phone. He was sure that someone from his family had tried to contact him. Once the phone was on the notifications went crazy. He saw that the last person he had spoken to was Dawne and that Dawne was going out of town. Kash text Calvin back like he was Steven and said he was going out of town for a couple of days with Dawne but, he would be back in time for the funeral.

Now it's the day of the funeral and no one has heard from Steven. Calvin didn't bother going to the house because he knew Steven was out of town. The funeral was starting. As much as the family didn't want to begin without Steven, they had to. The church was filled with old friends and church family. Even a few of the girls from The Spot came by once they found out the funeral arrangements. Then came time for friends and family to give words of reflection. The family wasn't really expecting anyone to get up since they had never met any friends of Aleese. Then a pretty young lady walked up to the podium, dressed in all black, wearing a black veil over her face. She began to speak. "I know you are all probably wondering who I am," stated the young lady looking at the family. "My name is Karina, and I was Aleese's lover. She was planning on coming out to you all after the family dinner. That's why she invited Pastor Johnson. She didn't know how you all would respond, so she figured he would be there for moral support. Me and Aleese were together for four years. She spoke so highly of all of you. There was nothing she loved more than her family. I'm sorry that this is the way that I get to meet you," she stops talking as the tears begin to come down her face. "I'm sorry, I can't do this." She starts balling as she walks back to her seat. Mrs. Thompson grabs her hand as she walks past her. She then stood up and gave Karina a hug. She then whispered in her ear, "Make sure you see me after the service, okay." Karina shook her head yes and went back to her seat. Before Mrs. Thompson sat down, she said, "Pastor Johnson, I think we've had enough reflections. It's time for the word." Mrs. Thompson wanted to laugh. She wanted to laugh and cry. As long as she joked with Aleese about being gay, she didn't understand why she felt she had to hide it. She just wanted to point at Joe and say, "Didn't I tell you she was gay?" Instead, she chose to be wise and save her laughter for home. But that little scene did make her forget for a minute that her son wasn't at his sister's funeral.

Pastor Johnson stood up and said, "Diane, I think you are right. It is time for the Word. If you have your Bibles this afternoon, I want you to turn with me to the Gospel recorded by Luke. I will be coming from the fifteenth chapter, beginning at the eighth verse. Can we all stand for the reading of God's word.

"And it reads, 'Either what woman having ten pieces of silver, if she loses one piece, doth not light a candle, and sweep the house and seek it diligently till she find it? And when she hath found it, she calleth her friends and her neighbors together, saying, rejoice with me; for I have found the piece which I had lost. Likewise, I say unto you, there is joy in the presence of the angels of God over one sinner that repenteth.'

"That was the King James version. I know some of you young people like things broken down a little simpler. So, I will now read the same scripture to you from the New International Version.

"'Or suppose a woman has ten silver coins and loses one. Doesn't she light a lamp, sweep the house and search carefully until she finds it? And when she finds it, she calls her friends and neighbors together and says, "Rejoice with me; I have found my lost coin." In the same way, I tell you, there is rejoicing in the presence of the angels of God over one sinner who repents.'

"If I had time to preach today, I would take the subject from the last verse. 'In the same way, I tell you, there is rejoicing in the presence of the angels of God over one sinner who repents.' My topic today is, God wants you to come back home.

"Everyone, bow your heads with me for a word of prayer. Father God, in the name of Jesus, I come to you one more time asking you to word my mouth. I want to thank you for this word that you have given me for your people. My prayer today is that someone is touched by this word right now and surrender themselves back to you God. Take me away and let your people only hear what thus saith the Lord. All these things I ask in that name that is greater than every name. Jesus! Amen.

"You may now take your seats. As we see in the beginning of this eighth verse, the writer is letting you know that this woman had ten coins. So, you may wonder, if she had ten coins, why does she care about losing one? And why was she so happy when she found this one coin. Back in my day, when I was a little younger, I was a collector of coins. I loved to find coins from other countries as well as old coins from this country. How many of y'all have even seen a buffalo head nickel? From the chatter, I can tell it's not too many of you. For years I collected coins and kept them in jar. Every now and then I would go back in my jar to make sure all of my coins were accounted for. Each coin was special to me. The old coins, the new coins, the shiny coins, the dull coins. All the coins were my favorite, because they each meant something different to me and they each represented a place or a time in my life. Every coin came with a memory. So, one day, while I'm going through my coins, I notice that one of my coins are missing. I go to my grandad and say, 'Grandad, one of my coins are missing.' My grandad looks at me and says, 'Well, how do you know that? You have a jar full of coins. It's impossible for you to know that you have a coin missing.' I look at him and say, 'It's not impossible. Each coin is special to me. Each coin tells a story and now I can't go to sleep until I find this coin.' So, my grandad looks at me like I'm crazy, but he helps me look for my coin. We search every room looking for my coin. And where do I find it? In the last place I thought it would be. My coin made its way underneath the cabinet in the kitchen.

"When I found my coin, I was so happy. When my grandad saw the smile on my face, he then realized how much this coin meant to me. He grabbed me in his arms, and we celebrated because of my one lost coin that I found. Yes, I still had all my other coins and if I lost them I would've felt the same way, but I had to get back one that I lost. The same way I felt about my coin, is the same way that God feels about your souls. Yes, HE's happy for the saints that come here Sunday after Sunday, but HE is more pleased about the soul that HE lost, that wants to come back home. I know everyone has a reason of why they don't want to be in church. The people are hypocrites, the church only wants your money, or my favorite, church services are just too long. It's too long for you to sit in service and give thanks and honor to the one who wakes you up every morning? It's too long for you to sit in service to give praises to the one who watches over you and keeps you safe during the day and night? What if God decided right now that we weren't important enough, that we didn't matter? We would be in a lot of trouble. people. It's only the grace of God that keeps us in our right minds. Some of us have encountered experiences that have left other people in mental institutions, but God gives us the strength to keep going and keep pressing. For I press toward the mark for the prize of the high calling of God in Christ Jesus.

"There is a blessing in the pressing. God is keeping us all here for a reason. Aleese died way too soon and she will be missed, but she lived her life. She was not perfect, for no man is perfect, but she did strive for perfection. Her death brought you all here today. Some are probably coming to church right now for the first time in your life. If you feel in your heart right now that you are that lost coin, that lost soul, I admonish you to come to the alter now. This may be your last time. Life is not promised to us. The only thing that is promised to us is death. There is nothing in the world that you could do that would make God turn his back on you. He loves the drug dealer, the same way he loves the deacon. He loves the alcoholic the same way that he loves the choir member. He loves the prostitute the same way he loves the ushers at the door. All God wants is your heart. Not your body, not your money, but your heart and your worship. You are all valuable to God and you are all his children. The doors of the church are now open. If there is one today, who is tired of living a life of sin and wants to try something new, I dare you to try Jesus. I dare you to step into one of these aisles right now and come to this altar. I don't care what you have on or how you look. All God wants is your heart. Sister Brenda, come up and sing I surrender."

Sis. Brenda got up and came to the mic and began singing, "All to Jesus, I surrender, all to Him I freely give. I will ever, love and trust Him, in His presence daily live. I surrender all, I surrender all. All to thee my blessed Savior, I surrender all." By the time Sis. Brenda finished singing the verse and chorus over again, there were about twenty people up at the altar ready to give their life back to God.

When Mr. and Mrs. Thompson saw Calvin walk to the altar they stood up and rejoiced, thanking God for one good thing coming out of this bad experience. "Sis. Brenda, can you repeat the chorus while I say this prayer.

"God, we first want to say thank you, for the souls that have come back to you. I ask you, God, to come into the hearts and minds of your people. God, you promised that you would never leave us nor forsake us. Some of us here at this altar right now have tried everything to help fill this emptiness that we have. Liquor can't fill it, getting high can't fill it, smoking can't fill it, sex can't fill it. Only you, God. You are the only one who can make us feel complete, make us feel whole again. Some of us have been betrayed by the very ones we hold the closest to us, and that pain from that betrayal has left us broken. I pray right now, God, that you restore the brokenhearted. That you dry every weeping eye, Lord. That you mend together the brokenness that others have left in our lives. Only your Grace and Mercy has the power to completely restore us. We want to be made whole again, we want to be able to love again, to trust again. We need you right now, God, like never before. I ask a special blessing on every individual at this altar right now, God. I ask you to hold them and let them experience what real love is through you, Jesus. All these things I ask in the name of the father, in the name of the son, in Jesus' name. Amen! Now hug the person next to you and tell them that you love them."

At that moment a wave hit the church. The Holy Spirit came by and showed out. People were praising God through dance and by mouth. After Pastor Johnson prayed, he came down with his oil and laid hands on everyone that came to the altar. He was especially happy when he saw Diamond was one of the souls that gave her life back to the Lord. She felt restored through that message and she knew from then that this is where she was supposed to be. After Pastor Johnson was done, he made sure that he had the name and number of everyone who came back to God that day. As he walked back past the casket, he touched it and said, "Aleese, you would be proud of how many lives were saved through your life."

As everyone made their way back to their seat, Calvin saw Dawne. He immediately had a bad feeling go through him. If she was here and Steven wasn't, then Steven wasn't with her. His parents immediately noticed the change in his face. They became worried as they began to think this sudden change had to do with their son Steven. As soon as the funeral was over Calvin jumped in his car and headed to Steven's house. He kept calling his phone, which had been going to voicemail since the day after he got the text from Steven. He pulled up to the house and saw Steven's car outside. He knocked on the door before kicking it in. There at the bottom of the steps laid Steven's body. He laid there with his eyes open, staring at the ceiling. He looked peaceful, despite the shot to his chest and abdomen. He felt numb as he called nine-one-one. He knew that this was far from over. As he waited for the police to come, he began plotting on his plan to catch Kashmere. He didn't keep his word and he would pay for that with his life.

To be continued...